Through the Mist

CECE FERRELL

COPYRIGHT

ISBN: 978-1-7329101-0-2

Cover Design by Sarah Hansen of Okay Creations
Editing by RJ Locksley
Proofreading by Judy's Proofreading

DEDICATION

For my mom and dad, thank you for always encouraging me to chase my dreams.

For Josh, thank you for being my rock.

MY LITTLE ONES,

I know, I know. You aren't so little anymore, as you all love to remind me, but it's how I will always think of you. The little loves who came along and filled my heart to bursting.

I started these journals so long ago, my attempt to commit everything that happened to paper, not wanting to rely on my memory for fear that once that began to fade, my story would be lost. I was also trying to make sense of what truly seemed impossible.

I never wrote these with the intention of you seeing them, but as the years passed and I realized how many secrets I was keeping—your father and I both were keeping—I knew that there was a chance that I would entrust my memories to you all.

I always felt that children had a right to know their parents' secrets. You never know when or how those secrets will sneak up and destroy, or change, a life, no matter how many generations down the line. We never wanted to keep our story a secret from you.

I hope that by the time you're reading these, if ever, that you are all grown with lives of your own. I hope you know enough of love, the true nature of it, to understand why I'm sharing my story. That love is never as black and white as people would like you to believe. That it's full of complexities, light and shadows, curves and turns. That the heart is capable of far more than we could ever imagine.

You are blessed if you get to love one person in your life, if you get to fall madly, deeply, with abandon. Many people never get to experience that. I pray that you get to feel that kind of love. I was lucky enough to find it, even if it wasn't easy or pretty, even if it nearly tore me apart.

I don't have answers to the whys or hows. It's still as much a mystery to me now as it was then, but writing this helped me make sense of things. This is my story, the truth about so many things. Well, my truth, at least.

ONE

GRIEF. It's an asshole. An insidious son of a bitch, and once its hooks are in you, it never lets go. It tricks you into thinking you're okay, only to hit you in the gut and make your knees buckle when you least expect it. It doesn't matter how long it's been. Weeks, months, years.

They say the pain lessens with time, but eleven years later I now knew that was a lie. The anniversary of my mom's death never got any easier, it never hurt any less. Grief still held me in its razor-sharp claws.

It wasn't like I could ever forget the day a piece of me died, but in those groggy first moments of the morning, reality hadn't caught up with me. One look at the date on my phone screen and all the pain and memories I'd managed to bury came rushing back.

My chest throbbed and I rubbed my fisted hand rhythmically against it, trying to force the pain away, knowing all the while it wouldn't work. It never did. My hands were incapable of touching the source of the wound.

I considered calling my husband, Dan, for about a minute before I changed my mind. He'd begun a new work assignment, one that had brought us both to this tiny island in the Pacific Northwest. He didn't need the interruption, and in my current state, anything I tried to say would be gibberish.

Even after all these years, I still hadn't found a way to talk about her death. It'd happened too fast for my teenage mind and heart to process. The terminal diagnosis and the rapid decline. I'd sat witness to the cancer as it took her life but never her spirit.

Within months my mom was gone and I'd been left with a father who never let down his walls enough to talk about all I had lost, all he had lost too. So I'd tucked those feelings and memories away, tried to act like they never existed in the first place. I'd thought my attempts were successful, even if I found myself drowning under the sudden crash of emotions at the most inopportune times.

Rubbing the tears from my eyes, I decided to do what I had done for the last five years. I set the timer on my phone for an hour, grabbed the box of my mom's things that I kept hidden in the back of my closet, and gave in to all the memories and grief.

Some years I let myself linger over the contents of the box for longer than the hour, some years I couldn't even handle that much time. I combed through the items in the box, crying over the cards and letters she had left for me, sliding on her favorite ring, a beautiful and dainty gold one that held both of our birthstones.

I even found myself able to laugh at some of the pictures in the box, ones from the vacations we had taken together. She'd always made sure we took two pictures— a nice, serious one that we could display in our home, and a goofy one of us posing funny or making silly faces. We always ended up loving the funny ones more.

I made it to the bottom of the box as my alarm began to sound, startling me. I wiped the tears from my cheeks and placed everything back in the box, sliding the ring off my finger last. I put the lid back on the box and on my emotions for the moment.

As an only child, I sometimes wondered if dealing with my grief would have been easier with a sibling by my side, someone else who knew what it was like to have her as a mother. Then again, living in denial the way I was would likely be impossible with a brother or sister to answer to.

———

I stepped out of the shower to my phone ringing. I ran,

attempting to wrap my towel around my body and slipping on the way to my bedside table. It stopped ringing right before I grabbed it, and by the time it was unlocked, the text alert dinged. Josie.

Jos: Wake up and answer your damn phone, Ros!!!

I smiled to myself as I pressed her name and waited for the FaceTime call to connect.

"Are you awake, or will I have to suffer through zombie Ros?" She sounded put off even though her voice was laced with humor as her gorgeous, ethereal face filled the screen, her light blue eyes alight with mischief. Josie was wild, didn't have a shy bone in her body, and lacked a filter between her brain and mouth.

My eyes flashed to my image in the little box on the screen. My tawny skin with cheeks tinged pink from the shower, freckles strewn across my face, hazel eyes, and dripping wet hair already starting to curl up couldn't be more different from Jos' face staring back at me.

"I've been up for a little bit." I winced, hating the way my voice cracked, the fact that I had been crying now obvious to Jos' practiced ear and gaze.

"Oh, babe. How long did you spend with the box?"

"Just an hour. I don't think I can stomach any more.

Maybe later. Probably not." I turned away from the screen.

"Want to talk about her?" Jos swept a piece of her platinum-blonde hair cut into an angular bob behind her ear.

"No. Not yet."

Jos asked me this every year on the anniversary. Sometimes she asked throughout the year when she could tell I was struggling. My answer was always the same. We had yet to talk about my mom's passing in any real way.

There were times I wanted to, but every time I tried to get the words out, grief wrapped its claws around my throat and applied pressure, making it impossible to choke out the words. Jos always seemed to understand, never saying much more, never pressing me to do more than I was ready to. So there we sat in silence for a minute or two.

"I miss her so much too, Ros. She was amazing."

I nodded my head. She didn't say anything else. I knew the loss wasn't mine alone, even if it felt that way most days.

Josie was my oldest, closest friend, and for years my only one. I remembered the first time I'd met her, this tall, gangly girl with her almost white-blonde hair cut into long, straight layers that I'd envied on sight. She'd been standing at the bus stop on our cul-de-sac, a fuck-off attitude radiating from her, even at the age of eight.

Immediately drawn to her, I'd inched closer, like a moth to a flame. She was the complete opposite of my short, crazy-haired, introverted self. For reasons I'd never understood, she'd found something in me she was drawn to as well.

Not five minutes after I made it to the bus stop, she'd sauntered up to me, her thumbs hooked in the straps of her neon Lisa Frank backpack, and said, "Hey, I'm new here. My name is Josie. What's your name?"

The bus had pulled up as she finished her question. She'd followed me up the steps and surprised me by sitting beside me.

"I'm Rosalind, but you can call me Ros," I responded in my whisper of a voice.

From that day forward we were inseparable. She had been there for me through everything: my parents' divorce, the loneliness and torture of getting bullied in elementary school, first loves and the inevitable heartbreaks.

Even when I had to move in with my father and switch to a different high school, we still saw each other several times a week. It was always Jos and Ros forever. We even decided to go to college together.

Until this move, we hadn't spent more than a month apart. She was the closest thing I had to a sister, at least what I thought it would be like to have one. And with her next question, she proved that she knew me better than anyone else.

"So what else is bothering you?"

"I don't know. I was so ready for the move to be done. Now that it is, I'm ready for things to… change."

The silence stretched between us as I debated what I wanted to say next, if I even wanted to say it at all. She just let the weight of my unspoken words sit there, waiting for me to decide. That was the thing about having a friend who knew you so well, someone who gave you what you needed when you needed it, and wasn't afraid to kick your ass and force you to face the truth when necessary. You could be one hundred percent real with them, no masks, no artifice. I knew I could leave things the way they were now, not even bring up the shit bothering me, and she would probably let it slide today. The words were out before my brain had even decided.

"Shit is so weird with Dan and me, Jos. I thought this process would bring us closer together, but nope, we're more distant than ever." I covered my mouth with my hand, shocked that I let the confession pass my lips.

"How long has this been going on? Maybe it's because you both have been going crazy trying to get shit figured out?" Her image on the screen went blurry as she adjusted her body to get more comfortable.

"It's been going on for a while and I ignored it. He's gone more than he's home. You know that."

"It's always been this way, Ros, even when you guys met. So what's different now?"

"I always thought I was okay with it. I worked a lot before we moved and kept busy to avoid dealing with it. I figured if I filled up my days it wouldn't leave time to miss him and be lonely."

"You're really good at avoiding the truth when it hurts, girl," Jos said.

"I know. Since we've been here I've had more time on my hands than I ever had before. And Dan's been gone more than he said he would with this project. I mean, the whole reason I came with him and gave up everything back home was for us to connect."

"And you guys aren't connecting? Are things getting worse?"

"No, not worse. But not better either. But all this time alone has given me time to think about us and how our relationship has always been."

I went quiet, unsure how to verbalize the thoughts racing through my head, the emotions running through my body. Without warning, the words spilled out of me in a rush.

"I'm not okay with it, Jos. This distance, this lack of communication. I always chalked it up to the physical distance between us. I figured I needed to just suck it up if I wanted to be with Dan because our relationship has always been this way from the very start."

"And what do you think now?"

"Now I think the distance wasn't it at all. We've both been complacent. But I'm not anymore. I fucking hate feeling like this, like I don't even know my own husband sometimes. Texting and occasional phone calls for nine months out of the year isn't working, I'm not sure if it ever did." My chest heaved with the need for air as my heart pounded.

"Ros, calm down. We'll figure this out. I promise—"

"No," I interrupted, shaking my head and trying to get a handle on my emotions.

"Maybe it's the seven-year itch?" Jos suggested, laughter in her voice.

"I'm pretty sure people are referring to a wandering eye when they say that, Jos. Plus, we've only been married for three years," I huffed in response, trying to keep a straight face.

"Yeah, but you've been together for seven years," Jos began, but paused after seeing the look on my face that clearly conveyed that I was done with both of these conversations. I didn't want to dwell on the loss my heart had yet to recover from, and I didn't want to talk about the issues with Dan anymore, not today.

"Random subject change needed?" Jos asked.

"Yeah, that would be great."

"Hmm... what to share that you don't already know?" She tapped her finger on her chin, probably the only nervous tic she had.

"Tell me about this new guy you're seeing."

She laughed and blew out a breath. "For starters, he is gorgeous and all wrong for me, and will utterly break my heart. I love him already!"

"Oh, God, Jos. Dramatic much? Think this will be the one to break the mold?"

"I hope so, but I'm not holding my breath. The guys here are a fucking waste. I know things are rough for you two right now, but Dan's one of the good ones. How you managed to find that here, I'll never know."

"I don't know how I found Dan. I got lucky, I guess. I really believe it's just hard to find the right person. It's so easy just to walk away when things start to go bad; no one wants to work on their issues anymore. It's like, oh, life sucks, and we fight, so we're done."

"I just want to make it to the fighting part."

My laughter rang out. Only Jos would *want* to argue with her significant other.

"What? I'd love to get to that point in a relationship. Plus, it's not like you and Dan ever fight." She had a point.

"We don't because Dan isn't around enough for us to argue. All of these separations keep us in the honeymoon stage. Arguing would be an improvement at this point.

Pray for us, Jos, we might need it." The chuckle that made its way through my lips was an awkward thing, my attempt to hide the worry chipping away at me.

"Oh, shut it, you guys will figure this out and we will be celebrating your twentieth wedding anniversary before you know it."

"We just need to figure out how to get you to meet someone you can celebrate a twenty-year anniversary with, Jos. Hell, even a one-year anniversary."

"I know, I know." She sighed. A moment passed, and then another. We both said nothing, just stared at the image of the other on the screens of our phones. "Ros?"

"Yeah?"

"I know you've only been gone a few weeks, but I fucking miss you."

"Me too, Jos. Me too."

Somehow, in spite of all the things we had talked about that day, just hearing how much she missed me made all the difference.

TWO

I WAS on my back floating in the water. The air was cold and crisp and sprinkles of water from the undulating waves coated my skin. I should've been terrified, alone in the expanse of ocean. Instead, I was filled with the sweetest, most liberating feeling. Like I was home, exactly where I belonged.

Time passed and I was content. Until something smacked at my leg, jarring me. I sat up and opened my eyes only to see a dark shadow below the water and a familiar-shaped fin above, circling me. I opened my mouth to scream but my throat constricted and all I could manage was a strangled sob. I was going to die.

I closed my eyes in preparation for my fate and instead a squealing sound hit my ears as something nudged my body. My eyes flashed open and instead of the shark I was expecting, I made eye contact with a dolphin. My head was filled with thoughts that were not my own, like the creature was communicating with me telepathically, urging me to climb on its back. So I did.

After a while other figures came into view, bobbing in the water. As we neared, I was able to make out the forms of two other people. We grew closer still, and I could see Dan. The dolphin stopped, letting me slide off his back before he swam away. Dan smiled at me and held out his hand, but I was hesitant to take it.

My skin began to heat under the weight of someone else's gaze. I turned, and there was another man, also floating nearby. He was incredibly handsome, and his gaze was penetrating. I had never seen this man before in my life—I would have remembered if I had. You did not forget a face like this, and you did not forget the emotions he brought out in me.

It was like gravity or magnetism, and I couldn't break the connection. It was as though deep inside some hidden part of me, I knew him, I recognized him. Something dormant in me woke up in his proximity.

I finally tore my eyes away from him and noticed his body was different from mine and everyone else's. I could almost see through it, and though he appeared solid, it was obvious he wasn't. My brain couldn't make sense of it. I looked back to Dan, and the difference between the substantiality of him and this other man only became more glaring.

They both reached their arms out to me, and against my will, I took both of their hands at the same time. My gaze kept ping-ponging between the two men I held in my grasp. I was drawn to both, as though there were magnets under each of our skin creating an actual, physical pull to my husband and the man I didn't know but recognized with every fiber of my being.

This was how I rode the gently swelling waves, me between these two men who were splitting my heart right down the center.

THREE

I WOKE WITH A START, completely disoriented. It took a minute for me to get my bearings and realize I was in our room in our new house.

I usually forgot the details of my dreams as soon as I woke up, but not this one. It was perhaps the most vivid dream I had ever had. I could remember every single part of it. It was strange and frightening and comforting, all at once.

I couldn't help but wonder who the man was. Had I possibly seen him in passing once, just smiled at him and forgotten all about it? No. I knew with complete certainty that if I'd ever laid eyes on this man, I would never have forgotten him.

I always hated when the lingering emotions of a dream stayed with me after waking, making it all seem so real. I never believed in past lives or fated connections that seemed controlled by the hands of God, but sometimes my strong emotional reaction to dreams made me consider the possibility. It often seemed like the only logical explanation as to why sometimes the emotions I experienced while dreaming felt so much more real than anything that happened while awake.

I sighed, turned on my back and slowly opened my eyes. My mind was still muddled with sleep, and I was having trouble disengaging from the dream world I had just woken from. I just couldn't forget the other man, his eyes, the way his body looked like I could almost see through him but still touch him at the same time. What struck me most was the intense look in his eyes, imploring me to go to him, to not look away, to not turn back to Dan.

"You okay, babe?" Dan's voice, still husky with sleep, cut through my mental haze. "Crazy dream?"

"I think so. I can't remember what happened. I just woke up feeling strange." The lie tasted terrible in my mouth, but I was still trying to make sense of it all.

"I'm sorry. The feeling will pass, it always does."

I simply nodded my head and tried to burrow my body further into Dan's embrace. My body shook and warmed with his laughter before he groaned, disengaging himself and rolling onto his back. I looked up at him and my stomach fluttered at the sight of him, as it always did.

He was attractive in that boy-next-door kind of way, a combination of handsome and adorable. The first time I saw him I remembered thinking he looked like the adult version of the surfers I'd grown up with: a little taller than average and lean with well-defined muscles. His hair was dark blond with hints of gold.

His symmetrical face held deep, blue eyes and his strong jawline that was almost always clean-shaven gave way to lips that were soft, full, and utterly lush. His teeth were almost completely straight, except for some crookedness on the bottom from years of forgetting to wear his retainer. For some reason, that imperfection made him approachable, though his charming, boyish smile didn't hurt.

"As much as I'd love to lie in bed with you all day, I've gotta get up and start getting ready, or I'm going to be late for my official first day. That's not the kind of impression I want to make." He got up and made his way through the closet and into the master bath.

Dan specialized in cryptanalysis and the creation and implementation of biometric technology. When we first got serious he tried explaining the basics of what he did, but science and math were never my strong points, and I always got lost and confused. It had something to do with making sure companies had the best and most advanced security in place to protect their highly confidential information.

So much of what he worked on was incredibly secret and often classified if he was on a government project. The details were protected by non-disclosure agreements, non-compete contracts, and a lot of other legal documents. It used to be really frustrating to not discuss his day at work with him because of how limited he was in what he could tell me, but I realized pretty early on that the information would be lost on me anyway, and I got over it.

While I couldn't explain to anyone asking what he did for a living in more than a few words, I knew that Dan was extremely good at what he did and one of the quickest at the firm to lead the number of projects he had. I was very proud of him and how far he had come in such a short time, but I thought a small part of him had been hoping he would have started his own firm by now.

He never complained, but we both felt this was in the cards for him, and that one day, possibly after this assignment, he might have the means and reputation to make the big move on his own. I wanted him to have all the success and opportunities he desired.

I dragged my body out of our warm bed and pulled the bench from the room into the entrance of the master bath so I could watch and talk to Dan as he shaved and got ready. I plopped down on it, leaning against the back, pulling my legs up to rest underneath me.

"You've been going to the office for the last week and a half, hasn't the first-day-jitters ship already sailed?"

"That was all just prep work and meetings to finalize my paperwork and create a general plan for the project. Today is the day I meet my team and I find out exactly who I'm working for. I haven't actually gone to the office yet. We've been meeting around town."

"That's so weird to me. Where will you be working? Which village is the office located in?" Dan wet his face with warm water and began applying shaving lotion.

The island we were living on was broken up into little villages, each with their own unique characteristics and personality.

"Wait, why are you shaving? I thought you were going to keep the beard?" I asked in dismay.

He laughed his deep, warm laugh as our eyes met in the mirror.

"I thought about keeping the beard, but I think I'll make a better first impression if I shave. Plus, in a day or two, I won't be so clean-shaven."

We both knew I liked him best a little rough around the edges. It made his good looks a bit more approachable, made him come off less preppy and perfect.

"I'm not sure where the office is or if I'll even be working in one. Rogers said they were sending a car for me this morning."

He stopped talking, contorting his face to get the

closest shave possible. I didn't miss the pensive, slightly troubled look on his face.

"I'm actually kind of nervous."

"Really? Have you ever been nervous starting a new project?"

"Not since I first started. It's strange walking into a project completely blind and I don't know what to expect. You know me, I work best when I have all the information."

"True. This is the first time you've been completely on your own too, right? That can't help either." I readjusted my body, pulling my knees up to my chest and wrapping my arms around my legs.

"Yeah, it is. It's strange not having a team from the company here. The level of secrecy surrounding this project is beyond anything I've experienced. I don't know… I think most of these feelings will go away after today," he said almost to himself.

I wasn't used to him saying so much or expressing so much uncertainty. This was the most vulnerable I had ever seen him.

"Do you ever get the feeling you're on the verge of something big? Something that will make your life unrecognizable?" he asked, putting his razor down before placing his hands palms down on the counter, leaning over slightly, and turning his upper body in my direction.

I got up and walked toward him, slipping under his arm, wrapping myself around his bare waist, leaning the small of my back against the counter. I lifted my head and looked him in the eye.

"I do. I know exactly what you mean. And just so you know, I feel it too."

I placed a kiss on his chest over his heart as he leaned down and rested his forehead against mine for a moment before placing a light, sweet kiss on my lips. I couldn't bear to tell him that the change I felt coming didn't necessarily feel like a good thing.

"Thank you for always being there for me, for always supporting me. I know it can't be easy feeling like you always come second to my career." He pulled me into a tight embrace. "It's not true, you know. You don't come second. I would choose you over this every time," he whispered in my ear before pulling away and turning his attention back to his shaving.

I settled back on the bench and felt the weight of Dan's eyes on me again. I looked up at him smiling at me with affection in his eyes. I smiled back at him, but I knew it didn't reach my eyes.

I knew he believed what he had just said, but years of experience had told me it wasn't true. His job always came first. *Always.* The birthdays, anniversaries, and holidays I spent alone only reinforced this.

The decline in communication during previous

projects did too. I had no reason to believe it would ever be any different, though I never stopped hoping. This move, this leap was made with the last bit of hope I had in me.

I didn't even blame him. This was his passion, his dream. He loved what he did. I'd known this about him when we met, when we started dating, and when we married. This wasn't a surprise to me. I had never asked him to change or put me first, always believing it was a selfish thing to do to him.

As the veil of denial I'd been living under cleared, I realized we were nearing a breaking point. The cracks in our foundation were becoming fissures, and I was holding on to the hope this time together would repair them before the damage became irreparable.

FOUR

AFTER DAN LEFT FOR WORK, I sat out on the balcony outside our bedroom for a while considering what I wanted to do with my day. I thought about driving around the island, checking out shops and galleries, but I just wasn't into that idea. This was the first time in my adult life that I didn't have a job and the free time while I figured out my next step was a novelty.

I only knew I didn't want to spend the day alone like I'd done since arriving. Marie, the owner of the B&B Dan and I had stayed at when we first got here, had extended an open invitation to visit her, and I figured today was as good a day as any to take her up on the offer.

I got into our Tesla Model S and drove to the Madrona Bed and Breakfast. As the scenery passed by my window I once again couldn't help but be in awe of how beautiful everything was. Massive trees and hills in more shades of green than I had ever seen surrounded me, magnificent and lush.

I drove for a little bit before turning off onto a smaller road. While not very well paved, it was well taken care of. I soon pulled up to a large house with a barn not much smaller than the main house. Several cars were parked in front of a short picket fence which might have been white at one time but was now varying shades of brown. While in most cases it would make the fence look decrepit, the distressing made it look charming. Shrubs and tulips ran all along the bottom of it, and the simple beauty made me smile.

The main house of the Madrona was a lovely light blue shade with lots of windows trimmed in white and a large covered porch area in front through the gate. The property was bordered by trees that looked as though they had been there forever.

I made my way into the living room with comfy-looking chairs, a fireplace, a table with games stacked underneath, and the wall opposite taken up by a large built-in bookcase holding more games and hundreds of books. I made my way over toward the books and ran my hands along the spines as I read the titles. The room filled with scents of fall: pumpkin, cinnamon, and utter deliciousness.

I walked through the rest of the living room into a

good-size dining room and called out to Marie before I hit the door leading to the kitchen.

"Hey there, Ros! I was hoping you'd stop by one of these days," Marie responded cheerfully as I walked into the room.

My jaw dropped a bit that she remembered me before I caught myself. She was standing at the huge island kneading dough, the sleeves of her blouse pushed up past her elbows, her hands covered in flour.

Marie looked up, smiled, and blew a strand of her straight, ash-blonde hair out of her face. There was something about this woman that made me feel at ease. Maybe it was the warmth of her smile or the kindness she seemed to radiate.

"I hope this is a good time." I sat down at one of the stools lined up in front of the island.

"It's a great time. How have you been? How are you liking things here on Orcas Island?"

"I'm liking it. I actually haven't gotten out much. I was starting to feel a bit stir-crazy and figured I'd stop by."

Marie nodded her head at that, looked up at me and laughed. It was a musical sound. It lightened up her entire face and made her look younger than her sixty years. "Well, we need to change that then, don't we?"

It was more a statement than an actual question, and

she went on to tell me about the island, the places I didn't want to miss out on and all the hidden gems only a local knew. I had a feeling this was something incredibly important to her and if given a chance, she likely could have spent the rest of the day telling me the history of the island.

It finally hit me why I liked this woman so much. The warmth toward strangers, the baking, the joy and passion evident in every word that passed her lips. She reminded me of what I imagined my mother would have been like had she lived long enough.

Ideas began to flow through my head about how to turn Marie into a friend. Then I started to feel self-conscious about the schemes I was hatching up. The forgotten feelings I'd had in high school started to emerge. I'd been the new kid at school trying to adjust to not knowing anyone, trying to find my way in an unfamiliar place, not having my very best friend there with me to help ease the transition. The new, awkward girl attempting to deal with the fact that my mom was gone and I would never see her again. I would never hear her voice or feel her arms wrapped around me.

Like Marie, my mom had had a musical laugh. She had also been an amazing baker and more times than not had something delicious and warm waiting for me when I got home from school each day. I hadn't realized until I was older what a treat it was, how rare and special.

I'd become adept at pushing the memories of my

mother down to the darkest recesses of my mind. I could go most days without even a thought of her entering my consciousness. Sometimes all it took was something small like a scent or an image to spark a memory. It wasn't ever just one or two. It would be several, dozens sometimes, flooding me until I was drowning in them.

The way she combed my hair gently every night, careful to not pull on it when one of the curls became knotted. The way she would then braid it into pigtails, not so tight that it would hurt my head, and not so loose that it would be a mess by morning.

The way we would read our favorite books together, her reading to me when I was younger, then us taking turns reading to each other as I got older, snuggled in my bed, each reading a chapter a night.

The way she would always ask with genuine care and interest how my day was and what had transpired when I got home from school. She always listened intently, first at stories of bullies and teachers, and, as I grew older and entered my pre-teen and early teen years, stories about which boy I had a crush on and who was dating whom, always without judgment.

Most teenagers don't realize how good they have it, but I always knew and appreciated her. She was my closest friend. Losing her was something I knew I would never recover from, and the best I could do was bury the hurt, anger, sadness, and memories so deep they almost never were able to surface and come out on their own.

But here I was, standing in a stranger's kitchen, starting to drown in the memories prompted by the sweet woman in my midst who reminded me so much of what I'd lost. I asked for a restroom and excused myself. If I stayed any longer, the waves would overtake me and I would surely drown in front of a stranger.

I stared at myself in the mirror and tried to find my mom in my face, in the few features we shared. It got harder and harder with each year that passed. I only pulled out her photos a handful of times a year—it was all I could bear. They'd become worn with age and from my touching them for so many years. They were fading the way my memory of her face was beginning to in my mind.

I could always see the resemblance between my father and me. It was there in my nose, the darker tone of my skin, in my high cheekbones, the hazel eyes we shared. If I looked hard enough, if I focused hard enough through the hurt, I could see glimpses of my mother: the sprinkle of freckles across my cheeks, the tilt of my eyes, our same stubborn chin.

Every now and then I would meet or see someone

who knew my mother while she was alive. They would say such nice things about her and tell me how much I looked like her. I know they were trying to be polite.

I always wanted to ask my dad about it, see if he saw as much of her in me as others seemed to, things I just couldn't see myself. I wondered if perhaps that was part of why there was so much distance between us, but I knew I never would mention any of it.

Even after all these years, and a new marriage under his belt, my mother was still a sore subject for him. He was likely the only person who could give me an honest, truthful answer about it, but she was not something either of us ever found ourselves able to talk about. We always tiptoed around the subject.

I shook my head and realized I had gotten lost in my thoughts and I had no idea how much time had passed or how long I had been in here. I turned on the cold water and splashed my face with it, and looked at myself again. Nothing was going to hide the red around my eyes, a sure giveaway I had been crying. A knock rapped on the door.

"Ros, are you okay?" Marie called out.

"I'll be out in a second."

Thank God my voice somehow sounded steady and even. I opened the door to Marie leaning against the opposite wall. My mouth opened to give some kind of explanation for why I'd been in there so long, but she took one long, searching look at my face and pulled me into her tight embrace before I could even utter a single word.

"Shhhh, it's okay. You don't have to say anything," she whispered in my ear as I returned the hug.

Just like my mom would have, she somehow knew exactly what I needed in that moment and gave it to me without question or explanations. As I fell into the warmth and comfort of her arms, the arms of what was basically a stranger, I couldn't help but feel grateful this woman had come into my life.

FIVE

"THIS MOVIE AGAIN, SWEETIE?" Dan breathed into my ear as he pressed a soft kiss to my neck.

I groaned, turned, and stretched out, reaching up to link my arms around his neck, pulling him closer to me. I glanced at the TV and realized I had drifted off watching Shirley MacLaine racking up dead husbands in *What a Way to Go*, one of my favorite movies. I had a serious addiction to classic films, something my mom had fostered in me.

"I missed you, babe, how did your first official day go?"

He leaned over, placing one knee on the bed next to me and both hands on either side of my head, caging me in.

"It went well, all things considered. I'm sorry it's so late," Dan murmured against my mouth.

He kissed me again lightly, sweetly, and ran his tongue along the seam of my lips. I granted him access, stroking his tongue with mine. As we continued to kiss, I shivered as desire coiled low in my belly, heat gathering between my thighs.

I moaned into his mouth, running my fingers through his hair, lightly tugging, my signal to him that I wanted to play. He groaned, lowering his body to mine, and began kissing a trail down my neck to my collarbone.

I loved this, missed this. The feel of him in my arms, the weight of his body against mine. I needed this connection with him, needed the noise of us to quiet all the thoughts in my head. While his frequent absences had created an emotional distance between us, I always knew we could connect physically, that there was a comfort found in losing ourselves in each other.

I arched my back as I ran my hands down his sides, reaching for the hem of his shirt, wanting more of his skin, to feel his warmth against me. He took the hint and sat up a bit, reached back, and tore his shirt off with one hand, a boyish grin lighting up his face.

He grabbed the hem of my shirt and said, "Off, now," his voice rough with desire, the sound of it sending a shiver down my spine.

I sat up, crossing my arms, and pulled my shirt off. Before I could get it past my hair, Dan slipped a hand behind my back, pressing my body up toward his. His lips wrapped around my nipple, sucking it into his mouth.

I moaned again and rolled my hips up to meet his, silently begging him to cut to the chase and put us out of our misery. He laid me back down, switching his attention to my other nipple, running his tongue over it the way he knew I loved, lightly biting it in the way he knew would make me wet almost instantly.

I whimpered and moved my hips faster, trying desperately to get some friction, anything to ease the growing ache between my thighs. Or ramp it up, I wasn't sure at this point.

I moved my hands between our bodies and ran them down his chest to his flat, ripped stomach. I reached for his belt buckle, impatiently tugging to loosen it and work his pants off, first with my hands, and then with my feet. He laughed. I returned his smile. He stood up and finished taking them off, tossing them to the side.

Dan stopped and stared at me with a look so full of lust and love, my breath caught. Before I could breathe again, his hand slid down my body, caressing as he went: the side of my breast, a whisper against my ribcage, a feathering on the curve of my stomach, a quick grip on my hip, the light pressure of fingers on the inside of my thigh. His hand then dipped between my legs, tracing my center through my thin pajama pants.

"Shit," he groaned. "You're already so fucking wet, I can feel you through your pants."

Dan was normally so reserved, but I loved how filthy his mouth got when we were intimate. He slid his body down mine until I could feel his warm breath between my thighs.

"Fuck, I can even smell you. So good, baby. I've missed this."

He pulled my pants and panties off with a firm tug and dropped them to the floor as I quickly wrapped my legs around his waist and tried to pull him down on top of me, wanting him inside of me, feeling like I would die if he didn't fill me right then.

He moved down my body, spread my legs further with his wide shoulders and looked up, giving me a devilish smirk that made me even wetter, if that was possible. His head dipped down as he licked my slit with the flat of his tongue.

My back arched so hard in response, I almost screamed. He continued at a steady pace, sometimes focusing his attention firmly on my clit, lapping at my wetness, drinking my desire.

"Dan, this feels so good, but I want you inside me," I managed to groan out through my panting.

He said nothing but gave me a look I recognized. One that said he wasn't going to stop until he was good and ready to. Before I knew it, I arched off the bed again, back bowed, grabbing at his hair as I forced his face right up against me, exploding on his tongue as his mouth continued to devour me.

As I came down, he pulled away, smiling at me, and I couldn't help but giggle. I loved that about us, that our lovemaking was always full of smiles and laughter along with the passion.

He climbed his way back up my body, kissing me roughly on the mouth and grinding his thick, hard length against my overly sensitive bundle of nerves. I could taste my arousal in his kiss, and I felt how ready he was for me.

I wrapped my legs around his waist again, crossing my ankles and resting them on his tight ass. I began to grind against him, my wetness making us both slippery.

"More. I need more. I need to feel you inside me now," I begged, still breathless from my orgasm and his kiss.

He reached up and pulled my hair, not gently, just rough enough to send another flood of wetness to my core, and plunged inside me with one hard push.

This. This was what I missed so much all the months he was gone. Every. Single. Time.

He began thrusting into me slowly, setting his rhythm and pace, my hips matching it. I closed my eyes, my head rolling back. I could feel my muscles tightening and knew it wouldn't be long before I shattered again. It wasn't always like this, but things were always more intense right after a long separation.

"Fuck, I don't know how much longer I can hold out, you feel so fucking good," he whispered harshly in my ear.

I kissed him hard, forcing my tongue into his mouth, wanting to taste him and myself mingled together. Our bodies were so in tune, years of experience guiding us to the rhythm that would guarantee our mutual release, like a dance we had done so many times it was muscle memory, despite all the time we spent apart.

Our pace increased to the music of our bodies meeting, my moans and panting, his groans. Our sounds sang out a chorus of harder, faster, more, deeper, right there.

I fell apart again, the breath I'd been holding rushing out. I contracted around his length, feeling him harden and pulse, groaning out his release moments later. He dropped his forehead to mine as I collapsed backward, spent and exhausted.

"I so needed this. I missed it. I missed you. I thought you would be around more with this project, but I've barely seen you over the last few weeks," I said, laughing from the relief of release.

"I needed that too, baby. I hope after we get the new

project kinks worked out that I'll get to be home more. How was your day? What did you end up doing?" Dan rolled us onto our sides, pulling me close, throwing his leg over mine.

"It was good. I spent some time with Marie at the Madrona. It was nice to get out and actually have some human contact."

"Who's Marie?" he asked in a faraway voice. He was much closer to sleep than I was.

"Marie is the owner of the Madrona, the B and B we stayed at when we first got here. Sweet, older woman?"

I didn't know why this surprised me. Dan had proven time and time again that if it wasn't on his immediate radar, he forgot about it, including things that had just happened. This was another reason I'd spent so many birthdays, anniversaries, and holidays alone.

I turned over to continue the conversation, only to see he was already asleep. As I snuggled back into his hold, attempting to find a comfortable position so that I could fall asleep, I envied his ability to pass out at the drop of a hat.

⎯⎯⎯⎯

Hours later, I was still wide awake. I disentangled myself from Dan's embrace, grabbed the blanket from the bench in front of the bed and made my way out onto the balcony.

The air was chilly and it was lightly misting, but I could hear the crashing of the waves along the shore below and found a certain peace in that. I wrapped the blanket tightly around my shoulders and sat on the outdoor sofa, cuddling into the cushions and pillows, finally finding a comfortable position.

I tried to calm my brain down, using some of the meditation techniques Jos had tried teaching me. As I decided to try a different breathing exercise, the hairs on the back of my neck stood up and it felt like someone was standing behind me.

"Dan, is that you?"

Nothing. He was still in bed and I was completely alone out here, though it didn't feel that way. I turned back around, figuring it was paranoia getting to me.

Then it happened again, the sensation that someone else was here. I looked around, got up and walked the entire length of the balcony and back. No one was there, but I couldn't shake it.

Probably an animal or something.

Settling back into the chair, I closed my eyes, taking deep breaths to calm down. Rationally, logically, I knew I was alone. I had to be imagining things because it was more remote out here than I was used to. I'd gone from having neighbors shouting distance away to having to drive a couple of minutes to reach the closest.

I finally calmed down when a breeze started to stir. It was almost like a caress on my neck, as though someone gently ran their fingertips along the nape.

As the sensation warmed my body and sent a shiver down my spine at the same time, I got the scent of something warm and masculine and divine. There was no other way to describe it. My eyes fluttered closed as the scent of sandalwood, something sweet like tobacco, musk, and salty ocean enveloped me.

It was quite possibly the best thing I'd ever smelled. Comforting, slightly arousing, a heady combination. As the scent and the caress of the wind faded, I opened my eyes and looked around one more time, hoping to find the source of the airy touch and intoxicating scent. I came up empty.

I went inside after and tried to watch TV and then read, all in an attempt to distract myself from what had happened on the balcony. It sat there in the back of my mind, needling at me, like a puzzle my subconscious was trying to solve. I tried to brush it off to some lingering discomfort in a new house, but I knew it wasn't true. This place already felt like home.

I couldn't forget that scent, or the sense of someone being out there with me, the caress. It brought back the dream from last night. What had happened out on the balcony brought out the same emotions the dream had. The windblown touch elicited the same excitement as when the man had touched me in my sleep. It made absolutely no sense and I realized the only thing I could do was try to ignore it all, push it out of my mind.

SIX

THE SENSATION of being watched never went away. A month had passed since it first started, and I should have been used to the feeling of featherlight caresses on my neck and hands, as often as it happened.

Every single time I would look around the property, inspect every room of the house, and double-check the security system, but I was always alone. It should have creeped me out or scared me—that would have been the reasonable reaction to what was going on—but it never did.

I hadn't mentioned it to Dan, because what was I going to say? "Hey, honey, it feels like someone is watching me or stalking me, even though I don't know anyone here, and our closest neighbor is at least a mile away, and it makes no logical sense."

CECE FERRELL

I decided at least that could be a safe topic to broach with Dan. One that wouldn't make me seem so crazy. The last thing I wanted was for Dan to start worrying about me while he was in the midst of what could be the most important project of his life.

Nearly two months here on the island and three weeks into the new job, and Dan was already working crazy hours. He often wasn't home before midnight and was gone most mornings before the sun had fully risen.

Toward the end of the week, he had finally made it home in time for dinner, so I decided to broach the topic. I just wasn't sure how to insert it into our conversation.

Did I just throw it out there? Get it on the table and out of the way? I nibbled on my nail, considering the best way to do this without looking like I had lost my mind. Because really, it felt like I was losing my mind.

"Hello? Hello? Anybody in there?" Dan waved his hands in front of my face.

I shook my head to regain focus and looked up at him. "Huh?"

He laughed, shaking his head at me. "You were on another planet, babe. I must have asked you the same question a few times. You were staring off into space. You okay?"

"Yeah, yeah, everything's fine. I was just thinking about stuff and guess I got a little caught up in my thoughts. Sorry. What were you asking?"

"I was asking how your day was. I know I've been working crazy hours and we haven't been able to talk, let alone spend any time together."

"Things are okay. I haven't explored as much as I would like yet, but now that we have a pretty good idea of what your schedule's like, I will."

"Sounds like a good plan. I know you're not used to being cooped up in the house."

"I'm not, but the little break was nice. And yeah, I'm not crazy about all the hours you've been working, but it's nice not having to go to bed alone every night," I said before taking a bite of my food.

I leaned my head to the side, my thoughts returning to what I wanted to ask him. I decided to just go for it. He already knew my style of crazy, why not add a little more to the mix?

After another couple bites, I launched into it. "So, this may sound kinda funny, but do you ever get the feeling you're being watched?"

"Yep. Every single morning." He tried to hide the smirk but failed miserably.

"Ugh, you're the worst! You know exactly what I mean. I know you haven't spent much time in the house, but when you're alone, do you ever get the feeling like you aren't alone?"

He sat for a minute, chewing his food and considering my question. He swallowed and took a drink of his water.

"No. But like you said, I haven't been here much. Maybe it's an animal? Or maybe it's just living in a new place and the fact this house is a little more isolated than you're used to? I don't know, babe. But I haven't felt it."

"Yeah, maybe. Have you ever suddenly smelled something? Like a sudden strong smell of sandalwood and tobacco?"

"No, are you sure it's not my shower wash?"

"No, this doesn't smell like you. This is a very distinct scent. I smell it when I get that feeling someone might be nearby or watching me." I whispered the last thing, moving the remaining food around my plate with the fork before looking up at him.

"Are you trying to tell me you think there is a ghost or something living in this house? A great-smelling, male ghost, perhaps?" he asked, no longer able to contain his laughter.

"Of course not! I was mostly just trying to pinpoint where the scent was coming from. If I could, I would bottle it and make a fortune. I dunno, I'm probably just not used to the scent of nature."

Even I could tell I was trying to convince myself more than him. We continued to eat in silence, me trying to figure out a way to change the subject and forget about this entire conversation. Dan looked like he was spacing out a little, so I had no idea what was going on in his head at all.

"So how's work going?" I asked awkwardly, leaning back in my chair and rubbing my hands over my full stomach.

"It's going well. The first month is usually just the planning phase anyway, identifying what we need to accomplish, figuring out a timeline, planning ways to accomplish everything necessary in the time allotted."

"Hmmm." Dan knew this was code to continue.

"A lot of team-building happens early on too, making sure we're all on the same page and working well together." He leaned back in his chair, rubbing the muscles at the nape of his neck absently.

"So, what's this project all about? Have you met the owner of the company yet?"

I knew he wouldn't be able to tell me much because of the highly confidential nature of it. His job title on his business card was a very vague "IT consultant." Yep, that was it.

He grinned at me before responding. And while I could see the humor in his eyes at my question, I could also see them start to shutter, closing down the way they did any time I asked for more details about his work. "There's not much I can say, babe, as much as I would love to. I've only met the owner of the company once. My new boss is Liam Maris."

"Wait, you're working for MarisCorp? Seriously?" I nearly jumped out of my seat at the mention of the mysterious billionaire.

"Yeah, I was just as shocked. Sorry I didn't mention it sooner."

"So, what's Maris like?"

"I don't really know. He's extremely reclusive and I've only met him twice."

"That's it? That's all you've got for me?"

"He owns an island nearby and he boats or choppers to and from the small facility here when necessary. Most work outside of administrative tasks happens at a facility on his island, so there is a pretty good chance I will spend most of my time working there."

I knew I wasn't going to get anything else out of him, so I changed my line of questioning. "You haven't talked about your team much. Tell me about them."

"There's only four of us. There's two other guys, Ben and Rashad, and one woman, Kelly. So far, they seem nice, and more importantly, very smart and hard-working. I have a good feeling about this, Ros."

"I'm excited for you, Dan. And really proud of you."

His answering smile warmed me from the inside. "Thanks, babe."

He grabbed both of our plates off the table and

walked to the kitchen. I stood up and walked over to the island, leaning over and resting on my crossed forearms, watching him as he rinsed our dishes and placed them in the dishwasher, so happy to just have him here with me.

"Hey, want to watch a movie?" He dried his hands off, a signal that he was done talking about work.

"Sure, what are you in the mood for? Wait, bedroom or living room?"

"It's still pretty early, and I don't want to go to bed just yet. How 'bout we watch in the living room? Let me just go get changed first."

I walked into the living room, sat down, turned on the TV and got comfortable as I sifted through all of our saved movies on our Apple TV. Nothing looked remotely interesting, so I put the remote down and decided to let Dan choose. I knew what I would have chosen, and I was pretty sure he didn't want to see one of my classics.

He came back a few minutes later in a gray t-shirt and loose gray lounge pants that hung on his hips in a seriously distracting way. He grabbed the remote off the table, slouched in the corner of the couch, getting comfortable, and opened his arms up for me to snuggle against him, wrapping his arms around me once we were settled.

"Did you find something for us that was filmed after 1970?" His laugh tickled my neck, sending a shiver down my spine. He continued to nuzzle into my neck, inhaling my scent as he waited for my response.

"Nope, it's your turn."

I barely suppressed my moan as he pressed featherlight kisses along my neck, my jawline, the corner of my mouth. This was quickly turning into something other than movie-watching.

I turned to face him fully, only to have him crash his lips into mine, at first hard and demanding, then slower and more seductive as I responded by gasping and turning my body flush against his. I could feel his growled response against my chest as he thrust his tongue into my mouth in a rhythm matching what I wanted him to do to my body.

The remote control crashed against the floor as it slipped out of his hand. I jumped up in surprise, which Dan took full advantage of by twisting us until he was sitting slightly slouched down. He pulled my thigh over his lap, so I was straddling him firmly.

His kisses alternated between passionate and harsh, and sweet and slow, leaving me breathless and gasping. Delicious pressure built between my thighs, desire and tension making me grind myself against him for relief. It didn't make anything better, it never did. It only succeeded in making me burn hotter, want him more.

We continued at that maddening pace, not slowing

down or stopping until our climaxes had crashed through us.

It was always like this. No matter the distance between us, the amount of time spent apart, we always came together without skipping a beat.

Frantic, desperate, familiar.

Even when all the other parts of us seemed to be tearing at the seams, this was always right. Maybe it was because things always felt both new and fleeting.

Until now, we never knew how much time we had together to enjoy each other, but it was never much. Our time together was always more famine than feast. My mind wandered, and I couldn't help but think back to the night before we moved here.

We had just sat down to dinner, and I looked down into my food, avoiding eye contact until I could figure out what I wanted to say. I couldn't ignore the tension anymore and I couldn't pretend. How did I communicate that things were just not feeling right between us when communication was our biggest issue? Dan took it out of my hands.

"What's up, babe?" he asked in a concern-laced voice.

"So," I began and let the word hang for a minute. "I don't know if it's just me, but things have been feeling off between us lately."

Dan's smile faded, some of the light left his eyes, and it made me regret even bringing it up. My hands started to feel a little clammy as nervousness set in. This was so absurd. He was my husband, not some guy I had only been dating for a few months. The realization why hit me like a punch in the gut.

The disconnect, the unease all pointed to years of shitty communication, which we ignored and covered up with false intimacy and great sex. He was coming and going so much, our time together almost always felt a little like a honeymoon: reunion, elation, reacquaintance, the beginnings of getting comfortable together again, only to be halted by another separation.

I sighed and started again. "I hate to bring this up, but I just don't want us going any further into this new start with any negative shit between us. You feel it too, right?"

He looked down a moment, and then looked back up. "Yeah, I've been feeling it the last couple weeks, but I didn't want to bring it up and ruin anything," he said.

"I'd gotten my hopes up so high and the reality of the situation began to creep in. We don't know how much time we will actually get to be together and we don't know how us living together will affect things. What if it doesn't work?"

The minute the words left my mouth, I wanted to take it all back. I'd never pictured myself as an emotionally needy wife. I was used to being second place. It had always been fine because I knew Dan loved me. Lately, I couldn't help but wonder if he would ever choose our marriage over work, if he would ever put us first. I knew there was nothing more I could say tonight without causing damage to us.

Dan grabbed my hand across the table and intertwined his fingers with mine.

"We don't know what's to come, and while it could be crazy and stressful, it could also be amazing. I never want to be the source of your unhappiness. I promise I will try to balance time at home with you and time spent on work as equally as possible."

Tears welled up in my eyes and I tried to will them away. The first one slid down my cheek, then another, and another, before so many were falling, I couldn't stop them. All the pent-up tension, worry, and emotion of the past few weeks just took over me, and I was a ball of emotions too out of control to handle.

Dan stood up and walked over to me, kneeling down beside my chair. I turned to him and he wrapped his arms around me, resting his chin on the top of my head. My arms gripped his waist, and before I knew it, I was crying again.

"Shhh, it's okay, babe, I promise," he said, rubbing my back. He lifted my chin up with his hand until my eyes met his. "I know things have been crazy recently, but everything is going to work out," he said, looking me in the eyes, trying to be as reassuring as possible.

I rested my cheek against his chest, rubbed my face on the soft wool of his sweater and nodded. While I didn't feel certain, he seemed sure enough for the both of us, and I realized it was going to have to be enough for me.

I knew not to get used to it. To not get my hopes up

that we could build on this for the next six months or even year. I knew not to put full trust in what he had said that night or assume we could use our physical connection to help sew back together all the other parts of our relationship coming apart.

I knew not to, but God did I ever hope for it.

SEVEN

"SO I DID what anyone in my situation would do. I burned the place down when he went to work the next day," Josie said.

"Wait, what?" I shrieked, pressing the phone closer to my ear.

"Seriously, Ros? What is going on with you? You've been so out of it this entire conversation, I just started saying the most ridiculous things to see if you were listening."

"I'm sorry, Jos, I've just had a lot on my mind lately."

I didn't even know where to begin. I'd pretty much been avoiding all of my friends and hadn't talked to Dan on more than a superficial level when he was around, which wasn't often.

He kept saying things would calm down soon, but I was starting to think he was just telling me things to keep me thinking and feeling positive about all the changes and sacrifices we'd made to do this.

"So why don't you start at the beginning and tell me about it. I know it's different when we aren't a ten-minute drive from each other, and I can't just pop by unannounced to eat your food and drink your booze, but that doesn't mean I'm any less here for you."

"I know, I know." I sighed.

"Actually, bitch, why aren't we FaceTiming anyway? We can drink wine and bitch about how much you hate it there and how there's a particular circle of hell for friends who fuck your boyfriends," she said, obviously joking, but I knew her well enough to recognize the underlying sadness in her voice.

My phone buzzed in my hand. I looked at the screen and saw it was her wanting to connect to FaceTime.

"Did you just use FaceTime as a verb?" I asked as I answered the call.

"Damn straight I did. It's an action, right? Hell, give it a couple of years, and I bet it will make its way into the dictionary! Anyway, I've got my wine." She held up what might have been one of the biggest glasses I'd ever seen. "Where's yours? C'mon, grab some, I'll wait. We both need this girls' night."

I knew there was no way I was getting out of drinking something with her and it was feeling like a Jim Beam and Coke kind of night anyway.

"Hey, I'm gonna grab my iPad while I'm getting a drink, I'll call you back when I get back outside, okay?"

I hung up before she had a chance to respond. I walked back out to the balcony off my bedroom a few minutes later, my iPad and stand tucked under my arm, a mug containing my drink in my hands, along with the bottle and an unopened can of Coke, just in case I wanted a refill. And to convince Josie I was, in fact, drinking something stronger than tea in my mug.

"Thatta girl," she said when I called her back after setting my iPad up in its stand on the outdoor coffee table. She saw the table beside me with what I was drinking, and raised her glass up in the universal gesture for cheers. I half-heartedly mirrored her gesture.

"Okay, so let's start with what crawled up your ass, and then I will retell my story of romantic woe, just without the embellishments. And go!" she said, taking a huge gulp.

It looked like she drank a quarter of her half-bottle-sized glass in one huge swig. I sighed and took a sip of my drink. "I don't know, Jos. Nothing is really wrong, but things just don't feel right, ya know?"

"Like what?"

"I think I need to get out more, meet more people. I've spent too much time alone in this house." I paused and took another drink, staring off at the water below.

"I know how much you struggle with that, how hard it can be for you to come out of your shell."

"I'm still in this creative rut. I thought I'd get here and instantly be moved by the environment to create new art." I stopped and took a drink, trying to collect my thoughts into something coherent. Jos let me do my thing and didn't try to interrupt. "I let my lack of inspiration keep me from creating a collection at home. So I stayed at the gallery helping Cindy, teaching classes for far longer than I should have. But now I don't have that excuse and I just feel…"

"Stuck. You feel stuck," Jos answered for me, seeing through my ramblings and finding the right word when I couldn't.

"Yeah. And then Dan hasn't been home much and is mentally wiped when he is. He says it'll ease up and get better after this phase is done in a week or two."

"Do you think it will?"

"I don't know. I hope so." I shrugged, trying to brush off what I was feeling. "I'm just disappointed things aren't going as I expected. And I miss you guys so much."

Josie looked at me, sipping her wine, attempting to stare into my soul or something through the screen. It was unnerving. I started to fidget and was about to say something when she started talking.

She always had some weird ability to see through my

bullshit and the walls I put up, but I guessed it was one of the benefits of knowing someone almost all your life.

"So, all that shit makes sense. Being surrounded by trees all day every day by myself would probably drive me up a wall. But what else is bothering you? And don't tell me nothing. I can see it, and you know it's no use lying to me anyway. Spill." She gave me her "I'll cut you, bitch" look.

"Ugh, this is going to sound so stupid and ridiculous. Sometimes, and by sometimes I mean almost all the time when I'm the only one in the house, I get this feeling like someone is watching me."

"What do you mean?"

"Sometimes it feels like someone is standing right behind me, other times it feels like someone is walking by and lightly brushing their fingertips against my arm or my neck or my hand. Sometimes there's a sudden breeze when there shouldn't be."

"Okay, that's strange, but continue," she interjected as she took a sip of her wine.

"You wanna know what's even more strange?"

"There's something stranger than what you just told me?"

I ignored her sarcasm and pressed on. "Every single time this happens, I smell the best scent ever. It's masculine, and crisp, and clean. I almost drool a little, it's that good. I only smell it when I get the feeling that I'm not alone," I finished, trying to take a sip of my drink, only to realize it was empty.

I refilled my mug while Josie looked at me curiously like she was trying to figure out if I was serious or not.

"Did you talk to Dan about this?"

"Yep."

"And what did he say? I'm guessing his response was less than satisfactory if you are here reluctantly talking to me about it and all freaked out. I don't know why you haven't brought this up before now. We talk about everything, even anal sex!" she exclaimed.

"No, you talked about anal sex, I sat there uncomfortably trying to ignore you, wishing I was somewhere else."

"I don't understand what your issue with anal is. You shouldn't be afraid of the back door. I bet you would love it if you tried it."

"Okay, first of all, you have no idea whether I've tried it or not. Second, just because I don't want to talk about something doesn't mean I have an issue with it. Can nothing be sacred? Just because I won't have detailed conversations about my sex life doesn't mean I'm not having sex. I'm not a prude, there are just some things I think would be weird to go into detail about."

"Yeah, yeah. You think I don't know all this by now? It's why we work, babe. We're just different enough and similar enough not to want to kill each other," she responded sweetly.

I laughed into my drink as she continued to look at me innocently, batting her lashes at me. She was right though. I was definitely the more reserved of the two, always more introverted and introspective, while she was hilarious, often crude, and utterly lovable.

"But really, what did he say?"

"He said it was probably nothing. It was likely an animal nearby, and the smell was probably the ocean, or his body wash. I don't know, he pretty much brushed it off, and I already feel kind of stupid about the whole thing," I said, shrugging my shoulders.

She didn't say anything for a while. We each just sat staring at our screens, drinking our drinks, contemplating if I was indeed going as crazy as I felt I was. Well, at least that was what *I* was contemplating.

"I call bullshit on that explanation," she finally said. "You would know if it were an animal watching you. You would hear them, or see their eyes or something. He was probably trying to calm you down." Jos took another drink and tapped her finger on her chin in contemplation. "Or he was being a dick by disregarding you. Could it be a neighbor? Maybe you have a peeping Tom or some creepy teenager watching you through his bedroom window." Sometimes it was so hard to keep up with her train of thought.

"No, he wasn't being a dick. You know how oblivious Dan is when he's in his own headspace. And nope, we don't have any neighbors within sight. It's pretty remote up here. Although the idea someone is creeping around and watching me is even scarier than a wild animal watching me or it being all in my head." I shivered, looking around and rubbing the goose bumps that rose up on my arms.

"Oh, stop. There's no one there right now, silly. You'd have felt it. You're just getting weirded out by our conversation," she scolded, and then went quiet as a look crossed her face.

I recognized that look. It meant an idea was brewing. It was never good when she got it. It usually led to us embarking on "adventures" which ended in me hurt or scared and telling her I was never trusting her hare-brained ideas again. "No, no, no. You can stop right there with whatever idea just popped into your twisted little mind, Josephine Mae Davis. The last time you gave me that look, I ended up with a broken foot and nearly got arrested!"

"Hey, it could've worked! I didn't know the rocks were so slippery. Or that your top would come undone as you fell. Or that there was a family with kids within view. Man, will you ever forgive me and let it go?" she asked in a huff, crossing her arms over her chest.

"Nope, never. My foot still hurts on really cold days."

"Yeah, but it was kind of worth it, right?"

I groaned in response, taking a drink. I knew there was no use in me trying to argue with her. And it had been kind of worth it at the time.

"Anyway, I know exactly what it is!" she nearly shouted, excited by her theory.

"And what would that be? An android or something?" I asked, unable to suppress my snarky retort.

"No, but it actually isn't a half-bad idea. But it's really wet where you live, so that doesn't really make any logical sense. It's a ghost. You have a ghost following you around."

"Seriously, Jos? A ghost makes more logical sense to you than an android? Also, I'm pretty sure androids are waterproof. A ghost? This is the last time I confide in you about anything like this. Pfft, a fucking ghost," I murmured to myself, taking the last sip of my drink.

"What? It's possible! Just you wait. When you find you are living with a hot ghost, you can let me know, and I'll make sure a pottery wheel is delivered, and I won't even say I told you so."

At this point, she couldn't contain her laughter. My shoulders began to shake, and I couldn't hold it in any longer either. Before I knew it, we were both laughing hysterically, tears streaming down my face.

"So, are you going to tell me what happened with Jason? I want the full, honest truth. Not this dramatic retelling you try to pass off as the truth. I'm sure it's spicy enough without needing embellishment, knowing you."

"I've pretty much just finished off this entire bottle of wine on my own, and your stuff is so much more fun to talk about. Can we just skip my shit for now?"

"Nope, no way. You've intrigued me, and I am sick of focusing on myself. Talk."

"Fine, but you are getting the super-condensed version of it. It's really not interesting anyway. Remember I had that seminar I needed to teach? Oh, wait, no, you don't, because you've been MIA, bitch!" she began, going off on a tangent.

I was used to reining her back in and leading her back to the conversation we were supposed to be having. "Yeah. I'm sorry, okay? Now, back to the seminar."

"Oh. So yeah, I was supposed to teach it, and there were probably a good hundred people signed up, which is the biggest group I've been scheduled for."

"Okay," I said as I gave her the gesture to hurry it along. It was useless, Jos would tell the story at her pace.

She rolled her eyes before continuing, "So I asked Veronica to help me. She agreed, but then texted me a couple of hours before it started saying she was sick, food poisoning or something."

"Uh-huh. What does this have to do with Jason?"

"I'm getting to it, will you please stop interrupting?"

She shook her head at me in exasperation. "I'd tried to make plans with Jason for after the seminar, but he had some important meeting he needed to prep for. So I show up at the studio only to find out there had been a small electrical fire and everything was soaked when the sprinklers went off. We had to cancel the seminar."

"Holy shit, Jos! Is everything okay?"

"Yeah, no one was injured and the damage to the studio was minor," she said, waving her hand to brush off my concerns. "Anyway, I figured I'd surprise Jason with some dessert and hang out for a bit since it was still really early."

She stopped and poured herself the last of the wine, swirling it around in her glass. She normally wasn't one to stall, but I had an idea where this was going, so I let her.

"Well, he'd given me a key to his place a couple of weeks earlier. I know it was kinda quick, but he assured me he was serious about us. He must have forgotten I had the key. I entered and he wasn't in the living room, but I heard noises coming from the bedroom. I decided to surprise him, so I stripped down naked in the living room and threw open the bedroom door saying I had dessert and *was* dessert."

I laughed out loud at the move that screamed Jos. "What happened?"

"Well, it would've been pretty epic if I hadn't walked

in on him and Veronica sixty-nining. Wanna know the worst part of it?" I couldn't hold in my gasp, but Jos kept right on going.

"There is something worse than walking in on your friend and boyfriend simultaneously rounding third base?"

She sniffle-laughed, and it was heartbreaking to see her so upset over the douche. It took a lot to upset or rattle her.

"The worst part was when they both looked up, he smiled and asked me to join them! And Veronica just looked at me and shrugged, like, why not? I mean seriously, who the fuck does that?"

"Your douchey ex? What did you do? You didn't call me from jail, so it wasn't anything too crazy, right?"

"I did what any normal person in my position would do. I dumped my dessert over the custom suit hanging on his closet door and let him know she'd just tested positive for herpes a month ago. It was a lie, as far as I know, but the look on his face was priceless. I don't know if he was more pissed about the thousands he would have to spend to replace that suit or potential exposure to genital sores."

"Wow. I don't think I would've had the forethought to do anything more than walk out. And Veronica? That was beyond a cunty thing to do to a friend. I'm sorry, babe, it just fucking sucks. See, it's times like these where I wish I could just drive over with booze and hugs."

I hated being so far away while she was going through all this. She deserved to have me there with her to hug her and get her wasted on wine and ice cream and popcorn while watching old movies.

"I'll be fine. I really liked him, but it wasn't like I was full-blown in love yet. Anyway, you telling me about your ghostly suitor when he finally makes his appearance will make up for all this drama," she said as she smiled and brushed a tear away. I shook my head and rolled my eyes at her.

"What if it's a woman?" I asked, laughing with her at the silliness of the whole thing.

EIGHT

I WAS STANDING on my balcony, leaning on the railing, looking at the trees and water below me. It was that fleeting time of day where it wasn't quite daytime and wasn't quite dusk, but you could feel the change in the air. It was misting so heavily it was almost drizzling.

I thought I saw someone at the water's edge. A slight form dressed in white. It wasn't a child, but they almost looked too small to be an adult. I watched as they leaned over to touch the water.

They must have lost their balance because all of a sudden, they began to slip. It was so hard to see though, I didn't trust my eyes, but I leaned forward and started shouting, shouting until my voice was hoarse. I pushed myself away from the balcony edge so I could run down and help.

In my haste, I tripped. Next thing I knew, I was

falling over the edge of the balcony. I opened my mouth to scream, but I had no voice left, even if I could get a sound to make it past the absolute terror paralyzing me.

I flailed my arms.

I tried to remember what lay directly beneath the part of the balcony I had fallen over. Was it soft grass or was I destined to leave a broken body on the paver stones below? Just as I thought the ground was upon me, I was caught up quick and tight. I opened my eyes and cautiously looked around to see what had been my salvation.

The first thing I made eye contact with was a beautiful, expressive pair of green eyes. I gasped as butterflies rioted in my stomach at the same time this intense feeling of comfort came over me. I was tucked firmly in the man's arms, and he was holding me like he was about to carry me over the threshold. I breathed in deeply, leaned my head back slightly, and took in his face.

It was the same man who had been in the dream I had before. It all finally clicked in my head, though my body had been clued into this fact the minute he touched me. I somehow knew this man, intimately and soul-deep.

Before I could move or say anything, he leaned his head toward mine and whispered in my ear in an impossibly deep, soothing voice, "I've got you. You're here with me now."

The man pulled back and I closed my eyes for a moment. When I opened them, his lips were only a breath away from mine, and my insides swooped and freefell, as though I was on a roller coaster.

Just as our lips made light contact, I jerked awake.

I placed my hand on my heaving chest as I tried to get my breathing to calm down. I didn't know how a dream could affect me this way, but it was becoming a frequent occurrence since moving to the island.

Some nights I had no recollection of the details, but the vivid, stirring emotions took hours to dissipate. The few I did remember were all different, but this same man always appeared.

Dan stirred beside me, stretching and groaning.

"Everything okay, babe?" he mumbled in his gravely, sleep-filled voice.

"Yeah, yeah. Everything's fine. It was just a dream."

"Then come here."

I lay back down and let him pull my back to his front, his arms wrapped tightly around my waist. He fell back asleep pretty much instantaneously, but no matter how hard I tried, I just couldn't. I couldn't shake the feeling the dream brought out.

After over an hour of tossing and turning, I decided to get up and do something to try to distract myself. I went downstairs to make myself a cup of tea and grabbed my notebook and pencil. I curled up in the comfy armchair and stared outside.

It was so dark and misty I couldn't see anything. I doodled and drank my tea, trying to think of something, anything other than the dream.

I closed my eyes, resting my head on the back of the chair. My thoughts drifted to the things Jos and I had discussed, the other things bothering me.

Something had to change. I needed to change. Somehow, I'd allowed myself to become a hermit up here on this hill. I had to start getting out, exploring, making friends.

A couple of months was more than enough time to get adjusted to a new place. Now it was time to start living. I decided that in the morning I would venture out and explore the island more.

I finally felt my body start to relax when a slight breeze moved past me, even though all the doors and windows were closed. Then came the sensation of fingertips brushing over my hand, followed closely by that scent.

Before I could stop myself, I inhaled deeply. I really loved that damn smell. The sensation that someone was standing close to me, watching me? Yeah, I did not enjoy the feeling. Dan's joke about it being a ghost and being haunted slammed right back in my mind.

"Hello?" I called out in almost a whisper. "Is anyone there?"

There was no response. I looked through all the windows in the room to see if I could see anyone or anything out there. Nothing. The scent was already starting to dissipate.

"I'm seriously losing it, aren't I? Talking to ghosts." I laughed to myself, shaking my head. I decided to head back to bed.

As my foot hit the first stair, the scent washed back over me with renewed strength, and again something whispered across the palm of my hand and down my fingers. I shivered, my skin instantly covered in goose bumps.

"Hello?"

Again, I got no response, so I headed the rest of the way upstairs. I usually only bought into logic. Try as I might, I could not seem to find a reasonable explanation for any of this that made sense and felt right in my heart.

But ghosts? There was no way. I know some people believed they existed, but I was not one of them. No, there was obviously some explanation I was missing right now, but I was certain it would come to me eventually.

This day was already making me its bitch.

I couldn't stop the thought from going through my head as I dragged my body downstairs and into the kitchen. I considered turning around and heading right back to bed. I had missed too much sleep the night before and ended up sleeping in, causing me to miss watching Dan get ready for work.

It had become a nice morning ritual I loved and needed since it was really the only time we got to spend together now. His work had picked up, not slowed down.

The project was a couple of months in, and the planning phase would be complete this week. I hoped it meant he would be around a little more, but if experience had taught me anything, especially recently, I knew not to get my hopes up too much.

I made my way down to the coffee pot knowing today called for something stronger than my usual tea. There was a note right next to the pot from Dan, letting me know he hoped I got to sleep in, and that he loved and missed me. I smiled as I traced my fingertips along his bold, clear writing.

I went about making my coffee, had breakfast standing at the counter flipping through a magazine, and turned back to grab the note from Dan. I had a box I kept little things like this in.

For some reason, the note wasn't next to the coffee

pot where I had left it, and I spent the next fifteen minutes tearing the kitchen apart trying to find it. It was gone, had disappeared into thin air. I was a little sad about it but figured it would turn up later, and even if it didn't, it wasn't the biggest deal.

Until I found it in my notebook at the coffee shop.

"How was your day, babe?" Dan headed to the couch with our beers while I trailed him with our dinner plates.

"It was great. I got out of the house and I really like it here so far. Strangely enough, it kinda already feels like home."

I paused to take a bite and shrugged, then looked up and smiled at him. Dan returned the smile and we both sat in slightly awkward silence as we ate our dinners. I suddenly remembered the note from earlier.

"Sweetie, I saw your note this morning. Did you happen to write two of them?" I asked, aware as it came out of my mouth how silly it sounded.

"Two notes? You mean two different ones? Are you talking about the note I left near the coffee pot this morning?"

"Yeah. But no, I mean two of the same."

I could tell by his questions he had not, in fact, written more than one version of the note.

"Why would I do that?"

"I don't know. I saw the one you left at the coffee pot but it was gone when I went to put it away a few minutes later."

"Okay, but I don't get why that would make you think I wrote two of the same note, Ros."

I bit back my exasperation, knowing it wouldn't get us anywhere. "Because I tore up the kitchen looking for it with no luck. Then I found it tucked in a notebook I hadn't even touched this morning when I was at the coffee shop!"

I'd done a terrible job of hiding my frustration, which was reinforced by the incredulous quirk of Dan's eyebrow.

The more I tried to explain, the more confused I became. If he hadn't written two of them and I hadn't moved the note, I had no idea how it had ended up in the notebook.

"Strange. I don't know, babe. I only wrote the one."

"Hmmm. I guess it's not important. How was your day? Any new developments on the project?" I was eager to change the subject and get the focus off of me.

"We're having some issues and I've been spending more time at the island facility during the day. If we're going to fix this without falling behind, it's going to take some long days and me staying overnight just makes more sense."

He continued to talk and tell me what little he could, but I found myself drifting off, trying not to drown in the frustration and discontent surging inside me. I knew this was his career, and while I would never interfere, with each setback it became harder to believe him when he said that our marriage came first.

Two days later I woke up alone again. This was quickly becoming routine, and I hated it. I missed watching him get ready in the morning. I missed the intimacy of the sweet, small shared moments.

The loss of what I had started getting used to left me feeling lonely and sad. As I began getting ready for the day, considering what I wanted to do, I padded down to the kitchen.

I found a pencil with a book lying open on the island next to it. I leaned over to see what it was. An underlined quote instantly jumped out at me off the page: "I wish you to know that you have been the last dream of my soul."

An unexpected shiver ran down my spine. I'd never read A Tale of Two Cities, but I couldn't help but believe its placement here and on that page was deliberate.

As much as I would have loved to assume it was Dan

who left the message, it wasn't likely. He wasn't big into the classics. Or reading. I shot him a text anyway.

> **Me: Hey, sweetie, I'm sorry to bug you at work, I just had a quick question. Were you reading *A Tale of Two Cities*?**

I waited a few minutes for his response, and when it didn't come right away, I set to brewing my coffee and pulling together breakfast. I rechecked my phone ten minutes later to find he had replied.

> **Dan: No, I don't think I've read it since college. Why?**
> **Me: It was out on the kitchen island when I got up today.**
> **Dan: I didn't even know we had a copy of it in the house. Sorry.**

Exactly what I thought. But if not him, then who? How?

> **Me: That's OK. I love you, will you call later?**
> **Dan: I'll try to, but I'm swamped, and I can already tell you I'm probably going to be stuck here the next few days.**

This was crazy. Books didn't just appear out of nowhere. They didn't just move on their own. Neither did notes. Or really, any of the other random objects I had noticed in different places than where I had left them.

The jewelry, my phone, the TV remote control, my wallet. All things I'd chalked up to either Dan or me moving without realizing it. But the more I thought about it, the less likely it seemed. I found myself searching for an explanation. Something rational, logical. I came up empty. It was getting weird, and I was frustrated there were no answers to be found. I didn't mind mysteries, but I was notoriously impatient for answers to them.

My conversation with Josie came roaring back.

Ghost.

She was a lot more open-minded about supernatural, paranormal, and inexplicable things than I was, but she didn't really believe this was a ghost, right?

I thought back to how strange I'd been feeling since moving into the house. The feeling of being watched, the scent that would come and go, the feeling of a breath or touch on my skin when I was alone, hearing whispered words I couldn't quite make out, objects being moved.

I could totally see how a more superstitious person would believe it was a ghost. I just couldn't believe it. I loved a good ghost story as much as the next girl, but this didn't feel the way I pictured a haunting would. Plus, if the house were haunted, wouldn't Dan be experiencing things too when he was around?

So I was back at page one. Back to searching for rational ideas or explanations for what was becoming increasingly illogical and inexplicable.

NINE

"HOW ARE you enjoying island life, Ros?" Marie asked as we sat at her kitchen island drinking tea while I watched her knead dough for dinner rolls.

"I really like it here so far. I've just begun to explore and I haven't met many people, but the ones I have are all so welcoming and kind."

"That's good to hear. If you're interested, we hold a book club here at the inn once a month. There's a pretty good mix of ages, and we aren't too serious about the actual reading. We mostly use it as an excuse to get together and drink wine."

"Oh, I'd love that! I used to do one with my friends back home, and I miss it. What kind of books do you guys read?" I settled onto one of the stools at the island.

"Oh, a little bit of everything." She continued to knead at the dough, pushing and pulling in a hypnotic rhythm. I shook my head to break the trance I found myself in, and decided to ask her what had been on my mind.

"Marie, I remember you saying you knew a lot about the history here. I would love to know more if you have the time."

"Of course, I have the time, let me just get these into the oven," she said as she finished with the dough and slid the pans into the oven. She wiped her hands off on her apron as she closed the door with her hip. "Okay, so I wouldn't say that I'm an expert or anything, but I've spent most of my life here. So where did you want me to begin? Or did you have something specific you wanted to know about?"

Yes, yes, I do have something specific I want to know about.

"How about the beginning? Some general history with anything interesting thrown into the mix? I'd love to know whatever you know."

Marie's face radiated with her excitement to share one of her passions as she sat down with a fresh mug of tea. "Orcas Island is the largest of the San Juan Islands. While there were obviously natives living here long before any Europeans made it over, settlement on the island began in the mid to late 1800s," she began.

Before I knew it, an hour had passed while she told me the basic history of the island along with some fun and interesting stories thrown into the mix. My time

CECE FERRELL

with her today was coming to a close, and there was no better time to throw out the questions heavy on my mind.

"I'm kind of curious, and I know this might be a silly question, but are there any good ghost stories?" I chewed on my thumbnail, a nervous habit I usually managed to contain.

"There are most definitely ghost stories. I don't know all of them, but there are a few well-known ones."

"Which places?"

"The Orcas Hotel is well known to be haunted by the former innkeeper." She paused for a moment to take the rolls out and slide some pies into the oven. "Rosario Resort has some colorful stories. The wife of one of the former owners is said to be kicking around the place. She was known to be quite the party girl and people claim they can hear her heels clicking down the halls, or that they see her in her red nightgown atop her beloved Harley. Some even said they've heard a bed squeaking and moaning come from an unoccupied room."

"What have you experienced living here?" I asked, hoping she had some great firsthand tales to share.

"I haven't experienced anything out of the ordinary, but there's just too many stories floating around for me to think there isn't some truth to them. Have you seen anything interesting since arriving here?"

I knew I wasn't going to get a better opening, and she

seemed to be open-minded, so I just hoped I didn't sound completely foolish.

"I'm going to preface this by saying I don't believe in ghosts. I love ghost stories, but I've always considered them complete fiction. Lately, I've been experiencing weird things in my house."

"What kind of things?" Marie stopped wiping down the countertop and looked at me curiously. The beginning prickles of heat started at my neck and rose to my cheeks, my body making my embarrassment obvious.

"It started with feeling like I was being watched, accompanied by a masculine scent. Then it was feeling like I was being touched when I was completely alone. Most recently things are moving and showing up in places they have no business being."

"As a non-believer, what do you think is going on?"

"I've tried coming up with rational, logical explanations for all of this, but I'm at a loss. My best friend joked about it being a ghost, and while I brushed her off initially, I can't get the idea out of my head now," I finished, laughing self-consciously, feeling foolish and vulnerable at my honesty.

"You live on the land the Breckenridge family owned ages ago. I haven't heard of anything happening there as far as weird occurrences or hauntings go, but that doesn't mean it's impossible. The family's story is a sad one, too."

"What happened?" I asked, intrigued by the potential answers Marie held.

"I don't know a lot. The Breckenridge family was this very wealthy family who lived mostly on the mainland, based in San Francisco and Seattle. If I remember correctly, they dabbled in quite a few different businesses. The youngest son in the family was quite a prodigy, from what people say. He was also quite handsome and sought after. It sounds so silly and antiquated now, doesn't it?"

"I'd agree, though if that were true, shows like *The Bachelor* and matchmakers for zillionaires wouldn't be so popular, would they?" I joked back.

"Good point. Anyway, the son had bought the land where you live now with the intention of building a home for his fiancée. I'm not sure why he chose Orcas Island, especially since it wasn't a widely inhabited place at that time." Marie shrugged as though that were answer enough.

"Did he ever build the house?"

"No, he died in a steamer crash on his way from San Francisco to Seattle. And his beloved fiancée? She married just a few months after his death."

"That's so sad. How old was he?"

"I don't remember, somewhere in his late twenties, I think."

"When did he die?" I asked, enraptured by his story.

"In the early 1900s."

"Oh, wow. So, whatever happened to the land? Did the family ever build on it or did it just sit vacant?"

"They never did build on it. It was eventually sold, and a home was built on the lot. That home fell into disrepair and was torn down about a decade before the house you're now living in was built."

"This is all so interesting. It doesn't sound like I'm being haunted, based on what you just told me." My stomach tumbled in a weird way, making me slightly nauseated. I couldn't tell if it was from relief or disappointment.

"I wouldn't immediately say it is haunted, but I wouldn't rule out the possibility either. I guess that could be said for every chunk of land here, though," she finished, laughing to herself.

Marie had given me so much to think about and consider. I wanted to know more about this family, more about this man who'd died so tragically. I looked down at my phone and saw I had missed a call from Dan before realizing I had spent well over half my day with Marie.

"I just noticed the time! I'm so sorry to have taken up so much of your day."

"It's all right. It was nice having someone here to spend the day with and talk to. Steven is in and out of here so much, and we don't really get the chance for any quality time until late into the evening. Sometimes the guests will sit and talk, but they usually are out exploring or don't want to bother me. I've really enjoyed having you here, and it helped my work go by much faster."

"I should be going. It looks like I missed a call from my husband, and a middle-of-the-day call from him is probably important," I said, as I hopped off the stool and went over to Marie to give her a quick hug.

She wrapped me in her arms, giving me what might be one of the best hugs I'd had in a while, squeezing me extra tight at the end. I could smell sugar and lavender on her skin, and it was all so comforting.

"Please come by anytime, sweetie. I mean that."

She walked me to the door, we said our goodbyes again, and I drove off with a quick wave, thoughts of the Breckenridge family on my mind, and trying not to worry what Dan's phone call was about.

TEN

I TEXTED DAN, then called, and waited. And waited. And then waited for him to come home. At least that was how it felt.

I convinced myself maybe it wasn't so important if he hadn't called me back yet. I wasn't even sure if he was going to be home that night anyway. It seemed like at least half the week he ended up spending the night at work, and he often didn't know until the day of if he would be home or not.

I decided to go home and prep dinner as though he'd be home, a bit of wishful thinking on my part. I looked over at the clock over an hour later to see how close to dinnertime it was, and still no word from Dan. I poured myself a glass of wine and stirred the nearly done pasta sauce.

I was lost in my thoughts when a strong arm

wrapped around my waist and soft lips kissed my neck below my ear. I jumped and screamed, knocking my wine glass over and sending the wooden spoon I was stirring the sauce with flying in the process. Dan's deep, rumbling laugh sounded in my ear.

"Hello to you, too," he rasped in my ear, still getting a good laugh out of my reaction.

I spun around in his arms, smacking his chest as he pulled me close. I gave him a lingering kiss before pulling back.

"You know not to sneak up on me and scare me!" I nearly screamed, pushing at him again.

"I'm sorry, when I saw you there daydreaming I couldn't help it."

"I wasn't even expecting you home tonight. You called in the middle of the day, which you never do, so I figured the call was either important or you were trying to let me know you wouldn't be home tonight."

"The call was pretty important, but we can talk about it later. I miss you, and I just want to hold you for a minute. Is dinner almost done?"

"Yeah, let me turn it off." I reached around and turned the burner off. "I miss you too. I feel like I never see you anymore, and you call much less than you normally do."

He looked away from me for a moment before turning back and running a hand through his hair in frustration. He began to talk but was avoiding eye contact. I guessed he didn't want to put off the conversation after all.

Anxiety spiked in my blood, a crushing pressure in my chest. It felt like the beginning of a panic attack. I took deep breaths, trying to reassure myself he had said it was only "pretty" important.

"This project's kicking my ass. I wish I could go into detail, but you know I can't. There's problems left and right, and the minute we solve a problem, a bigger, more complex one pops up." Dan stopped pacing and rubbed at the back of his neck, trying to loosen the corded muscles. He cursed under his breath. I knew that whatever words passed his lips next were ones that I wasn't going to like. "It's been crazy, but if we can pull this off, it'll make me seriously consider taking on fewer projects at the firm or finally starting my own company. I just need to get through this one."

"Okay, I feel like there's something else."

"So, with that all said, it's looking like this project is going to take closer to a year to complete."

"Whoa." I took a couple of deep breaths and felt my body relax. That wasn't so bad. "That all sucks and I'm sorry we can't talk about it. I know you're more than capable of kicking ass on this and I don't mind staying here longer, so don't worry about me." I walked over to Dan and placed a kiss to his cheek.

Instead of relaxing with that confession off his chest, his body remained taut and tense. It was in that moment I knew there was more he hadn't told me yet.

I set the table and made plates for us, waiting for him to work through whatever it was in his head he needed to work through so we could finish this conversation. He came and sat down at the table across from me, still silent while eating his pasta. Finally, he made eye contact and gave me a smile that didn't reach his eyes.

"Remember when we talked about having Josie come visit sometime after the new year? What do you think about her coming a little sooner?"

"Oh, hmmm. I could ask her what her schedule is like since the holidays aren't too far off. Were you thinking of having her over for the holidays?" I asked, more than a little curious as to why he wanted her to come sooner.

"Well, yeah, if she could do it. I don't know, it was just an idea, something to think about and run by her," Dan replied before focusing on his dinner.

We sat in silence for the rest of the meal. This time, it wasn't so comfortable. The unsaid words between us were a weight pulling us down, and the only way to lighten the load was to throw the words out there and free them. But we continued to sit in silence, waiting.

Finally, he slid his plate out of the way, and leaned forward, resting his forearms on the table, steepling his fingers.

"I suggested you have Josie come for the holidays because I have more news. Maris wants to increase the parameters but he still wants us to maintain the same timeline. To do it, he's making the team move to the island facility where the work will be done."

And just like that the other shoe dropped. Dan couldn't or wouldn't even meet my eyes, though his shoulders slumped and something that looked like guilt tightened the features of his face.

"Fuck." I could feel the tears begin to gather in my eyes, and I closed them tightly, willing myself not to cry, not to make this harder than it already was. When I finally felt I could talk without losing it, I asked the questions floating around in my head.

"What does that mean? Will I be living here alone then? Will you be able to come home for the holidays, even just the day?"

"Yeah, you'll pretty much be alone unless I can manage to get away for a day here or there. I know this wasn't part of the plan. If you aren't comfortable being here by yourself, you can always go back home."

The disappointment and guilt in his voice was obvious—he didn't even try to hide it. I wanted that alone to ease my own disappointment, but it didn't. I'd just sat witness as our plans, our chance crumbled before me. I took a deep breath and did what I always did. I sucked it up and tried to bury my feelings.

"I'll stay." The words barely made it through my tight throat. I coughed and swallowed reflexively, hoping I could convince Dan with my words alone. "I'll be okay here. I'll call Josie tomorrow and see if she wants to come a little earlier." I managed to sound more resolute and I nodded my head vigorously as though that would reinforce my point.

He smiled tightly back at me, not believing me for a second. The one thing I couldn't help but wonder was, would he ever choose me, choose us over his career?

———

Two weeks had passed, and I still hadn't called Josie. The day after our conversation Dan was packed and ready to go. He was allowed to take a half day to get his things together, so we slept in, holding each other tight and not wanting to let go or talk about what this meant for our already shaky foundation.

We ate breakfast together, and I watched him shave and prepare for his day. We showered together, making love in a melancholy, subdued way. It felt like goodbye. Hell, it was a goodbye.

I watched him drive off in the town car that came to pick him up, feeling shell-shocked about our plans having changed so much in what felt like the blink of an eye.

One thing hadn't changed: the strange shit going on at the house. Sometimes I could hear my name whispered on the breeze, like a faint caress. So quiet, over so quickly I often thought I'd just imagined it. Random breezes flowed through the house when all the windows and doors remained closed.

Objects still moved and showed up in places they weren't at before, places they didn't belong. One time I found my phone in the shower. I had no explanation for that one.

The stereo system would turn on, playing different songs. Sometimes it was songs I enjoyed and had played on repeat in the house, sometimes it was songs I'd never heard before but ended up loving.

The books still showed up, almost always open to a page that contained some passage that automatically jumped out at me. This did not seem random to me at all.

I still felt light touches on my skin, always accompanied by that now familiar scent. I knew when that scent surrounded me, something else would follow, whether it was a touch or the sense I wasn't alone. Strangely enough, these events were happening with such regularity I was getting used to them.

The weirdest and perhaps worst thing were the dreams. They were happening nearly every night now. They were all strange and surreal, not at all like the dreams I was used to having. I was floating, or falling, or swimming. There were mystical, mythical creatures.

The one thing all of these dreams had in common was the handsome dark-haired man with the beautiful green eyes and unnerving, penetrating gaze. What got to me so much was the fact he seemed so familiar. Like I had met him before, like I knew him better than I knew anyone. Like I loved him more than I had ever loved anyone. There was always this strange magnetic pull between us. A pull so strong, as if no matter what, we were destined to touch, to be together in some way.

It was also strange that now, even days after having one of these dreams, I could still remember them. I was retaining every single detail. I'd been lucky if I remembered any of my dreams before moving here. Now I couldn't escape them, even when I was awake.

I considered journaling them, but I realized I didn't want to commit them to paper. I wanted to hold on to the feelings they elicited as tightly as possible, keeping them only for myself.

"Seriously? You wait three weeks to call me and act like that's okay?"

The humor in Josie's voice was evident, but there was no mistaking the underlying disappointment.

"Well, I'm not the only one with a phone. You could have called me too," I retorted with no bite.

"True, true. I've been busy. Things have been crazy here at the center. We lost a couple instructors and I've been teaching classes and hosting seminars along with all my other responsibilities. It's been exhausting, but things are starting to slow down with the holidays around the corner, so I'm almost caught up." She sighed.

"It's funny you say that. Things have changed here and I was wondering if you wanted to maybe stay with me for the holidays?"

"You do know we're like a week away from Thanksgiving, right? Is Dan okay with this?"

"It was actually his idea. The truth is, I don't even know if he will be here for the holidays."

"What the hell are you talking about?" she practically shouted at me. It was one of the things I loved about Josie. She always supported me, always had my back.

"Jos, calm down. Everything is fine. His project is screwed up and it was expanded. The entire team had to move to a neighboring island for the duration of the project."

"Wait, so you're living there by yourself?"

While she wasn't shouting, she didn't sound calm in the least.

"Yeah, I am. But I'm okay with it. I just miss him. With Thanksgiving and Christmas coming up it would be nice to know I'm spending them with at least one person I love."

"Well, I just spent the last week nose deep in my schedule and we decided to close the studio down for most of the holidays, so you can have me until January third. Are you sure you don't want to come home, sweetie? Wouldn't that make more sense?"

Josie ran a popular studio that was sort of new age-ish. On top of fitness and yoga classes, they also ran seminars in things like meditation, tantric sex, and couples' therapy. She had somehow made this odd mix of offerings usually targeted at the hippies, hipsters, and crunchy mamas who lived in the area also accessible and desirable to the more moderate and mainstream residents.

"No. It feels like this is where I need to be. Plus, I haven't talked to the girls much since being here. We've been playing phone tag and we've texted a little, but I feel a bit disconnected from Santa Barbara right now."

"Are you sure, Ros? You know the girls won't care. We all miss you and would be happy to have you home."

"Yeah, I'm more than sure. Plus, there's always the chance Dan will be able to come home for a day or two for the holidays, so that alone would keep me here. So, yay! I'm excited and I can't wait for you to see everything. Just send me the day you want to come and I'll arrange your ticket."

Even if Dan was a no-show for the holidays, I knew with Josie here, everything would still be festive and feel like home. A part of me also knew this was a test.

I wanted—no, I *needed*—to see what she would experience here in this house. I needed confirmation or I needed to let it all go. If Jos experienced any of the things I had, she could provide that confirmation.

ELEVEN

"HOLY SHIT, Ros! The photos do not do this place justice. At. All." Josie gasped as we stepped out onto the balcony off the master bedroom.

I gave her a tour of the house and her jaw remained suitably dropped for most of it. I had to walk up to her at one point and close it for her. It didn't remain that way for long.

"I thought I knew what to expect, but there was no preparing for this."

"I know, I felt the same way."

My mind drifted back to the first time we came up the drive. The towering Douglas firs, pines, and cedar trees gave way to wood shingling, red brick, and glass-paneled French doors on the most beautifully modern Craftsman-style house. The rustic yet modern interior and furnishings perfectly fit its exterior.

"I love it here and I don't know how I'm going to leave when the time comes," I murmured as my mind cleared from the memory.

"You're okay here, by yourself? I was never worried about you back home because you had us. But here? I'm worried." Jos stopped to take a breath and I opened my mouth to speak, but she beat me to it. "Then throw in all the weird shit you were telling me about. I hate to say this, but as beautiful as this place is, isn't this how most horror movies begin? A young woman by herself in a peaceful yet remote location? Everything appears perfect at first—"

"Oh my God, Jos, stop being so dramatic!" If I didn't stop her, she would keep going until we ended up in this ridiculous place, with neither of us knowing how we ended up there.

"Okay, okay. But I will say, I'm not getting a weird or creepy vibe at all from this place. You know when people talk about the hell they went through living in a haunted house, they always, always talk about how they knew from the minute they set foot in the place something was off, that something didn't feel right. I don't feel it here at all. I can see why you love it."

"I know. It's why I don't agree with the haunting theory of yours. I think you just want it to be something exciting. I'm sure the real reason is much more mundane."

I turned and walked back into the house.

"Well, on to the *real* important matter at hand, what are we doing for turkey day? Is Dan coming? What are we eating? I need to know these things, dammit!" she said as she practically skipped through the house to the kitchen, grabbing the bottle of wine and glasses I had left out on the island, and making her way back to the balcony off the living room.

"I haven't done any planning. I don't know if Dan is coming or not. Marie is throwing a potluck-style family meal and invited us, so I was thinking maybe we should go there." I ticked off the answers to all her questions on my fingers.

"You know what, if it means we get more time together and less time stuck in the kitchen, I'm down for it. Now, let's drink, and you can tell me all the gossip about this place and your ghostly roommate."

I side-eyed her and couldn't miss her lips twitching in an effort to hide her smirk. What she couldn't hide from was the pillow I threw at her face.

"Hey, asshole, don't spill the wine!" she yelled at me, sloshing wine onto herself before launching the pillow right back at me.

Before I knew it, we both had dissolved into endless giggles.

It felt like the time Jos had here was slipping through my fingers. Thanksgiving had been a blast. Josie and I had spent it with Marie and her family, and a few of their friends who also had no one else to spend the day with.

Dan had called the night before to let me know he wouldn't be able to make it, some mishap they ran into. I could hear boisterous laughter in the background during our five-minute call, including that of a woman. I mostly brushed it off, as I knew there was a woman on his team.

I didn't really understand how an emergency at work that kept him from spending a holiday with me led to what sounded like a social gathering at eleven at night, but he was working so hard, I would never have denied him the need and opportunity to relax. I still couldn't help but be disappointed by his absence.

Jos and I had spent a lot of our time since she arrived vegging out, shopping, and hanging out with Marie. The only thing we hadn't talked about was researching the Breckenridge family.

"Hey, I was thinking about checking out the island historical museum today, see if I can find anything out about the family who used to own this land. Are you up for playing historian with me?" I asked her while we were enjoying coffee after breakfast a week into her trip.

"Sure, what do you know already? Did you Google them?"

"Ummm, no. I kind of put it all on the back burner."

"You said he wasn't from Washington at all, right?"

"Yeah, I think he was from San Francisco, though I'm not sure how accurate the information is."

"Well, it's a place to start. Hold on a sec." Jos grabbed her phone, clicked and swiped a bit before putting it to her ear. "Hey, hon, how are you? Yeah, I'm still here with Ros. I know, I know, I'll have her call you tonight, I promise. Oh, we can do a FaceTime wine night!"

She explained what she needed help with while I sat listening to her side of the conversation, wondering which of our girls she was talking to. Finally, she said her goodbyes, ended the call, and pulled my laptop in front of her, beginning to type in a flurry.

"Sooooo…" I began, trying to get her to tell me what was going on.

"Oh, that was Scarlett. She's good with this kind of research. She did this whole genealogy project for her family a couple of years ago. I figured she would know where we should start looking, and I was right!" she exclaimed without looking up from what she was typing once.

"How did I not know?" I asked, feeling like a shitty friend.

"I don't think it was something she talked about. We only discussed it once. Okay, Ros, so what was his name?"

"I don't know actually. His last name was Breckenridge. He died in the early 1900s, and he was in his late twenties to early thirties when it happened. He died in some boating accident or crash or something."

"Okay, well, we'll just start with the family name and San Francisco."

Two hours later we were surrounded by papers she had printed off from various websites. I had tried at the beginning to grab back my laptop and read what Jos had pulled up and help her, but she was so in the zone researching I didn't want to bother her, other than bringing her drinks and snacks. After the fourth time of me trying to look over her shoulder, she swatted me away.

"Go find something else to do. I'm having fun and I want to reveal what I'm finding all at once," Jos said distractedly, still trying to shoo me away.

"Fine, fine." I threw my hands up and walked away. I knew better than to argue with her.

Once my stomach started growling loud enough for Jos to hear in the other room (or so she claimed), I decided it was time for both of us to take a break for lunch. I walked into the dining room she had since taken over, and found her in the middle of chaos. She looked up with the biggest grin on her face, and I knew then she had found something.

"Hey, my stomach is starting to feast on itself, you ready for lunch?" I asked.

"Sure. We can talk about all the info I found while we eat."

"Do you want to eat here or out in town?"

"Ohhh, out in town for sure! Can we try that one restaurant you were telling me about? The place with the lavender ice cream? I can't stop thinking about it since you mentioned it yesterday."

She gathered up a stack of papers and shoved them into her purse as we left. Once we were seated and had ordered our food, she leaned forward in her chair with the biggest grin on her face, the excitement radiating off her in nearly tangible waves.

I wanted to wait her out and not say anything, just to drive her a little crazy, but I knew she wouldn't say anything without me asking first, and I could tell she would not be contained if her fidgeting and inability to sit still was any indication.

"So, what did you find out?" I finally asked, unable to hide my smile.

She pulled the stack of papers out of her purse and placed them in front of her. The first page was a picture. A copy of a very old picture, taken with one of those vintage cameras.

Though I guess it wasn't vintage back then. I tried to lean over so I could see it better, but she pulled it closer to her first, smirking at me.

"I think this is the man you've been looking for," she stated dramatically as she presented the picture to me with a flourish.

I took it from her hands, looked at it, and gasped as the picture fell from my shaking hands. The blood drained from my face and a dull pounding started in my temples.

"What? What's wrong? You look like you've seen a ghost."

She rose from her chair, but I put my trembling hand up, gesturing her to stop while I shook my head repeatedly. I glanced down at the photo again at an absolute loss for words.

"You're seriously freaking me out right now, what the hell is wrong?"

"Nothing, it's nothing. I want to hear what you found out first," I replied in a hushed voice.

My hands were on my lap in tight fists, my attempt to stop them from shaking or at least stop it from being noticeable to Jos.

How did I tell her the picture she'd just presented me with was the same man who had been showing up in my dreams for the last few months? How did I even rationalize it? It wasn't logically possible.

It was no wonder I looked like I'd seen a ghost. I just had. How I was even able to breathe steadily at the moment was beyond me.

She looked at me like she wasn't sure if she should continue talking or press me for more information. Her eyes narrowing and brow furrowing as her mind worked. Her face smoothed out, the tension gone when she'd made her choice. She shrugged her shoulders and went on.

"Okay, so his name was Archer Breckenridge, and he owned the land your house sits on. His family was from San Francisco and they were very prominent in various businesses and banking."

"That's pretty much what Marie told me."

"Think you can let me get this all out without interrupting?"

"Ugh. Fine, fine. Go on." I sighed deeply, trying to give her the impression of being incredibly put out. Jos' mischievous smile let me know I failed.

"He was the youngest son but was known to be incredibly intelligent and gifted when it came to business. A business opportunity came up in Seattle they couldn't pass up, so they sent Archer to manage it. Coming from a family with this kind of wealth and prestige, he was a highly sought-after bachelor. And seriously, from looking at his picture, I can't blame them. He'd have women throwing themselves at him now if he were alive. Look at the intensity in his eyes. Panty-melting."

I glared at her with that statement and she shrugged and giggled.

"I digress. While in Seattle, another family in the same circles, the Averys, introduced him to their daughter. It seemed to be a love match, and they were quickly engaged. She was also quite lovely." Jos paused to hand me a copy of her picture.

With what looked like pale blonde hair, light eyes, a heart-shaped face and a small but pretty smile, she was classically beautiful, and also looked quite young.

"Archer was almost twenty-eight years old, which at the time was a little older than most getting married. Soon after they announced their engagement, he bought the land you live on with plans to develop it into an estate. No one knows why he chose a place so far from Seattle, especially a place so uninhabited."

She stopped as our waitress appeared with our food. We both ate in silence. Josie enjoyed her meal, while I picked at mine and contemplated what I now knew about Archer.

To say I was still in shock would be an understatement. Maybe if I had seen his picture before, I could understand how he had ended up in so many of my dreams. But this was my first time seeing him, other than my dreams, and it scared me.

The sane, logical world I thought I knew no longer made sense. Josie began waving her arm in front of my face, which finally broke me out of my intense thoughts.

"Earth to Ros. Where'd you go? You're so out of it, I practically shouted your name! If the arm-waving hadn't worked, I was about to start screaming out obscenities to see if it would get your attention," she joked.

I would love to say she would never do it, but I knew Jos far too well to make that bet. She wouldn't have minded the attention she would draw.

"Sorry, I just kinda zoned out for a minute there," I replied shakily. "So, was there anything else you learned about him?" I asked, eager to have the attention off of myself.

"Oh, yeah. He died in 1906 in a steamer ship accident. He wasn't initially supposed to be on the ship at all, he never even appeared on the passenger manifest. His fiancée happened to be on the ship though, and she was one of fewer than forty people who survived."

"If he wasn't on the manifest, how did they know he was on the ship at all?"

"The only reason they knew he died in the wreck is because Helena survived and was able to give her account. There were a few other survivors who remembered seeing him before he died and backed up her story. Archer and Helena were only a few months away from getting married," she said, taking the last bite of her food. "So yeah, that's pretty much all I know. Care to tell me what has you so freaked out?"

"Can we wait until we get back to the house? It's nothing major, I promise."

"Okay." She simply nodded her head, keeping the question in her eyes to herself.

"Thanks for taking the time to research all that."

"I enjoyed doing it. It was fun getting to know more about the person who would have lived there before you, if he hadn't, you know, died."

I couldn't help but laugh at her honesty. It was maybe my second favorite thing about her. My first? Her undying, unquestioning loyalty. She called me out on my bullshit all the time, but there was never a question of whether she would have my back.

TWELVE

"SO, you want to tell me what had you so spooked back there?" Josie asked right after we stepped into the house, before I even had a chance to shut the door.

I wondered if I could come up with a convincing lie in the next thirty seconds that would both pacify her and shut the conversation down. Jos leaned on the kitchen island, tapping her phone on the countertop, an exaggerated sign of her impatience. She quirked up one brow and gave me a knowing look.

Fuck. I was stuck. She obviously knew I was trying to think my way out of this. Jos read me better than anyone, so I would have already needed to have had a good excuse at the ready.

"Fine, I'll talk, but let's take it to the balcony."

I began making my way to the balcony off of the living room without giving her a chance to respond and without checking to see if she was following. I grabbed one of the pillows off the outdoor sofa and sat down, wrapping my arms around it and hugging it tightly to my body.

"Remember how I was telling you about all those strange dreams I've been having? The dreams that began the minute I stepped in this house?"

Jos didn't say anything, probably afraid I would stop talking if she did, and nodded her head.

"Well, do you remember me telling you about the man who has been in every one of those dreams? The one I seem inexplicably attached to? The one I can't get out of my head, even when I'm awake?"

I took a deep breath, trying to calm myself down. I was feeling far too close to hysterical for comfort, and Jos could sense it too.

"Well, it's him. Archer is the man I've been dreaming about."

"Whoa. Wow. Fuck." Jos loudly exhaled. "I mean, maybe they just look similar, or maybe you've seen his picture before somehow? Maybe somewhere here in town?"

She was grasping for an explanation, just like I had been in the restaurant.

"No, Jos. I've never once seen any picture of him. I'd remember. I know this man, Josie. How the fuck is that possible? I can tell you things that aren't in the picture. I can tell you the top of my head barely reaches his chin. I can describe to you how damn good it feels to be in his arms, like I belong there. And I can describe in perfect detail what his eyes look like. They're green. The most vivid, clear shade of wet grass with a hint of gray around the edges. I've never seen anyone with eyes that color."

"I get that you believe all this, but how is this possible, Ros?"

"I don't know, Jos. I've been trying since lunch to come up with some kind of answer, and I keep coming up empty. I fucking. Have. Nothing."

I laughed hysterically, and before I could stop them, the laughs turned to sobs. I was completely and utterly wrung out.

"Shh, shh," Jos said as she came to sit next to me and wrapped me in her embrace. "You're not crazy, I believe you." She held me for a few minutes, rubbing soothing circles on my back.

"There was an article I read, some gossip column where they talked about Archer's hobbies and social habits. There was special mention made of the odd color of his eyes. His green eyes," she said, her voice barely above a whisper.

When I looked up her face was as pale as mine felt and she had a shaken look in her eyes. We continued to hold and comfort each other, not knowing what else to think or do.

"Well, at least we know your ghost is a hottie," Jos joked eventually, hugging me closer and kissing the side of my head.

———————

Before I knew it, the holidays were over, and Josie was on her way back home. We had spent most of Christmas Eve with Marie and her family and friends, eating, drinking, exchanging small handmade gifts, and singing carols.

Dan wasn't able to come home for Christmas, and a five-minute FaceTime call was all I got with an explanation that made sense, but fell short. I had never been so thankful to have Jos there, and at least he had had the foresight to arrange that.

We'd only talked about Archer Breckenridge once after that lunch. Josie never did end up experiencing the things I did. She never got the feeling someone was watching her, never caught a hint of the scent I'd come to love. It happened once or twice while she was staying with me, but never, ever when she was around.

At the end of her stay, I begged her to stay. I loved it here, but she was like my sister, and I missed her. She asked me if I wanted to come back home with her, saying she would extend her trip if I wanted to move back, that no one would blame me.

I wished I could say it was even a consideration, but it wasn't. I was meant to be on this island, in this house for a reason, and until I figured that out, I couldn't leave.

Over the month that had passed since the holidays, Dan had only come back to the house once for a night. He was stressed out and exhausted, a shell of the man I knew. His phone calls dropped to once a week, and in those few minutes I could hear the terseness in his voice, and our conversations, even through texts, were stilted. I didn't think either of us knew how to fix things when we were more distant than ever.

I realized him being away from home during these long projects was probably the best thing for all involved. Trying to maintain the workload and stress from a project that wasn't going as planned was exhausting, and he just didn't have it in him to be physically and emotionally present for us.

After his last visit, I came to the conclusion I needed to ask him to focus on getting the project done so we could be together because the time we spent when he managed to get away was full of distance and awkwardness.

He wasn't happy with the conversation or my idea, but he finally caved, and I would be lying if I said I couldn't see the hint of relief in his eyes when we had the conversation over FaceTime. By the end of the call, he was reassuring me he loved me, but I could see his shoulders lighten with a burden no longer weighing on him.

The weird occurrences in the house only increased. They had slowed down quite a bit while Josie was here, but once she left, they picked up again and began occurring more frequently.

I had gotten used to books showing up randomly, hearing my name whispered in the wind, the unexplained breezes, feeling gentle touches, and no longer feeling alone most of the time.

I tried to take comfort in the moments it happened. I still was unsure of what exactly the cause was, but it felt like a little bit of magic in my otherwise very ordinary world, and I couldn't help but revel in it a little.

Sometimes late at night while lying in bed, staring out into the sky as the fog crept up from the water and trees and onto my balcony, I would start to think of Josie's theory of Archer being the ghost and the house being haunted. She still joked about it during our phone conversations, asking me to say hello to Archer for her.

I always brushed the jokes off, laughing along, but when I was all alone and felt the soft sweep of fingertips on the back of my hand, or smelled sandalwood and tobacco and salty ocean, I couldn't help but think for a moment maybe I was being haunted.

Everything came to a head when I experienced all of these things in one day, which had never happened before. It led to a nearly sleepless night where I was lucky if I got a few hours of fitful sleep, and I realized something had to change.

I couldn't continue to live this way, barely sleeping half the time from fear, always worrying and wondering about the things going on in this house, if it was all in my head, a way for my mind to ease the loneliness that especially hit at night, or if I was being haunted by Archer or some other unknown entity.

I'd reached my limit. On the porch, as I was about to pull the door closed, I leaned my head in and called out to the empty house, "If you're there, if there is someone or something here, please either let yourself be known or stop and leave me be. I can't stand this anymore."

I waited a few minutes for something to happen, but nothing did. I closed the door, shaking my head and laughing to myself, feeling far sillier than I had ever felt before.

THIRTEEN

I CAME HOME LATER than usual that night and walked right into that now familiar scent. I closed my eyes and inhaled deeply, a sense of comfort washing over me before the prickly, slightly nauseating feeling of unease set in.

I waited for the sensation of being watched to hit, but after a few minutes, I felt nothing. I made my way to the balcony off my bedroom, putting away my things and grabbing some tea and a blanket on the way.

I sat down with my legs curled under me and snuggled under the blanket. With the mug clasped tightly between both hands, I stared off into the fog. It was exceptionally thick, so much so I could barely see past my balcony, and definitely couldn't see the water or trees below.

I didn't think about anything while I was out there, my

mind pleasantly and surprisingly clear and free. I reveled in the feeling, letting all the stress and worry that had taken up residence in my body drift away. I finished my tea, set the mug down, and curled up against one of the pillows, half lying down, just enjoying the cold, fresh air around me.

Sometime later I startled awake. I stretched, looking out into the night sky, wondering what had woken me up, knowing I hadn't dreamed.

Through the mist, I began to see a shape take form. I rubbed at my eyes, shook my head, and then looked back as though the movement would clear my eyes or change what I was seeing, but there standing before me was a man.

He was almost completely opaque, but not fully solid. His back was turned to me, his posture straight with an innate confidence radiating off him in waves. I could tell by his clothing he was not of this time.

Ghost. You are looking at a ghost.

My brain screamed these words and I shook my head, refusing to believe what was right in front of my eyes, what my mind was already trying to process. A part of me wanted to run, to slam the doors to the balcony and leave the house as quickly as possible.

I couldn't, though. I was rooted to the spot. I should have been terrified, my heart should have been pounding through my chest, but I wasn't.

All the weird occurrences in the house over the last several months began to play out in my mind, ending with my call-out to the unknown occupant of the house this morning. When Josie and I had joked about the house being haunted, it might have freaked me out, but I'd never really believed it to be true.

As I continued to stare, I began to question what I was seeing. Maybe I was seeing what I wanted. Maybe my intense loneliness was playing tricks on my eyes, on my mind. That had to be it.

I didn't even realize I was holding my breath until a strangled gasp escaped my lips, the heat from my breath creating a steamy trail in the frigid air. The sound I made must have been louder than I realized, as the form began to shimmer and move.

He stiffened as if startled and began to turn. I stood up clumsily, grasping at the arms of the chair to keep myself from stumbling. My mind willed me to move but my body was utterly unwilling to comply.

Something in me wanted to see him, see his face, to finally know who I had been sharing this space with. As he turned I took a sudden, involuntary step back and the air pushed out of my lungs in an audible *whoosh*. This was most definitely not a hallucination or my imagination taking over. There was an actual ghost standing in front of me.

He's so much more attractive than his picture or how he looked in my dreams.

That thought was the first thing that popped in my head. *Archer*, my mind whispered, the name never passing my lips.

He was wearing a suit that looked like it was from the late 1800s, maybe early 1900s, but I wasn't an expert. A long suit coat, trousers with a crisp crease in them, a matching vest, shirt and tie with a chain attached to a pocket watch.

It was too dark and foggy to tell the color or any other details. My eyes drifted back up to his face, all of his features arranged into a fashion far too familiar for comfort. He was clean-shaven, had a slim, angular nose, a tiny cleft in his chin, and full lips in proportion with the rest of his features.

His hair looked to be dark brown, trimmed short on the sides, a bit longer on the top, but not quite reaching his ears. There was a slightly off-center part, and it was slicked back nicely. It was a pretty stylish cut and it was slightly jarring to think it had been popular all those years ago too.

His gaze was what got me. It wasn't the vacant or distant look I had expected. He really saw me, met my look, and his eyes instantly filled with warmth and something that looked a lot like affection. A slight smile touched his lips.

My own mouth dropped open in shock, and I was still stuck where I was, unable to move, unable to even look away. His mouth broke into a full smile at my reaction, amusement now dancing in his eyes, and I smiled back in spite of myself.

Before I knew it, his form was shimmering again, moving closer to me. The icy current of panic flooded my veins, a scream got stuck in my throat, and my brain was telling my body to run, but I was paralyzed, rooted to the spot.

Within seconds he was right in front of me, mere inches away. I shivered at his proximity. But looking into his eyes, I could see uncertainty and shyness there, nothing evil, no ill intent. The rush of the panic I was feeling seconds before receded.

Now that he was closer I could see him in more detail by the porch light. His hair was dark, dark brown, almost black, but with hints of lighter brown throughout. He had tiny wrinkles next to his eyes and mouth, a sure sign this man had laughed a lot in his short life. For some reason, it calmed me further, tempered my fear.

He was slim but well built. It made me wonder if he had done a lot of labor while alive to give him the muscles he obviously had. Men born during his time didn't really exercise for vanity or strength, right? It wasn't like they had a gym on every corner the way they did now.

His suit was obviously well made and well tailored. Just like in my dreams, he was much taller than me, definitely over six feet, which had to be rare for the time. I always pictured men as being shorter at the turn of the century, but there were obviously exceptions.

His eyes were a deep, piercing green rimmed in gray. I had never seen eyes like this before.

Except I had. Every single time I had a dream with him, I looked into those eyes. A wave of familiarity and comfort washed over me. He smiled tentatively and I nodded my head, as though answering a question.

"Well, finally," he said in a deep, melodic voice.

I was expecting it to be like a whisper on the wind, but I could fully hear him like he was alive and not a figment of a man. I was utterly speechless. I didn't even know how to respond.

After what seemed like forever, I managed to squeak out, "What do you mean 'finally'?"

He laughed then, and I smiled at the sound, warming me from within as it settled over my body. "I've been trying to get your attention for quite a while. It's not easy making myself visible."

His voice hit me then, like a punch in the stomach. I knew that voice, recognized it deep within. This really was the man I had been dreaming about since arriving. I couldn't believe it.

The face, the smile, the voice. It was all the same.

"So, if you've been trying to make yourself visible, if you've been the one doing all these things, why now? Why didn't you just show yourself sooner?" I asked, completely confused and baffled.

"I wanted to see if you were open to the idea at first, if you even believed. I suppose I could have presented myself to you sooner, but I didn't think it was a wise course to take," he replied with a shrug of his shoulders.

I shivered and rubbed my arms absentmindedly. He reached out to me, but stopped himself just shy of making contact with my arm.

"You look like you're freezing cold, we should take this inside."

"I don't even know your name, and you've been with me this entire time and probably know mine," I replied, not bothering to respond to his statement.

I needed to hear him say it. I needed the confirmation that he was indeed Archer Breckenridge and I hadn't imagined everything. He smiled fully again and I was struck by how captivating his smile was.

"My name is Archer, Rosalind," he stated.

Another chill down my spine, followed quickly by a shiver. He did indeed know my name. What else had he seen and heard since I had moved? Instead of responding, I turned and walked into the house, realizing I was probably being rude.

Wait, how can you be rude to someone who isn't even living?

I laughed to myself, feeling like I was going crazy. I was having a conversation with a ghost, of course I was going crazy. I guessed my loneliness and the strange things happening around the house had finally taken their toll.

I made my way toward the couch closest to the fireplace. Archer suddenly materialized in front of me and stood in front of the other sofa.

"How do you know my name?" I asked in a much harsher voice than I had intended, realizing how stupid that question was the minute it crossed my lips.

He chuckled, and I swore I could feel the reverberations in the atmosphere around us. "I've lived in this place for decades, Rosalind. I'm slightly embarrassed to admit I've watched you a little since you arrived." He looked away from me shyly as he said this. He at least had the decency to appear embarrassed.

While a part of me wanted to say something snarky or sarcastic in return, I realized his admission didn't bother me nearly as much as it maybe should. I couldn't think of anything at all to say in response. I just stood there a moment, trying to process all of this.

"Have a seat, I guess," I said, waving toward the sofa he stood in front of.

He lowered his body onto it, so it looked like he was sitting, though I guessed he was just hovering.

"Does it take a lot of energy to sit like that?" I asked, my curiosity winning out.

He smiled, a twinkle of humor in his eyes. "No, not really. Not any more than standing or walking takes."

There were so many questions racing through my head, but leaving just as quickly, too fast for me to grab onto one long enough to formulate the words out loud. I closed my eyes, laid my head on the back of the sofa, and took a deep breath, exhaling a moment later. When I opened my eyes, he was still there, the same smile on his face.

"Is this really happening?"

With that question, he laughed, a rich, deep laugh. "Yes, Rosalind, this is really happening, as difficult as it must be to fathom. I take it you've never conversed with a spirit before?"

He sat back on the sofa, as though he were getting comfortable, and threw his right ankle to rest over his left knee.

"No, this would be a first for me. And if we're going to have a conversation, you might as well call me Ros."

"If it's all right with you, I would much rather call you Rosalind."

"Okay." I nodded my assent. "Is there another name you go by? A nickname perhaps?"

"Yes, my friends and family often called me Archie when I was alive."

"Would it be okay if I called you Archer? And when would that have been, exactly? When you were alive? How old are you?" I had a pretty good idea what his answer would be, but again, I was seeking confirmation.

"I'm twenty-eight years old, I suppose."

I sat quietly, willing him to continue with my eyes. After a moment or two, he must have figured I wasn't going to ask anything else until he went on.

"I was born in 1878. I died in 1906," he finished.

"You don't really sound like what I thought someone from the nineteenth century would sound like," I observed out loud, more to myself than to him.

As a ghost, he must have been able to hear anything spoken anywhere near him, no matter how quietly it was said. Well, that was my assumption, at least.

"Well, I'm not sure exactly what you were expecting. I think there's often the misconception we talked much differently during my time, but we didn't. Perhaps a bit more formally at times."

"Oh," I muttered, unable to form any other words.

"I've also been observing the inhabitants here for almost a century. I picked up the idioms and manners of speech over the years. It makes me feel more relevant, more alive."

I was slightly taken aback by this. I'd thought a ghost

was a stagnant, unchanging thing, completely stuck in the time he or she lived in when alive. I found I liked the fact he tried to adapt, with his speech at least.

"So, does that mean you've stayed current with music and books as well? Actually, can you even read?"

I had so many questions now, it took everything in me to refrain from spitting them all out at once. Archer steepled his fingers together and looked at me as though seriously considering my questions.

"I do get to listen to music, which has made things feel less lonely. As for books, I can move them and manipulate them, as I'm sure you've noticed." Archer chuckled at his joke. "I greatly enjoyed reading while I was alive, but I find it consumes too much energy to try to manipulate the pages to read for any length of time. Each time I've tried, I had to give up the endeavor after a few pages."

"I'm so sorry, Archer. I don't know what I would do if I couldn't read."

He nodded, and I swore I saw a flash of sadness in his eyes for a second before it disappeared. "I sometimes consider all the great books I must have missed over the years. Do you know what I've found unexpected joy in?"

"No."

"Films. I have found I really enjoy them. Well, many of them, that is."

He looked at me with a question in his eyes. I got the

feeling he was inviting me to ask more questions. I was stuck processing and taking in what he had just said.

"So, the books around the house were you then?"

"Yes, I remember many passages I loved or had great meaning to me. Those were the books and passages I shared with you."

Some time must have passed without me saying anything at all. Out of the corner of my eye, I caught him shift. I looked up at him, not sure where to go next and struck silent by the strange energy filling the atmosphere between us.

FOURTEEN

"SO, ROSALIND. HOW OLD ARE YOU?" Archer asked after a few minutes of electric, tension-filled silence.

"I'm twenty-seven." It was so strange to talk to someone practically the same age, but whom I was separated from by almost a hundred years.

"Your husband, Dan. How old is he?"

I was startled by Archer's use of Dan's name. It was like he had thrown ice water on me, made this all feel more real.

"I'm sorry, Rosalind, it wasn't my intention to upset you. Your ages are one of the few things I wasn't able to figure out."

"Um, yeah. I understand. He's thirty-three years old, so a bit older than me. Though I guess I've always felt older and more mature than other people my age and I never really noticed the difference that much."

"How long have you been married? How did you meet?"

He had a smile on his face, but I detected an undertone in his voice. It was almost melancholy. I leaned forward a little, trying to look deeper into his eyes, searching for any changes in his facial expressions.

He gave nothing else away, and I wondered if I had imagined it. I was wondering if I was imagining this all, if I would wake up from this like I had all the other dreams where I had been with him. I sat back and sighed, feeling somewhat reluctant to talk about Dan with him, but not sure why. This all was beginning to feel a little ridiculous.

"Hmmm. We began dating about seven years ago, and we've been married for three years."

"How did you meet him?"

"We met while I was in college. We just happened to be at the same restaurant on the same night. We were each there with our friends. It was late, and it wasn't a place my friends and I usually went to. I don't remember much of the night."

I stopped there and pulled my knees up to my chest, wrapping my arms around them and hugging them to me. I looked out the window, though all I could see was the fog still rolling around. The faint glow of the moon sometimes broke through the haze of mist.

I closed my eyes and went back to that night, to the

things I could remember. It was strange to me how much you could lose or forget over such a short period. I sighed again, opened my eyes, and looked back at Archer, smiling.

"Would you tell me about it, Rosalind?"

"I remember laughing at something one of my friends said, my head thrown back. I wore my hair down, something I almost never did. I could feel my hair tickling my lower back, which only made me laugh more."

I stopped and looked over at Archer, giving him a chance to ask any questions he might have had. He gave me a look that conveyed that he wanted me to keep going. So I did, getting lost in the memories.

"I looked across the room and our eyes just met. Mine and Dan's. It almost took my breath away, and I remember thinking this only happened in movies or books. But it happened. I couldn't look away, and I guess he couldn't either. He has the most beautiful blue eyes. They are this brilliant aqua color, with hints of gold in them, if you look closely enough. They are just unreal. But that isn't even what got me. As our eyes met, he smiled, a real, genuine smile. The skin around his eyes crinkled, and I could see the smile in his eyes. I can't even begin to tell you how rare that is, how rare it is to see a man's smile in his eyes. But Dan, he gave me the most breathtaking, authentic smile. I guess that was probably it for me."

Archer continued to sit there as I recounted my story, never once interrupting me, just letting me dwell in the memories. He nodded his head, telling me he wanted to hear more.

"The rest of the time we were at the bar, I kept looking back. He was looking at me too. I could feel his gaze on me. Dan and his friends were finishing up dinner before we even left the bar area. They came up to us and introduced themselves and ended up inviting us to some party they were headed to. I can't tell you one thing about that party. But I remember how it felt to have Dan's hand in mine when he introduced himself. I remember how it felt to have his hand on my lower back at the party, how warm and safe it seemed. I remember how his faint breath felt on my neck when he was talking in my ear so I could hear him over the music. I remember what his kiss was like at the end of the night, tentative and brief, but sweet and warm with the promise of something that didn't feel so safe. I think maybe I even fell a little in love with him then, even though I never believed it was possible." I stopped, remembering who I was talking to, and blushing.

"This must all seem very forward and scandalous to you, doesn't it?" I asked, not quite ashamed, but feeling some unnamed emotion I couldn't put my finger on and wanting to move away from this conversation that now felt awkward and wrong.

"No, I know some things are different now than they were when I was alive. More casual. But scandal wasn't unheard of or new, even then. Things did happen. We may have been more discreet, but life wasn't as different as you believe."

I could tell he didn't want to embarrass me in any way. He sat considering me for a moment or two before he continued. "Do you miss him now? I noticed he's been gone lately."

"He had this job before we met, so this is always how things have been. Well, I guess not always. This was the first time he had a chance to bring me along. Though it didn't turn out the way we expected in the end. So I do miss him, but I'm also really used to the time apart."

There was no sadness or longing in my voice. It was all so matter-of-fact. It troubled me, because in such a short time I'd begun to become numb to Dan's absence. Then I decided to push it out of my mind. It wasn't something I wanted to consider or explore at the moment, and not with Archer. It would do me no good anyway, I couldn't control the circumstances.

"Can I ask something a bit more... personal?" he asked suddenly, almost urgently.

"Well, you're on a roll right now, so why not?" I gave him what I hoped was a good-natured shrug.

"You've been married for several years now. Why have you not had any children?"

It wasn't the question I'd been expecting. Dan was already nearing his mid-thirties, and while it did seem a little soon to have children, it had never been a question of *if* I wanted to be a mother, but *when*. I realized I couldn't say it was the same for Dan. We kept putting the conversation off. I slowly lowered my legs back down to the ground, shifting to the side, and absentmindedly rubbed my arms, a failed attempt at keeping the growing cold within me at bay.

"I'm sure it must seem so strange to you. I bet I would've been considered a spinster in your time, being my age with no children yet," I said jokingly, my way to try to lighten the mood.

"Well, no, you're married, so the term spinster wouldn't apply to you, would it?" he joked back. "But it would be assumed at this point you were unable to conceive. Is this the case?"

"No, I don't think that's an issue. It's something Dan and I haven't discussed. And really, we haven't felt the rush to start a family. I do want children though, very much. I always pictured myself as a mother," I answered. "How about you? Did you have any children?"

A look of pure sadness and longing crossed his face, then disappeared, his eyes going blank with some effort.

"No, I died before I had any children. I died before I could get married," he said with regret and some other emotion adding an edge to his voice. It almost sounded like anger, but I didn't see it on his face or in his posture, so I couldn't be sure that was what it was.

"Wasn't it rare to reach your age without having been married?" I wasn't sure if my question would upset him, but I figured since he was already asking personal questions, this was fine, and I was curious anyway.

"I suppose in some ways it was rare. Though it was more common for men to wait longer than women. I was engaged once when I was younger, but it didn't work out. We were both young and thought we were in love. Our families were not happy with the engagement and insisted on a long one to try to prove our love false. Her parents then sent her to Europe to spend the summer with family. Not too long after she arrived she married someone else, an old family friend. I found I wasn't as upset by the news as I probably should have been if I'd truly loved her," he answered with a rueful smile. Before I could ask another question, he continued.

"After that, I threw myself into the family business for several years and was quite successful at it. It made me even more desirable to families in our social circle. A year before my death I met Helena. She was lovely, intelligent, and icy. It took no time at all for our families to arrange the engagement. I was happy with the match, but as time wore on and I got to know her, I began to feel maybe it would be a mistake." He stopped abruptly. I was about to ask more questions, now extremely curious as to what had happened and why he felt this way, but I stopped short at the troubled look on his face, his lips no longer smiling, but instead set in a grim line. I got the uneasy feeling there was more to the story, but it wasn't a happy story or one he was even willing to share at the moment.

"I'm truly sorry to hear that," I replied, slightly regretful my path to marriage seemed so effortless in comparison.

I began to get up then, deciding some background music was needed if we were going to continue to talk. I also thought I might be able to get an idea of what modern music he enjoyed and didn't like.

I refused to examine the reasons I was so interested in Archer, why I wanted to know his thoughts on every-thing, his likes and interests. The appearance of someone I could talk with, even if the person wasn't alive or didn't even exist, was a welcome relief from the loneli-ness I always felt at night. Even if it did make me crazy.

"I was thinking about putting some music on, is there anything you'd like to listen to?" I asked over my shoulder as I made my way to the hidden stereo system. I could have turned it on with the remote control and then just streamed from my phone, but I needed to get up and move around.

With a quick glance at the clock, I was taken aback by how much time had passed. Archer and I had already been talking for nearly two hours, though it felt like no time had passed at all. I should have been tired and ready for bed, but there was an edge of excitement running through me, almost like adrenaline floating through my veins, and I was wide awake. I opened the cabinet and went to turn it on. I glanced over my shoulder at Archer, waiting for his response. A frown touched his lips and I wondered what was wrong.

He stood up, and I knew I must have said or done something wrong, though what, I couldn't be sure of. I wondered if the talk about his fiancée upset or angered him. Before I could get a chance to ask and apologize again, he began to speak.

"As much as I would love to listen to music and continue our conversation, I think it's time for me to be going. I've used a lot of energy making myself visible and talking for so long, and I think I need some rest, for lack of a better word."

"Oh, I didn't even consider that! I'm so sorry for keeping you." My face warmed in embarrassment.

"No, no, it was quite lovely. I've never had a connection with someone still alive, let alone talked to them. To have you see me, *really* see me has been nothing less than miraculous. If it's all right with you, I would like to try again and continue our conversation another time?" he asked, the unmistakable undertone of hope and anticipation in each word.

"I'd like that," I replied quickly, probably much too quickly.

He smiled a breathtaking smile. His teeth must have been blindingly white and perfectly straight when he was alive. His smile had to have broken at least a few hearts. Mine fluttered a little, a brief weightless feeling in my chest. He took a step forward toward me and then stopped. That electric energy that seemed to surround us since he had appeared pulsed between us, growing stronger as he came closer. Neither of us knew what to say or do next. I smiled back at him, a little more tentatively than he had.

Before I could ask when I might see him again, he dissipated into thin air just as quickly as he had appeared.

FIFTEEN

I TURNED over for what felt like the thousandth time, punching my pillow before laying my head back down. I grabbed my phone from the bedside table. It was nearing four in the morning. I groaned and flipped onto my back.

I should have been asleep hours ago, but my encounter with Archer and our conversation kept replaying itself through my head. I was still finding it hard to believe this was all happening. Did ghosts really exist? I thought of all the things that had happened over the last few months, and I knew if this was all real, if Archer was a ghost, he had been there from the start.

The weird electrical disturbances, things turning on and off randomly. Items falling off tables or things being in the middle of the floor when no one had been in the room before. A breeze sweeping by and caressing my skin, even when there was a fire blazing and no windows open and no source for it. A whisper in my ear when I was alone. The feeling of being watched. That scent, which I now realized must be his. So many little things, moments most people would brush off—hell, moments I had tried to. Now I couldn't.

I threw the covers back, swung my legs over the side of the bed and stretched out long and slow, like a cat, and then pushed myself up and out of bed. I wrapped my long sweater around my body and padded downstairs to the kitchen to make a tea. I looked down and realized I was only wearing very skimpy underwear under my sweater.

My thoughts automatically strayed to Archer, and I walked back to my dresser, grabbed a pair of knit pajama pants and slid them up my legs. Normally I would have no issue walking around the house in just my panties, but realizing I wasn't exactly alone had me thinking twice about the wisdom of that.

After I finished making my tea, I made my way back into the living room and sat in the armchair closest to the fireplace. I wrapped the throw draped on the chair around me and reached for the book sitting on the side table, and without opening it, I rested my tea on it on my knee while staring into the fire I had started.

I couldn't even begin to calm my thoughts down. They were all over the place. A part of me was tempted to wake up Josie and spill what had happened. I wanted to hear her confirmation I was crazy.

Maybe then I could dismiss all that had happened as a hallucination and move on. A small part of me wanted to hold on to what happened though and not share it with anyone. I shook my head, wondering why I would even begin to feel this way.

Archer knew Dan's name and that we were married. How long had he been watching? How much had he seen? Did he know what I looked like naked?

Did he watch as I got ready for the day? Even worse, had he watched while Dan and I made love? I shivered at the thought and shook my head, attempting to dislodge the thought.

No.

Even after just one conversation, I couldn't believe it. Though really, what did I know? Maybe it was beyond his control. Maybe he had no choice as to where he could go. Maybe he had no choice but to witness all the things that happened in this house.

And then I wondered where he went when I couldn't see him or when he was trying to make his presence known. Was he just attached to the property? Could he go anywhere in the world he liked?

My mind came up with new questions before I could even finish forming the one before. So many questions.

I knew I was the only one he'd managed to make

contact with, but I wondered if he had attempted to reach out to Dan or anyone else. Why hadn't I asked him any of these questions earlier? Weren't those the kinds of things you demanded to know when finding out you were rooming with a spirit?

The one question I kept circling back to: why had Archer specifically chosen me as the person he wanted to connect with?

I finally managed to fall asleep on the couch, only to be woken up by a call from Dan in the morning. I was exhausted and the conversation was stilted, uncomfortable. He was just checking in with me, letting me know things were starting to improve, but he had no idea when he would get a chance to visit again.

I waited for the tiny stab of pain in my chest I'd started to get when he would tell me we wouldn't see each other anytime soon, but it didn't come. I wanted so badly to blurt out what had happened the night before, but Dan wouldn't get it. He would either laugh it off as a dream or overactive imagination, or he would start to believe I was crazy.

I knew by the end of our conversation this wasn't something I could share with him, and really, I didn't think it was something I could share with Josie either, no matter how open-minded she was.

I decided to spend the afternoon with Marie to get some space and distance from the house and the Archer situation. At first, I wanted to confide in her too, but my gut instinct telling me to keep this close to me won out.

Spending the rest of the day with her ended up being the perfect diversion. I helped her out in the kitchen, learning some tips and tricks about cooking and baking, and stayed to share dinner with her and Steven.

As I was driving home, all thoughts of my ghostly roommate returned. I wondered when I would see him again. The uncertainty filled me with a bit of sadness. When I got in the house I took a quick shower, put on some comfy, warm pajamas, and settled onto the couch, putting a movie on.

I was maybe ten or twenty minutes into the movie when my skin prickled at the shift in the energy surrounding me, a new tension in the air. I shivered, goose bumps rising on my arms as Archer appeared beside me, in front of the couch he was sitting on last night.

"I love this movie," he said with a smile in his voice. "Would you mind if I joined you?"

"Of course not, take a seat, if it's comfortable for you," I replied in almost a whisper.

We sat there in silence for nearly forty minutes, both

of us watching the screen intensely, though I kept looking at him out of the corner of my eyes, not daring to turn my head and get his attention.

I wasn't frightened by Archer—rather, I was strangely comfortable with him around. I had no explanation for the butterflies that took up residence in my stomach anytime he smiled at me.

I tried to maintain the appearance of watching the movie, but I couldn't concentrate at all. The magnetism and pull in each dream he was in was present between us now, seeming to grow with every minute we spent in each other's company. I was dying to ask him if he felt it too.

I found myself watching his every reaction to the movie as covertly as possible, enjoying every furrow of his brow and each grin. The expressions on his face when something happened that seemed to affect him emotionally, the joy and natural smile that would light his face when something humorous happened. I know he had seen this movie before, but he didn't guard his feelings the way most people did, making it a unique, novel experience for me.

I waited until the movie was over to say anything. I didn't want to interrupt Archer, as he seemed to be enjoying himself. Questions swirled through my brain, one right after another, but I also didn't want to interrogate him right off. I sat there deep in thought, almost missing it when he was the one to break the silence.

"Rosalind, please tell me you love this movie as much as I do," he said as he turned to face me, his gaze catching mine. The butterflies in my stomach took flight, the drop and swoop of unnamed emotions creating that weightless feeling again.

"I barely watched it," I blurted out before I clasped my hand over my mouth, which seemed to have a mind of its own. Archer's only response was a deep rumble of laughter. "I didn't mean to say that."

"What were you watching then, Rosalind?"

"You."

Shit. I couldn't trust myself around him. His laughter grew even louder.

"Okay, so I obviously have no control over what's coming out of my mouth."

"I find it refreshing. Why were you watching me?"

"At first, I just loved seeing your reactions. They were so unfiltered and honest. Then I zoned out thinking of all the things I should have asked you last night instead of talking about what we did."

"Well, then, let's rectify it now. What should you have asked me?" He shifted and changed his position, like he was settling in for a while.

I started biting on the tip of my thumbnail, considering which question I wanted to ask first. "So, I get you've been watching me, but how exactly does it work? Are you just around and watching all the time?"

He sat silent for a couple of minutes, looking at me thoughtfully, though I could tell by the look in his eyes he wasn't really seeing me and was more lost in his thoughts.

"I've never had to explain this to anyone, so please bear with me. I haven't fully worked out how this whole afterlife works, I only have my own experiences and beliefs to go on."

"Okay. What do you believe, Archer?"

"I feel as though I'm now merely energy. I can manifest myself physically at times. I can even gather enough strength, or energy if you will, to make physical contact with people or things. I can manipulate them, move them. But it all seems to take a significant amount of energy." Archer's brow was furrowed as if he was deep in thought about what he wanted to say. "When I'm not using this energy, I don't just disappear. I'm still here, in the air, around. I can leave the confines of this house, which I do quite often to ensure your privacy. Otherwise, my presence and spirit are just... here, around."

I must have looked as confused as I felt, because Archer rushed to explain.

"When I say I've watched you, it doesn't mean I'm sitting in a corner in the house watching your every move. I'm not watching when you're bathing or dressing, or being intimate with your husband. That would be a serious breach of trust and manners. Over time I have come to sense and understand when privacy is needed, and I respect it, for anyone who has lived in this home. Does any of that make sense, Rosalind?"

He was leaning over with his elbows resting on his knees, his face between his hands, deep in thought while trying to accurately answer my question. He turned his head and looked at me, smiling shyly, almost sheepishly.

"I think so. So you're saying if I want to just talk to you when I can't see you, you can hear me, you could respond?"

"Yes, I'm sure I could."

"Hmmm. Maybe I'll have to try it some time," I responded, giving Archer a silly smile. "I have so many more questions I want to ask you."

"Well, shoot," he said as he grinned. I found myself laughing. The use of the current phrase sounded so funny, but charming coming out of his mouth.

"God, I don't even know where to start. Hmmm. Oh, are you tied specifically to this house? This land? Or can you move around to other places?"

"That was a lot more than just one question." He ran a hand down his face, considering my questions. "I feel a deep connection to this place. I'm not sure if it's because I loved this land so much when I was alive or because I died so close to this place. Maybe it's the manner in which I died. Whatever the reason, I seem to be bound to the original boundaries of the land I purchased."

He looked away from me, but not before I could see the sadness lurking in his eyes, and that dark edge again too.

I looked over at my phone, only to realize it had been a few hours since Archer had appeared. Soon he would need to go wherever it was he went to rest, and I too needed sleep after the near-sleepless night I'd just had. I didn't think we'd be able to have the fun and light-hearted conversation I was hoping for, so I decided to end the night there.

"I'm sorry if I made you sad. Maybe we can continue this conversation another night? I'm drained, and I'm sure you must be too."

"Yes, I feel my energy starting to fade. And no, you have no reason to apologize. It all still seems raw, even though it happened a hundred years ago. I hope to one day feel comfortable talking about all of it, the details of my death," he said before looking outside and falling quiet. After a moment, he looked back at me. "I can come back tomorrow if you'd like?"

"Please do, Archer. Have a good night," I said as I watched his form begin to fade.

"And to you, Rosalind," he said before disappearing.

Thirty minutes later, I found myself still awake. I decided to try out his theory.

"You there, Archer?" I called out into the silence of my room.

"Yes, Rosalind," he responded.

His voice sounded like it was right in my ear and all around me, almost like surround sound, though I couldn't feel his presence the way I had all the other times before meeting him.

"God, that's so fucking creepy," I said, giggling to myself. Somehow his responding laughter reverberated through the air and into my body, shaking me with his mirth.

"Good night, Rosalind."

"Night, Archer."

SIXTEEN

"WHAT ARE YOU WATCHING?"

The atmosphere became charged with whatever this *thing* was that seemed to constantly hum between Archer and me before his words even hit my ears. I turned in time to see him form solidly before he settled into his spot on the opposite couch.

We had been hanging out like this for the last week, and you would think I'd have been used to the way his presence made me feel, but I wasn't yet. So I continued attempting to ignore it altogether.

"Hey! It's this old show I used to watch as a kid. For some reason, I thought of it today and decided to try it again. I've gotta say, it holds up pretty well."

I smiled at him before turning back to the screen and snuggling further into the plush blanket wrapped around my body.

"Holds up well? What do you mean? What's it called?"

I still forgot we weren't from the same time and that some things needed clarification.

"Sorry. I meant that I'm still enjoying it even though I'm older and the show is old. It's called *Daria*. It was actually my favorite when I was growing up. The characters and humor just spoke to me."

"All right. Tell me what's going on here. What did I miss?"

I explained the premise of the show and told him what was going on in the episode he'd walked into the middle of. It was hard for him to understand a bit, so much was out of context for him, but he appeared to enjoy it and didn't complain or ask once to watch something different.

"I think this might be the first cartoon movie I've ever seen," Archer said in the middle of our third episode. I glanced over at him and caught the smile on his lips and I couldn't help but return it.

"We'll have to change that. There are some really great animated movies out there."

"Was this really intended for children? I can't see this being appropriate for you to watch when you were younger."

I laughed and shrugged in a way that said, *Probably not, but not much I can do about it now.* "Watching as an adult, no, I guess it wasn't appropriate, but my parents didn't really monitor that closely. Plus, I turned out okay, so no harm, no foul."

We sat in companionable silence as we continued to watch. I snuck glances over at Archer, curious to see his reactions and if he was enjoying this or just being polite. His quiet laugh every so often let me know he was catching on quick to some of the humor. I smiled to myself, silently thrilled to be sharing something I loved with him. I refused to dwell on the reasons why.

"Oh, Jane," I whispered during the next episode.

"Hmmm," Archer responded, his body turning toward me, his eyebrow quirked in question.

"The girl with the black hair and red jacket?" I gestured to the TV, my eyes never leaving his. "She's my favorite character on the show. She was actually partially responsible for me getting into art and wanting to explore being an artist."

"You're an artist, Rosalind?"

Curiosity laced his voice and even after only a week of knowing him, I could somehow sense he wanted to ask more questions. I paused the show and then rearranged my body to face him more fully.

"Kind of, yeah." Archer might not have intended for that to be a loaded question, but my voice, my response was heavy with all the things I hadn't said.

"Can you explain that, please?"

"I went to school for art. I had the intention of getting out of school and making a name for myself in the art world. Then I realized it wasn't that simple, so I got a job at a gallery, helping run it and teaching occasional classes."

"It sounds like you're an artist, Rosalind."

"No, I'm really not. I graduated from college almost five years ago, and I have yet to have one gallery showing. I haven't even finished a single piece since I was in school."

I said the last sentence into my hands, unable to look him in the eye, ashamed at how far I had fallen, at how much I'd let complacency take over my life. When had I become this person floundering to figure out what her path in life was?

"Why do you feel that is?" Archer asked after a few moments of silence.

His patience with me, his ability to somehow discern what I needed in that moment was surprising and comforting. There was no judgment in his voice.

I bit on the tip of my nail, considering what answer I could give him that would be honest but wouldn't give too much of myself away. The vulnerability he managed to draw out of me was unnerving and painful. The walls I always maintained around Dan, Archer was dismantling, piece by broken piece.

I sat up straight, stiffened my spine as though it

might give me some strength and courage I wasn't particularly feeling in the moment, and looked Archer dead in the eye.

"I've always been the kind of person who needs to be inspired to work. It all feels too forced if I try anything else. And I haven't felt inspired in years. So long. Too long. I'm realizing now that I allowed this to happen. I got complacent and comfortable. And I somehow stopped looking for the magic in life. I stopped searching for the things that light up my soul and inspire me." The final sentence came out a scratchy, painful rasp that hitched in my throat before leaving my mouth.

A flurry of shimmering movement caught me by surprise before my eyes were able to focus and make out Archer kneeling right in front of me. The soft swish of air cooled my cheek as he reached out and brushed away the tears that had slipped down my face.

I gasped at the contact, at the feel of electricity that surged through my skin at his featherlight touch, the swoop and sudden drop in my stomach, that weightless feeling.

"So now that you know your truth, what are you going to do to change it?" he said in a voice just above a whisper, but ringing with strength.

His proximity and the weight of his words settled over me, rendered me speechless. We continued to stare at each other, the tension increasing with each passing second. He waited, giving me the time to consider his question, but not giving me the space that would have made me comfortable.

"I—I don't know," I managed to force through the emotion constricting my throat. Archer, God love him, simply nodded, stood up, and went back to his place on the couch.

I pressed play on the TV, hoping we could both get lost in the distraction and noise of it. I knew that his question would stick with me until I found the answer. As I stewed in my thoughts, trying not to let emotions pull me under, I started to wonder how he had figured out his life's purpose.

It couldn't possibly be that simple for anyone to figure out, right?

"Archer, how did you decide what kind of profession you wanted?" I asked, as I paused the TV again and turned to him.

"I didn't."

"What do you mean? You mentioned working the night we met."

"Yes, I did work. You already know my family was wealthy and involved in business. I started learning about the family businesses when I was very young. It was always assumed I would run them when I was old enough, so in that regard, I never had a choice as to what I would do with my life. Maintaining my family's legacy, ensuring the Breckenridge name and businesses continued to grow and flourish was my fate."

The undeniable regret behind every word he said bit into me, causing an ache in a deep, untouchable part of me. In that moment I felt so foolish, so ridiculous, feeling sorry for my lack of inspiration and progress in my career when he'd never even been given a chance to choose what he wanted to do with his.

"I'm sorry, Archer. I wish you had been given a choice."

"What is it I've heard you say? It is what it is? That's how I feel about it now. There's not much I can do about it anyway, being dead and all. Plus, it wasn't all bad." The smile on his face never reached his eyes.

"I'm curious. What kind of things did you do for work? What kind of businesses?"

"Hmmm, where to start? I can't really tell you my story without talking about my father's as well."

"I'd love to hear it, Archer. Whatever you're willing to tell me." I didn't want him to feel pressured to share anything he wasn't ready to talk about.

"My father was considered one of the original San Francisco Robber Barons. He came from a prominent New York family involved in banking, steel, ships, and railroads. He was one of six sons and he was also expected to take over one of the family businesses. He wanted more for himself, to establish himself on his own.

When he heard rumors about the Gold Rush, he decided to take us out west to make that name for himself. And he did."

The Gold Rush. Fuck. It was hard to wrap my head around the fact that he was even alive during such a pivotal part of history.

"Did your father have the same expectations of you?"

"Yes. I started in railroads before moving on to infrastructure. When I had done well with that, I then moved on to banking."

I sat there utterly transfixed by him, by the pensive look on his face, his brow furrowed and mind lost to the memory of his former life. The warmth of his deep voice worked its magic on me, wrapping me up like my favorite blanket until I was lulled into a feeling of comfort. I realized then that I could listen to him talk all night, it didn't matter what he was saying. So I considered ways to keep the enchantment going.

"I never knew about any of this. I'm kind of embarrassed to admit that I didn't look too deeply into your family when Josie and I were researching you." I shrugged awkwardly, a wordless apology for something I really didn't need to seek forgiveness for. "It's crazy to me how much you accomplished in such a short time."

"It was expected of me. There was really no other choice. And I was good at it. Great, actually." His body tensed as he said this and the sharp edge in his voice betrayed an underlying anger at the circumstances of his life.

"Was banking where you stayed?"

"Yes and no. When my father decided to expand into Seattle, I volunteered to go. I wanted a change and I needed the freedom. I had begun to feel stifled by the expectations of my family."

"You obviously loved it up there."

"Yes. I did."

The memories of another life a hundred years ago flashed across his eyes and the smile that graced his face was a thing of beauty. This time, the smile reached his eyes and they crinkled with what had to have been so many memories of better times.

"So what did you do for work there?" I asked, wanting to know every single thing about his life, especially the one he'd had in this place that meant so much to him that he was tied to it in death.

"I began by opening our first bank branch in Seattle. I was then responsible for us venturing into manufacturing. We were working on a prototype for what would have been our first automobile when I died. It was my idea from the conception, and I suppose it's the closest I ever came to loving my work." The sadness and regret in his voice nearly broke some small piece inside me.

"We are pretty far from Seattle out here. How did you discover Orcas Island?"

This was a question that had been on my mind since Jos and I started researching Archer. What had not only brought him so far away from civilization, but also compelled him to buy land with the plans to build a home out here? I wondered if uncovering his reasons would give me insight into who he was as a man.

"I was invited on a hunting trip out here by a client. Is that something that's still done?" he asked, interrupting his own train of thought.

"I dunno, actually. I don't think I know anyone who's really into hunting."

I shrugged and gave him an encouraging look, hoping there was more to it than just that. I didn't want to consider how quickly I had come to love listening to him talk. His deep voice full of warmth never failed to seep into my veins.

"All these years later, I find myself still trying to make sense of what happened. As we grew closer to shore, something came over me. This feeling of peace and contentment. It was something I'd never experienced before."

I nodded my head in understanding and my movement caught Archer's eye, making him pause.

"Like you were exactly where you were meant to be all along?" I said as my gaze met his, some invisible bond between us tightening, pulling us closer.

"Yes. As though I'd finally returned home after years

of being away. It scared the shit out of me, Rosalind. But that fear didn't stop me from returning several times until I found this piece of land. I knew this was where I was meant to live."

He stopped suddenly, his eyes unfocused, lost in the memory of his former life.

"And here you still are."

I whispered the statement to myself more than to him. After a moment, his gaze returned to mine. An emotion I couldn't name blazed in his eyes, burning me from the inside out with its intensity.

"Yes. Here I remain."

SEVENTEEN

"WELL, who is this on my phone?" I had to hold back laughter at the absurdly dramatic, confused voice I used once Jos' face appeared on screen.

"Bitch, don't act like you don't know, you called me!"

I dissolved into giggles at her indignant tone. "I just miss your pretty face. You've been MIA. I don't like it, especially when I can't just drop in on you to make sure you're still alive."

"Ugh, I know, I know. I'm sorry, babe. It's been crazy at the studio. Tracey quit and Melina's on maternity leave, which means I'm running their classes along with all the office work. I need a vacation."

I looked at the screen intently, and while she was as beautiful as ever, dark circles under her eyes were barely masked with makeup and her shoulders drooped in exhaustion.

"I have a solution!" I exclaimed, knowing she would never take me up on my offer.

"I can't come take a vacation. You know I would be on the first plane out there." She took a sip of what I guessed was green tea before turning her tired smile on me. "You look happy, Ros. Has Dan been home more?"

I couldn't help the frown that took over my face at her question. It hit me then that I couldn't talk about Archer with her, not yet, at least. Not until I found a way to explain his presence that didn't sound like I had gone off the deep end out here. Keeping this from her was going to be like walking on eggshells. We almost never kept secrets from each other, we knew each other too well. "No, he hasn't. He hasn't called much, either. He's so caught up with this project."

"Hmmm. You look much more content than you did during our last conversation. What's going on over there?"

"Nothing much, really. I've just been exploring, getting used to the place and spending time with Marie and some of her friends. I love it here, Jos. I don't know why this place feels like home, but it does."

That made me think back to my conversation with Archer a few nights ago. That feeling of rightness that came over me when I got here was so similar to what he described, it shook me a little. *We both belong here.* The thought flitted through my mind before I could stop it.

"What's that look for, Ros?"

Dammit.

Maybe a FaceTime call had been a bad idea. I sat for a minute considering how I could spin this to satisfy the curiosity I had piqued in my best friend. "I was just thinking about a realization I had the other day. About my career, or lack thereof."

"Oh, have you found inspiration yet? Are you creating pieces again?"

The change of subject perked her up. Jos was always encouraging me to just start working at my own stuff again, convinced that I would find my way once I lost myself in the creative process. I still wasn't sure.

"No, not yet. And that's the problem. I've been thinking that maybe I'm being my own worst enemy about this whole thing."

"I can see that. How do you think this happened?"

I'd been thinking about this for a while, trying to find answers, so my response came easier than I expected. "I got so stuck in my routine I stopped looking for the magic of everyday life. All those little things that used to inspire me in college? I think I stopped seeing them because I stopped looking for them."

Could it really be that simple? The words Archer and I had exchanged were on a loop in my mind, playing over and over again. Could it really be as easy as opening my eyes?

"Now that you know your truth, what are you going to do to change it?"

That one question kept screaming at me. The realization that I had all the control in this situation was a revelation.

"So, are you going to start seeing the magic again?" Jos asked, breaking through my thoughts.

"Yeah, I think I am." I straightened up my spine and looked her dead on through the lens of my phone's camera. "I've been letting life just happen to me for far too long. I think this is one area I can take back control. I have to take control of at least this."

A huge, breathtaking smile broke out over Jos' face. "That's my girl," she said. Heat rose in my cheeks and I couldn't help the blush her words, her love had brought out. "So, I hate to change the subject—"

I interrupted her with a groan. I knew I wasn't going to like the next words out of her mouth. "Is there anything I can do to keep you from finishing that? I see that look on your face, Jos, I have a feeling I'm not going to like whatever it is you have to say." I lay back and got ready for whatever it was she wanted to talk about.

"Nope, not a chance. Anyway, have you talked to your dad lately?" She almost sounded timid. Almost. The question hit me like a punch in my gut and I sat up quickly, making my head swim with dizziness in the process.

"No, I haven't talked to him since... damn, since the going-away party, I guess. Why?"

I thought back to the party.

The minute my eyes met a familiar pair of hazel eyes that were almost a mirror of my own, I openly sobbed, pulling away from Dan and running to throw my arms around my father.

"Oh, Daddy, I've missed you so much."

I pulled away slightly, trying to wipe away the tears now coursing down my face.

"I wouldn't have missed this for anything, baby girl."

His deep voice with just a hint of a Southern twang left over from his youth washed over me, soothing something in my heart I hadn't known needed soothing. While he didn't live far away, the nine-hour drive to Tahoe City always seemed like oceans away, and we didn't get to see each other as much as I would have liked.

The fact that he was missing the birth of his stepson, Marco's, first child made my heart ache in an unfamiliar way. His response when I asked him why he would miss the arrival of his first grandchild? "When is the last time I got to see you?" He was right, it had been far too long, and I couldn't deny how grateful I was to see him, even if I couldn't bring myself to say the words.

"I saw him the other day. He was in town with Maria, Marco, and his family. He asked how you were. Ros, he looked so sad. I know you guys suck at communication, I do. But he's not going to be around forever either."

She let her words trail off, but I knew what she was thinking. What she was always urging me to do gently, in her way: *Fix this. Fix things with your father.*

And I wanted to, I really did, but I didn't have the first clue how to go about doing it. We didn't suck at communication, we just didn't do it at all. It had always been that way, and as I considered that it became apparent that my issues with Dan stemmed from somewhere.

"Joooosss. I don't even know what to say to him. How do I fix this with one phone call, with a single conversation? How do I repair a lifetime of dysfunction?" I finally gave voice to the question on constant repeat in my head. In all these years, I'd yet to find an answer.

Jos looked at me like the answer was so obvious that she was disappointed I hadn't figured it out for myself already. "You don't, Rosalind. You don't fix it all with one conversation. You take that first step. And then you take another. Most changes in life don't happen overnight. They are little things you do every day until you wake up and realize your life has changed in a significant way. That's how life works. Little by little, piece by piece until you've created the world you want."

Long after our call ended, I thought about what she said, replaying her words over and over again. While so simple, it was a revelation to me. How could I have been so blind as to never figure this out on my own? The longer I thought about it, the more I wondered why she had never said this to me before.

A few days later it finally hit me. Until that day, I hadn't been ready to really hear the truth behind her words. Once I had, I knew I had to find a way to make them my truth.

EIGHTEEN

I COULDN'T STOP THINKING about my conversations with Archer and Jos. All their words were on repeat in my head, day and night. It struck me how similar their sentiments were, how they both somehow knew me enough to get right to the center of the issues holding me back—I was the main obstacle to having the life I wanted. I wasn't surprised that Josie knew me so well, and I wasn't ready to deal with how well Archer had gotten to know me in such a short amount of time.

My few trips out into town were already different. I was starting to notice more of my surroundings, the beauty of the island, the way the light would hit the water just right during my afternoon walks, the silhouette of the ever-present madrona trees quickly becoming one of my favorite views.

I wished I could say that I instantly found inspiration in the world around me and began creating again the next day, but of course that didn't happen. I did notice a change in the way my mind took in everything. My thoughts didn't manifest in direct ideas that would become new pieces, but there was a stirring of ideas, a new feeling of excitement and something I couldn't quite put my finger on, but felt right and good all the same.

After showering and getting dressed, I decided to head to Eastsound and explore before heading over to Marie's. My notebook and pencils were lying on the chair where I'd left them the night before and I decided to take them with me. As I drove through the village, I spied a cute bookshop with a cafe attached and decided to stop there first. I grabbed a tea and scone and found a cozy corner with an overstuffed chair that was calling my name.

I spent the better part of an hour slowly drinking and people watching through the window. A little girl walked by holding her mother's hand. She couldn't have been older than four or five years old.

I watched as she tugged her hand out of her mother's grasp, walked a few steps back, and then crouched down into the flower bed, picking up a perfectly oval, smooth rock. She held it up to the sky, turning it over in her hand as she looked at it, considering it. She then got the biggest smile on her face, slipped it into her coat pocket, and ran back, grabbing her mother's hand once again.

I couldn't help but smile and feel a surge of warmth from watching such a simple thing bring so much joy to the little girl and from the mother's patience. It reminded me of my own mom and how often she'd let me explore the world on my terms as a young child.

She'd always sat back, letting me discover things for myself, watching and ready to help or answer my questions, but never encroaching. Her demeanor, how she handled me always made me feel so special and loved, and watching the little girl made me miss the bond and long for the day I might have it with my child.

I dreamed of sharing little joys with my child one day. As an adult, it was so easy to lose focus on what really mattered, lost in the pursuit of things that didn't really matter. Children had it right. They so easily found joy in small pleasures, in the simple things in life. Children were able to recognize the simple pleasure of jumping in puddles after the rain or finding the perfect rock.

Something clicked for me at that moment. I could feel the tendrils of inspiration and the heat of creative spark I had found so elusive for years start to gather in me. The beginning of ideas that had been floating through my mind took root and grew.

I grabbed my notebook and pencil, wanting to get the thoughts onto paper before I lost them completely. Once

I'd gotten every last idea down I found I couldn't concentrate anymore. I knew I wasn't going to get anything else done in the bookshop, so I decided to walk around and explore some of the galleries and shops in the area.

Everything was so charming and comfortable. I could see this place being home for me for longer than the year we had planned on staying. There were several galleries and shops with amazing artwork, most of it local and representing the San Juan Islands. I was blown away by a lot of the work I was seeing, and I chatted with a few of the gallery owners, just getting a feel for each one, making mental notes of places where I might try to see if they were open to displaying my work, once I decided what medium I wanted to focus on. I loved my mixed-media pieces which merged painting and sketches, fiber and knit arts, but I hadn't created anything like them in the last couple of years.

As I continued to walk, I came across a small street leading down to the beach and decided to explore. The coastline here was so different from the long, sandy beaches of California I was used to, but no less stunning. Stone and shells instead of grains of sand, driftwood, and branches everywhere. I was enamored.

The wind whipped through my hair as I crouched down and began picking up branches made smooth by the water, fragments of sea glass, and polished rocks. As

I held these things in my hand, a canvas appeared in my mind, slowly being filled in with these pieces of the island, vibrant shades of green and blue paint splashed across, all merging to create a thing of beauty.

My fingers reflexively wrapped around these things in my grasp before I slipped them into my bag. I could visualize so clearly how my first piece in so long would come together, and a sense of contentment ran through me, a feeling of being exactly where I was meant to be at that moment.

I stood back up and left the beach, making my way toward the shops and my car. I turned up a street I hadn't been on yet, and halfway down I came across a little studio space with tons of natural, beautiful light. It was closed, but there was a flyer posted on the door letting people know the space was available for rent and how to contact them to set it up. I took a picture of the flyer with my phone as another idea came to me. I thought about the things I had picked up from the beach and then about the little girl from this morning.

As I looked in the studio window, a plan began to formulate. I had experience in teaching art classes from my time at the gallery back home. I wondered if there was a local art council or foundation I could work with in starting classes for children specializing in mixed-media art and using the studio space, if it was affordable.

I could do two sessions a week, one where we would

explore different areas on the island for inspiration and find a few pieces from nature to incorporate into our pieces, and then a second session where we would use the studio space to work on the art. I would start a new group each month, and it would take the entire month to create one piece of artwork.

I even considered an art show every six months where we displayed the work created, and the show could be a fundraiser to help pay for the expenses of supplies, so the classes really were free. The more I thought about it, the more excited I got.

As I continued to look through the window at the studio, a lightness filled my chest as my pulse started to race. Energy built up in me, something I hadn't felt in so long, years even. I felt like it was all about to vibrate out of my skin, that soon the frenzy inside me would be visible to anyone looking. I was on to something here, I just knew it.

It struck me then how strange this all was.

Seeing the mother and her child, the beach, finding the studio all on the same day.

A feeling of warmth and comfort came over me, making a home inside my body alongside the giddiness. It reminded me so much of what it was like on adventures with my mom and the thought crossed my mind that maybe, somehow, she was looking down on me right now, that she was with me in this moment and had a part in all of these pieces clicking into place.

I didn't feel her presence the way I had Archer's before I met him, I didn't believe she was around and present the way he was. But I couldn't help but *want* to believe that she was somehow responsible for all of this, for me being in this place at just this right moment.

NINETEEN

DO I CALL HIM? Do I not? Do I just try?

I had spent the better part of the afternoon and into the evening contemplating—fighting with myself, really —over whether I should call Dan to talk about what happened today. Once the floodgates had opened, I couldn't hold back the deluge of plans forming and then re-forming in my mind. I wanted to talk about this all, bounce thoughts off of someone. I wanted to talk to *Dan* about them.

Yes, I understood the ridiculousness of fighting with myself about calling my husband. But he wasn't an easy person to get hold of on a normal day, and since this project began our communication had dropped to all-new lows for us. I checked the time again. It was nine o'clock at night. I figured things had to have calmed down by this point and it would be safe to call.

I bit at my thumbnail as the ringing continued in my ear and I waited for it to connect. Eventually the voice-mail picked up and I listened long enough to hear Dan's voice, missing the deep timbre in my ear before I hung up. I pulled up the messages app and started to rapidly type out a text.

Me: Hey, babe, how's it going? I miss you and it's been a few days. Call me when you get a chance? I have something I wanted to talk about. XO

As I waited for a response I wasn't even sure would come, I debated what I wanted to do next. I could try calling again, but I knew if he hadn't answered the first time he was either busy working or sleeping. I paused for a moment, waiting for the long-familiar tightness in my chest, the cold feeling that would flood my veins, sure signs that the sadness I normally felt at being so disconnected from Dan was about to set in.

Nothing.

My shoulders sagged with the realization that in the absence of my usual feelings when I was let down, I felt a void. Nothing had changed recently, so why were my emotional reactions changing? I racked my brain trying to come up with answers but was left grasping at straws.

I pulled up the contacts on my phone again, went to

my favorites list, and let my finger hover over Jos' name. I needed to talk to someone, but I wasn't sure Jos was that person tonight. I didn't want to hear supportive words.

I could just imagine what she would say when I told her what I had brewing: *"Ros, fuck, that sounds amazing. Seriously. How did you not come up with this sooner? What are your plans and what can I do to help?"*

No. I didn't want to hear that right now, though I was sure on another day, a day I wasn't feeling so confident and sure of my plans, I would want and need to hear her beautiful words of support and love. But today wasn't that day.

Today I needed to hear doubt and questions. I wanted to hear all the obstacles and challenges that lay ahead of me if I took this path. Everything that could go wrong and wouldn't work. I needed to hear all those things so I could work out how to overcome them all. As amazing and honest and blunt as Jos was, she was also undyingly supportive. I needed Dan's brand of honesty and skepticism. His form of logic.

As I realized that nearly an hour had passed while I considered what I wanted and who I needed to talk to, it became obvious that I wasn't going to get what I wanted or needed that night.

I slumped down into the couch and rubbed my closed eyes. Frustration, elation, anxiety, fear, and trepidation. All of these emotions were waging a war inside my head and my heart, taking over my body until I was practically vibrating with it all. I sighed deeply, throwing my head back.

The energy in the room changed, a calm washing over my body before Archer's voice rang out in the room, deep, smooth, and refreshing as a dip in the ocean on a scorching day. No one had ever had this effect on me and I was ashamed and scared of this realization.

"Hello, Rosalind." His voice sounded from across the room.

"Hi, Archer," I replied, as I opened my eyes and forced some cheer into my voice and a smile onto my face.

I looked up at him as he fully materialized and sat on the sofa I'd come to think of as his. The smile strained my face, made it ache with the effort. Archer's brow furrowed for a second before smoothing out. He sent a smile my way, but I knew in that moment he was on to me and my attempts to pretend like I didn't have a million thoughts weighing me down.

"Care to talk about it?"

"No. Maybe another day, but not tonight." I turned away from him, grabbed the remote and turned on the TV. "Want to choose?"

I offered him the remote without looking back, but I lowered it when the movie selections flipped across the screen. It was still jarring to see and remember that he didn't need a remote, that part of his ghostly thing was being able to manipulate electronics.

Archer made a sound that sounded like a barely restrained groan of excitement as the movies scrolling by stopped suddenly on *Indiana Jones and the Last Crusade.*

"Do you mind if we watch this?" Archer practically begged. The pleading look on his face made him look so young, boyish even. "I love this movie and I can't remember the last time I watched it. The couple who lived here before watched these movies all the time."

"Your favorite? Even more than *Raiders of the Lost Ark*? C'mon, Archer. Really?" I knew there was no way I'd deny him his favorite, but that didn't mean I wouldn't give him a little shit first.

"Oh, Rosalind. I enjoy them both, but there is just something special about *Last Crusade* that I love."

He said this with such earnestness, such vulnerability and openness, that an unfamiliar warmth flooded my system, heating me until I could feel the warmth in my cheeks.

"You know, I've never really considered why I love this one more than the others. I was alive when the movie begins, and I think that's part of it. If I had been born a little earlier and into a different family, a different life, that could have been me. Indy's relationship with his father reminds me of mine, the constant effort to prove himself as worthy of his father's time. When I watch it, I can't help but hope that one day our relationship would have begun to change the way theirs had at the end."

He looked lost in thought as his voice trailed off. What was unmistakable was the now familiar note of melancholy in his voice, a remnant of regrets from a life cut so much shorter than it should have been.

A deep ache pinched in my chest for a heartbeat, an involuntary response that happened every time he was unable to hide the pain in his voice. I should have been used to this feeling by now, but I couldn't help but hurt for him at all he had lost and missed out on, at the loss of the man he was and the greatness he could have been.

As the movie continued, I snuck glances his way, some unnamed thing in me needing to check on him, to make sure he was all right. While his body appeared more relaxed, his arm thrown over the arm of the couch and his back slouched into the corner, the tensing of his jaw and the rigid hold of his fist betrayed the emotion in him.

I needed to take his mind off this. I didn't want him to leave with this cloud of anger and sadness hanging over his head. As we reached the book-burning rally in Berlin, I paused the movie, my decision made.

"Rosalind, is everything okay?" Archer asked.

"Yeah, it is actually. I'm ready to talk about what happened today." Even I could hear the determination in my voice. I looked up at him and was flooded with warmth at his encouraging smile.

"I was in Eastsound today. I found the cutest little bookstore with a coffee shop inside. I loved it." I turned more fully toward Archer, resting my head on my hand on top of the arm of the sofa, settling in to share with him. "I just hung out there for a while, drinking tea and watching people walk by. At one point, I saw this little girl. She was so cute and so enamored of her surroundings, of the nature around her. It was truly a joy to watch her picking up stones and sticks, seeing the happiness in something so simple."

"It sounds like you had a good day, Rosalind."

"I did, but that wasn't even the best part. Something started to click and I don't know, all of these ideas began of art I could create, canvases I could fill with art that combined elements from the island and my paintings or drawings. I've been to the galleries here, there's nothing quite like what I've been envisioning today." I stopped to take a breath.

"Rosalind, that's fantastic! Are you telling me you got your inspiration back?"

"Yes, I think so. But this wasn't even the best part of it all."

"Okay, go on."

"While I was walking around, I came upon this

amazing little art studio anyone can rent space in. That's when it all clicked!"

I looked up at Archer then and couldn't help but smile. His body was closer to mine, and he leaned forward with his arms resting on his thighs, head in his hands, and the most beautiful smile on his face. He quirked his brow at me as though to say, *Why did you stop?*

"I realized I could offer classes for kids in the kind of art I make. I would do month-long classes with a couple of sessions a week, and the kids would create one work of art during that month. Then every six months I could hold a fundraiser art show displaying the work. And it would be totally free for the kids. I still need to do some more research and get in contact with the local art foundation here, but I think this is special and could work. What—what do you think?"

I uttered the last sentence with trepidation. In this short amount of time I knew Archer to be kind, but also honest. I had a feeling that if he found too many flaws with this idea of mine, I would likely walk away from it.

He sat considering me. At first, I couldn't decode the look on his face, and it scared me. After a minute the biggest, brightest smile took over his face, and I sat back in awe of his beauty. His eyes filled with admiration and affection, and I couldn't help it, my cheeks warmed and flushed pink under his gaze.

182

"I think it's a great idea. I don't know much about art or setting something like that up, but if there is any way I can help you, even if you just need someone to talk to, I'm here for you, Rosalind."

The sincerity in his voice floored me, and I found myself speechless. I had no words for the support he was showing me, support I wasn't certain I would find in Dan. I also had no words for how quickly this man had become a good friend to me.

No, not just a good friend, but the kind of friend that you only encounter a few times in your life.

It wouldn't hit me until later that one day I was going to have to walk away from this man who was quickly becoming a part of me.

TWENTY

"WELL, HELLO, STRANGER," Marie said to me as I entered her kitchen and made my way over for a hug, a warm smile touching her lips and flour all over her hands. "Where have you been hiding your pretty face? You missed our last book club meeting."

I returned her smile as I hung my purse over the back of a stool at the island and sat down. "I've been home a lot. Busy. I've got some stuff going on I want to get your thoughts on."

It wasn't a lie exactly, but it wasn't the real reason I hadn't been around for the last couple of weeks. I was spending nearly every night with Archer, which meant I was trying to catch up on sleep during the day. I hadn't thought to ask him why he mostly only appeared at night, but it was something I noticed. Throw in the research I was doing on the art program, and I seemed to be busy all the time.

"So, what's been on your mind?"

I described my idea to her, all the things I'd been planning. Every time I said the words out loud it solidified my plan and my confidence grew. I knew this was the right move, I just needed to figure out the last pieces to pull it all together.

Marie sat and listened as she measured out the things she needed for what she was baking. Her face and body betrayed none of her thoughts. When I was done, I just looked up at her, trying to anticipate what her reaction would be, if she would find fault with what I had shared with her. The emotions running through me were what I imagined I would have felt if I was having this conversation with my mother, trepidation and hope that I was on a path that would make her proud.

"And what do you plan on naming this organization?" Marie asked. I studied her face for a moment, but still couldn't get a read on her or her thoughts.

"Wild Art," I replied simply, unable to hide the joy and hope I held in this idea of mine.

Marie smiled then, that beautiful, familiar one that sent warmth and pangs of loss coursing through me at the same time.

"I love it, Ros. How can I help?"

My answering grin took over my entire face, and I knew the final puzzle pieces were about to fall into place.

"I have nearly everything in place and I've started brainstorming the first show as well. I've placed flyers around town and I'm already booked up for the first month. The one area I'm struggling with is finding a contact with the local art council. I would love for this to be something that benefits the island, but the only website or information I could find for the council is outdated and incorrect. You wouldn't know someone on the council I could contact, would you?"

"Of course I do. You're right, it's difficult for a newcomer to get in contact with them, but I think they would love to be involved. I'll get you a list of names and numbers before you go."

I got up off the stool before my brain registered my heart's intentions, and I rushed up to Marie, throwing my arms around her and getting flour all over myself in the process. She giggled and hugged me back with warmth and love.

"Thanks, Marie. I can always count on you," I said as I disentangled myself from our embrace.

"You're welcome, dear. Now that you look like you've been baking, why don't you stick around for a bit and help me finish these?" she said as she bumped my hip with her own.

With Marie's contacts, everything else fell into place pretty easily. A week later, classes began. Aside from a few kinks here and there that needed to be worked out, it all came together pretty well.

We spent one session a week out in nature gathering leaves, branches, shells—really, anything that reminded us of this beautiful island we called home. The parents came along on the days spent out of the studio to help wrangle the children, and sometimes I even had people volunteer to join us and teach the class about the area we were in each session, telling us about the habitat or stories of those who lived here long before us. It was fun and educational.

The studio days were a blast, and not only did I find myself enjoying all the children who passed through the door, I even made friends with some of their parents. I was becoming more a part of the community.

As one week bled into another, my lost creativity crept back in, first appearing as ideas and dreams of half-finished canvases, which led to completed artwork and a new lightness and fullness in my heart I hadn't felt in years. On the days I wasn't working on things for the program or with Marie spending time in her kitchen or with her book club, I was creating my pieces in the sun-filled office turned studio at the house. A few of my works were in a couple of the local galleries and one on the mainland. I'd even sold a few pieces.

I was experiencing a level of independence and self-reliance I had never known. I'd met Dan before I finished college and moved in with him right after I graduated, so I had never lived on my own before. Dan continued to try to persuade me to move back to Santa Barbara in the few conversations we had. His guilt over abandoning me in some strange place was obvious, but time and again I tried to tell him that I was enjoying being on my own for now. I was growing, becoming stronger. It unsettled him, but I couldn't tell why, and he would never admit it.

I was happier with nearly every aspect of my life, aside from the gaping chasm between Dan and me. The handful of texts we exchanged each week and the random phone call here and there didn't help, and I realized the distance we had hoped to breach was growing impossibly wider.

Archer and I fell into a routine similar to the one that began the night we met. The days I wasn't home working on my own pieces, I was in the village working on the program or hanging out with Marie and the friends I made through her book club. I would come home, and after getting settled for the night, I would call out for Archer to join me. We mostly watched movies and then chatted for a little while after. We took turns choosing movies, and I was always surprised by what he would choose.

You would think a ghost this old would consistently choose silent movies or old classics. That would be far too cliché for Archer. His taste in movies was varied. One night we watched a classic noir, his next choice an old James Bond flick, followed by a more recent romantic comedy, then an indie drama. He invariably surprised and amused me.

Our conversations were mostly safe, regular topics. Most discussions were about the movies we watched, getting into debates about the themes or events within. We also listened to a lot of music. Our friendship, for lack of a better word, was simple, but it was nice. It was like I'd found a long-lost best friend, but I wasn't sure if he felt the same way.

The electricity and tension that always hummed between us, arcing and making my heart race whenever we came close to touching? That was still the elephant in the room that neither of us had dared to acknowledge.

My loneliness began to diminish, though it never entirely went away. I attempted to bridge the growing distance between Dan and myself, but on the rare occasion he returned my calls, he sounded extremely distracted, like his mind was somewhere else altogether.

I could often hear voices in the background, a younger guy and a woman with a husky, almost sultry voice. I figured these were his teammates, but couldn't bring myself to ask more about them, especially when we barely had a chance to talk.

My heart was hurting for us and the state of our relationship, but I became resigned to the fact we were stuck in this shitty place until this project was over and we were living together again. I secretly hoped this would be the last project he took on that kept him away from home for any length of time.

I just didn't think I could be the kind of wife who would ask him to choose between me and his career. I understood how much he loved it, just as much as I loved my art. Giving it up would be like losing a limb for me, and I couldn't imagine it was any different for him.

TWENTY-ONE

"ROSALIND, how has your work been going? We always talk about Wild Art, but we never talk about your own projects," Archer said as I shoved a handful of popcorn in my mouth.

We had stopped watching the movie I'd chosen a while ago, deciding to talk instead. I was curled up in a blanket on one side of the couch, while he was sitting on the opposite side of the same long couch. We'd finally realized it was easier to hold a conversation if we were sitting close together. We never touched—I made sure we never touched—but the ever-present energy between us crackled and sparked.

"Wait, haven't you looked at the canvases in my studio?" I sat up, upending the bowl of popcorn that thankfully was almost empty. I grabbed a handful off my lap and ate it.

"No, I haven't."

"Hmmm." I gave him a knowing smirk. There was no way he hadn't snuck a peek at my work that covered every available surface of the makeshift studio.

"I just wanted to hear you talk about it. Your face lights up when you speak about things you love. You positively glow, and to me, there is no more beautiful sight."

I gasped at his declaration as my gaze flew to his, wanting to see what truths lay in their depths, the need to decipher his feelings too intense to deny.

"You are, you know, Rosalind. You are the most beautiful thing I've ever seen," he said with a shrug, as though what he just said was a part of our normal conversations.

While I wasn't the most self-conscious person in the world, his words, compliments still made me uncomfortable. And all the old self-doubt came back, taking me right back to my childhood.

I was awkward and different from most of the other girls around me when I was younger. The area I grew up in wasn't very diverse, and I was bullied a lot. While my mother was French, Argentinian, and a bit of Sioux Indian, she had dark blonde hair and green-gold eyes. At first glance, we looked nothing alike, and the kids at school weren't old enough or aware enough to look for the nuances that made our relation apparent. What they were good at was making someone who looked different feel alienated and ostracized.

My mom helped out and volunteered at my school a lot. She was super crafty, and she shared her talent in my classroom. Every single time she was at school, the day would end with a large group of kids in my class cornering me behind the cafeteria to hurl insults at me.

"You're so ugly."

"You know your mom isn't really your mom, right?"

"You were adopted."

"You were such an ugly baby that your parents didn't want you."

"Your real parents left you on your new parents' doorstep."

During all this they would shove at me, pulling at my backpack, grabbing onto the sleeves of my shirt and stretching it out.

There are only so many times you can be told you're adopted and ugly before you start to question what you thought you knew to be true. At six, seven, or eight I had trouble seeing the resemblance between my mother and me. The hurt and confusion from the frequent bullying made me ask my parents on a weekly basis if I really was theirs or if they just didn't want to tell me the truth of my adoption.

My peers only ever knew my mother, with her green eyes, her straight blonde hair, her very European look. If they had ever met my father—saw his light chestnut skin, witnessed the *beautiful mix of his African-American and Italian features—they would understand my parents really were mine.*

There were so many days I came home and hid in my closet, crying until I was physically spent, praying to a God I didn't even know to change me. To make me just like everyone else. It can be so hard as a child to accept that your differences are something to value, not change.

I was never the most popular with boys in middle school and for most of high school. While I finally came into my looks, I was always different-looking, and there were times I still felt that old insecurity rise inside of me.

I had hazel-gold eyes, high cheekbones, full lips, dimples, a smattering of freckles, and long, heavy, loose, curly hair that was utterly uncontrollable. I wasn't short, wasn't tall, and I was fairly curvy. Over time I grew to be mostly comfortable with my self-image, but I never found a way to be comfortable with attention or compliments.

"Rosalind, are you okay? Did you hear me?" Archer's alarmed voice in my ear broke through my memories. I opened my eyes as his hand made contact with my face and I nearly jumped from the shock of it, from the warmth and ache that curled through my body at his touch and proximity.

The energy between us sparked and nearly ignited. We had always kept things between us so safe, on my end as an attempt to deny the connection growing between us. With Archer's body so close to mine, his hand absently caressing my cheek, my skin felt like it was about to catch fire. I realized I couldn't deny it anymore.

"Do you feel it? The energy, this strange pull? Is it just me?" Heat crept up my neck, into my cheeks, until the tips of my ears felt like they were on fire. Archer's eyes flared with so much emotion and tenderness it nearly made my heart stop.

"I feel it too, Rosalind. I've never felt anything like this."

"Like—" I began at the same time Archer did. I let him finish his thoughts.

"It's like I've known you all my life. Being dead and still present is solitary and lonely. You are the first person I've made any contact with, and I can't help but believe it's because of whatever this is pulling us together. So yes, I feel like there is something deeper here, and I hope this… friendship means as much to you as it has come to mean to me."

He looked at me with both a boyish shyness and a hint of weariness. He'd been so forthcoming with his feelings and I owed him a full explanation about my ties to him as well.

"I already feel like you're one of my closest friends, Archer. There are some things I need to tell you."

I took a deep breath and a step away from him, breaking the physical connection between us. I couldn't say what I needed to with him touching me. His touch was too distracting. It caused my pulse to skyrocket, the nerve endings in my skin to tingle at the current that arced between us.

"From the moment I stepped in this house, I began having dreams about you. I didn't know it was you at the time. I just knew I was having dreams about a man I had a profound connection with. Then strange things I couldn't explain began happening to me. Josie kept joking it was a ghost, but it seemed too crazy to be real or true. When I saw your picture, I started to put the pieces together, even if I still didn't want to believe ghosts existed."

I paused for a moment, taking a much-needed breath after the onslaught of words that just poured from my mouth. I looked down at my clasped hands, trying to buy some time to figure out exactly what I wanted to say.

"I don't know why I've been dreaming about you, but I believe it's where our bond began, for me at least. It's strange, and none of this should be possible. But it is, so I'm just going to roll with it," I finished and threw my arms out to my side in a gesture that showed I had laid it all out there.

He laughed, a deep, full, contagious laugh. I smiled in return, a little bewildered by his reaction.

"Rosalind, did you think I didn't know these things

already? This is all peculiar to me as well. The thought of finally having a friend, someone I can communicate with, someone I feel like I might have some common ground with, well, I don't want to walk away from that, so to speak."

I smiled at him, then laughed, and continued to laugh until tears streamed down my face. I looked up at Archer, and watched raptly as he leaned back on the couch, his ankle resting on the opposite knee. I glanced at his face in time to see curiosity and amusement written all over it.

My confession let loose something inside of my chest. A lightness that hadn't been there before crept in. It was a release, one I hadn't realized I needed. Once I stopped, wiping the tears from my eyes and clutching my stomach, which ached from the exertion, I felt a million times lighter, freer.

"Whew, sorry about that. Sometimes we all just need a good laugh, you know?" I asked him, silently begging him to understand. He scrutinized me for a moment before a wide, breathtaking grin took over his face.

"I do know what you mean, though before meeting you, I hadn't laughed in quite a long time."

I smiled back at him, starting to relax, feeling some of the burden of an untold truth lift off my shoulders while hiding my true feelings I wasn't ready to acknowledge under the guise of friendship.

TWENTY-TWO

"OKAY, FAVORITE AUTHOR, AND GO!" I exclaimed to Archer, grabbing the remote control from the coffee table, turning off the movie we hadn't been watching and putting on my instrumental rock playlist.

"I like this song."

"I do too, but you're changing the subject."

"Well, would you want to answer that question?" I couldn't help but laugh at the long-suffering look on his face.

"Of course not! I could never answer it. Maybe if I had to choose a top ten list, I could, but it would take me a lot of thought and time beforehand. It just isn't something I can come up with off the cuff."

"Then how do you expect me to do it?"

"Could you come up with ten?"

He arched his brow at me. "What have you been

reading lately?"

"I'm rereading one of my favorite series. I do it every year."

"Tell me about it." He didn't even know we could be here the rest of the night if I were allowed to talk about my favorite books unchecked. Well, at this point, he probably did know.

"Okay, so I had this mild obsession with young adult fiction at one time—"

"What is young adult fiction?" He cut in before I could finish my explanation.

"They're books written specifically for young adults. You know, older children and teenagers."

"We just called those novels when I was alive." Shit. Sometimes it was so easy to forget there was a century separating us.

"Well, now it's an entire genre. Anyway, I used to devour books in this genre. I got burnt out on them, but two of my favorite series were written for this segment of the population."

"Understood. What's the name of these?"

"The first series is the Mortal Instruments series and the next one is the Infernal Devices trilogy. They both deal with a group of teens with angel blood and special abilities. I'm sure it sounds pretty silly, but I love them."

He flashed his brilliant smile at me and it was impos-

sible to ignore the flip in my stomach, the rush of pleasure it brought me.

"So much so you read them every year." There was
understanding written all over his face. He got it. Of
course he would—we shared a love of books.

"Yes."

"So read them to me."

"Wait, what?" He couldn't possibly be serious.

"You know it's nearly impossible for me to read on
my own. If I attempted it, I wouldn't have enough
energy to be here with you, and that just won't do. If this
is something you love, I want you to share it with me."

He was serious. I was surprised. There was no way I
could deny him the one thing he loved more than most
others and couldn't have. I grabbed *City of Bones*, the first
book in the series, cracked it open, and I began to read.

I looked up what felt like a little while later, but upon
looking at my phone discovered was a couple of hours
later. Archer was utterly entranced, entirely lost in
the story.

"How do you like it so far?"

"I love it," he said. "It's unlike anything I've ever
read. So much imagination. I can see that world so
vividly in my mind." I beamed at him, his assessment

bringing me more joy than it should have. "Do you need a break? You've been reading for a while."

My mind was already on something else that had been bothering me. "No, I'm okay. Can I ask you a question? It's something I've been thinking about a lot over the last few weeks," I said, turning to Archer.

"Of course, you can ask me anything, Rosalind." His smile both warmed me and made me shiver at the same time.

"Do you ever think about going away, Archer? I mean, leaving for good?"

From the look on his face, from the tender, caring gleam in his eyes, I wasn't able to hide the sadness from my voice. I almost hated myself for asking the question and I didn't want him to answer for fear of what it would be, but I couldn't take the words back—they already sat between us, sinking like a dead weight in the ocean, threatening to bring us both down with them.

He raised his hand slightly; the movement was almost imperceptible. I think anyone less connected to him wouldn't have even noticed it, but I did. I could see the war in his eyes, the desire to reach out and touch me he was almost able to hide. Just as quickly as I saw his true intentions, his mask was back up, making him unreadable.

"Rosalind," he sighed finally.

He fell silent again, contemplating how much of his

truth he was going to reveal to me. It was so funny, even after only knowing each other for the short amount of time we had, we already knew each other so well. We read each other like our most worn, favorite books.

I tried to push down the want to caress him the way I often did my most beloved books, sought to deny the desire to have him caress me in the same way. Heat began to rise from my chest, up my neck, and into my cheeks. He would notice my blush soon, and I only hoped he wouldn't ask what caused it. I didn't think I had the strength at the moment to not answer honestly. I clasped my hands together, looking at the delicate lines and veins in my hands instead.

"Before you came along, yes, I considered finding a way to leave this place behind. I'd grown tired of being alone here, even when there were occupants. I grew to hate not being able to make contact with the people I shared this space with, or not wanting to make contact."

Archer closed his eyes and his features pinched, as though his confession was causing him physical pain. I wanted to say something, anything to comfort him, but I couldn't find the words.

"I put so much thought into what I needed to do to put my spirit at ease so I could leave. Then I saw you step through the doors of this house and for the first time in both my mortal life and my afterlife, there was genuine peace in my soul. I felt a pull to you, as though there was a rope binding us together. I—I couldn't leave. I had to try to get to know you, to see if it was solely over a century of bone-deep loneliness that made me feel this way."

"And was it?"

"I can honestly tell you now, it was not. It was the person you are, the person I am. I don't know why we are so connected. I only know I cannot, do not want this connection severed."

We both sat there in stunned silence. Archer looked surprised and baffled by his words, seemingly unsure how he allowed such honesty to spill from his lips. I was shocked by how deeply his truth resonated within me.

This connection should feel wrong. But it didn't. It had brought peace and an inexplicable sense of comfort when I walked into this home, when we first met. I couldn't deny those feelings had only grown since then. Until now, this thing between us was something we had mostly avoided and ignored, as though speaking of it would make us complicit in something wrong and dangerous.

Neither of us knew what to say or where to go from here. So we both sat there, nearly touching, but not. His fingertips danced along the back of my hand, along my cheek. I hadn't realized I had closed my eyes, but when I opened them and looked up, there was not even an inch separating his face from mine.

My eyes fluttered closed.

His lips brushed against mine for a second, the sensation over so quickly, I contemplated whether I had really felt it at all. It didn't feel the way a typical kiss felt. It was light and airy, like whispered words breathed across my lips.

I swallowed hard and willed myself to breathe calmly and deeply. When I opened my eyes, he was gone. I touched my lips with my fingers, again wondering if I had imagined the kiss, if I had secretly wanted it so badly I made it real in my mind. I opened my mouth to call out to Archer, to ask him if I had imagined it, but the words got stuck in my throat.

As long as I didn't acknowledge what might have happened, I could continue to deny it. The denial came so easily it scared me, but I didn't know what scared me more: that I was able to so easily convince myself it had never happened, or that I found myself wishing it really had.

TWENTY-THREE

A WEEK HAD PASSED since the maybe-kissing incident, but neither Archer nor I had brought it up. I continued to act as though it never happened while I dreamt about it almost every night. I instead chose to focus on work as a diversion.

I had just begun a new session of my art program with a new group of students. I had also decided to add a second class to my schedule to continue working with the kids who had taken my first session. It was incredible and surreal that my waiting list far surpassed the amount of time I would be here.

This felt like my baby, something dear to me I had created and nurtured. Something that continued to grow and surpass all my expectations and fulfilled me in a way nothing else ever had. I started making notes about how to build the program, including rotating teachers in

different disciplines, adding more classes, and potentially adding more fundraisers to help support the
growth. I knew I had something great on my hands.

I also knew that my time here had an end date. I
didn't want to walk away from the program I'd created
but knew I couldn't stay forever. I realized that with my
resources and connections back home, I could create a
similar program in Santa Barbara.

Anytime I started to consider making new plans in
Santa Barbara, my thoughts also went to all I had left
behind. I'd been avoiding contact with my friends back
home, including Josie, and I was starting to feel guilty
and shitty over it. I knew the girls had been planning to
visit soon, which meant I needed to stop being a crap
friend if we were going to solidify those plans. Instead of
calling Jos right then, I decided to call her the next day.

My mind was so scrambled with all the things going
on between my art stuff, spending time with Archer, and
the fact that Dan and I hadn't even talked on the phone
in the last week and a half. The last text he had
responded to was almost a week ago. Our anniversary
was the following week, and though it wasn't something
we typically got a chance to celebrate, I found the desire
to do so this year growing with each day that passed
without any contact from him.

I pulled my phone out and tapped his name before I
could overthink it and second-guess myself. It rang a few

times before going to voicemail. I hung up, and pulled my knee up to my chest and rested my arm on it before laying my cheek against my arm. I stared off into space, trying hard not to get upset. A few minutes later I was startled by the buzzing of my phone in my hand, and even more shocked to see Dan had called me back so quickly.

"Hey, babe!" I answered in a slightly high-pitched voice. I cringed. He would be able to hear something was off.

"Hey, you called? Is everything okay?" he responded in a gruff, tired voice that held an edge of annoyance.

"Yeah. Yeah, everything is fine. I just realized it's been almost two weeks since we last talked, so I just wanted to see how you were doing, see how things were going."

"Has it really been so long?"

"It has, but I know you've been busy. I've been swamped too."

"I'm sorry," he replied before falling silent.

He sounded so different, exhausted and maybe frustrated, but there was something else in his voice that sounded so different from the Dan I had spoken with last. It sent up a red flag and kicked my anxiety up a notch.

"Shit, Ros, I was just looking at my phone and realized it's been a week since I've even texted you. I'm so sorry, baby. We're working all day and night. Sometimes it's over twenty-four hours before we notice a whole day has passed. Are you sure you are okay?"

"Yeah, I'm fine, I promise. I wanted to ask you something, but now it seems so silly."

"You know there is little you ask that isn't worth it. What is it?"

"So our anniversary is next week, and I know we don't usually do much of anything to celebrate, but I was kind of hoping maybe we can do something together. Do you think it would be possible?" I asked, hearing the uncertainty in my voice, but also noticing the absence of hope.

The silence seemed to drag on. Then Dan groaned. In an instant, my heart fell. I knew his answer wasn't going to be the one I wanted to hear.

"Ros, I wish I could, you know I'd rather be with you than here working, but we are so far behind, and there is just too much to do. I don't even know when I'm going to be able to come back and visit."

The silence now sat heavy and tense between us. I was sure Dan could feel my disappointment, even through the phone and the distance. Tears gathered in my eyes, my throat ached with the effort of trying to hold them back, willing them not to fall. I didn't want to cry; I didn't want him to feel shitty or upset for letting me down.

Dan remained silent on the other end of the phone,

and he knew me well enough to guess I was fighting tears. Before I fully exhaled my next breath, a light breeze wafted by me despite all the windows and doors in the place being closed, closely followed by the masculine, musky scent of sandalwood and ocean.

I turned my head and saw Archer standing across the room from me. He gestured with his hands, a silent way of asking if I wanted him to leave and have privacy for the rest of the conversation. I shook my head slightly, without a second thought. I somehow knew he'd come to comfort me, something I didn't realize I needed at this moment.

"Dan—"

"Ros—" We both spoke at the same time. Before either of us could try to continue, I heard a feminine voice in the background, but not close enough to hear what the woman was saying.

"Ros, hold on a sec," Dan said, not giving me a chance to reply.

I heard the muffled sound of Dan pulling the phone away from his ear and covering it so the conversation couldn't be overheard. I turned and looked at Archer and could tell by the look in his eye he suspected something was up.

There was more muffled movement through the phone before a woman said, "C'mon, Dan, you promised. The movie is set up and ready to go and the popcorn is popped. We've been working for eighteen hours straight, let's unwind a little before we go back at it, okay?"

Just as before, her voice was husky and one hundred percent sexy. I recognized the voice from previous phone calls and knew this was Kelly, the lone woman on his team. I looked over at Archer and caught him staring at me with a look of worry and something that looked a lot like anger on his face. I knew then he was hearing everything being said, and I turned away from him quickly, again willing the tears not to fall.

A rush of air moved past me, Archer's scent lingering after. I turned to find him sitting right next to me. A tear escaped down my cheek, and before I could wipe it away, I felt his hand grasp mine, lacing our fingers together before he gently squeezed once, shocking me for a moment with the contact.

"Ros, you still there?" Dan asked, resuming our conversation.

"Yeah," I was finally able to force out through my aching throat.

"Look, I've gotta go. I'm sorry I can't make things work for our anniversary. I'll see what I can do on my end to try to get over there sooner than later though, okay?"

I nodded my head, forgetting Dan couldn't see me, and murmured a few words as the call came to a close.

I hung up and looked down at the phone in my hands, not knowing what to say, not even knowing how I felt other than emotionally wrung out and confused. I leaned my head down on what should have been Archer's shoulder and gasped when I made contact with something solid. I turned my head and found I was indeed resting on his shoulder.

I looked into Archer's eyes. He brushed back the hair that had fallen in my face and placed an airy kiss to my temple, resting his chin on my head and wrapping his arm around my shoulder, pulling me closer to him. I snuggled into him, getting comfortable, not even beginning to understand how being physically comforted by him was even possible.

"Rosalind, I know it doesn't seem like it now, but everything will work out. I promise. There is a good explanation for what's going on, I'm sure," he said before I even had a chance to say what was on my mind.

It was crazy to me that he knew me so well already, he was able to anticipate what my reaction to the phone call would be. I sighed deeply and curled even further into his body. It somehow felt warmer than any embrace I had felt before. I knew it would only last a few more minutes, but those moments of comfort were exactly what I needed and more than I could have hoped for.

I realized in those moments in his embrace that Archer had become more important to me than I could have ever imagined. How, in such a short amount of time, had a ghost become my best friend? I didn't have an answer, but I knew things for me could never go back to the way they were before.

The next day I sucked it up and called Josie. I'd been avoiding her for too long and knew I needed her too. I sat on my balcony with a cup of coffee, tapping my fingers on the side table nervously.

"Hello," she answered.

"Hey, Jos."

"Who is this? The voice sounds familiar, but I'm just not sure who this is," she said. I was caught between wanting to laugh at her snark and feeling guilty.

"I know, I know. I'm an absolute shit friend, I deserve to rot in hell, and I'm sorry. Are you happy now?"

"Well, as far as apologies and groveling go, I'd give it about six or so, but it'll do for now. I'm glad to see you're alive. What's going on? Why the disappearing act, bitch? I was about to call a search team!" God, I'd seriously missed her overly dramatic ways. How had I seemed to forget she could cheer me up like this?

"Ughhh, I'm sorry, Jos. The program is taking up most of my time."

"How are things going with it?"

"Amazing. So much better than I expected. I'm going to be seriously sad when I have to leave. I'm already making plans to keep it going once I go, plus I'm starting to research creating a similar program back home."

"So what is it you aren't telling me? You know we don't keep secrets. Spill."

And this was why I had avoided calling her. Even over the phone without her seeing my face, she could sense I was withholding information from her, that I was keeping secrets. It was easier to be open and get it all out there than to attempt to keep things from her.

The problem was, I wasn't ready to talk about Archer with her. I wasn't sure I ever would be. She likely wouldn't believe me and would think I was crazy, as anyone would.

My friendship with Archer was something special I wanted to keep to myself. I didn't want to share my thoughts or feelings or the experiences I had with him with anyone else, and I really didn't want to even begin to analyze my reasons.

"Things with Dan are just... rough right now. Jos, I have no clue what is going on with us." Sharing my issues with Dan, while uncomfortable, was the best way to avoid talking about Archer.

"Okay, tell me what the problem is. Do we need wine and FaceTime for this conversation?"

"I don't know, maybe. But it's only like ten a.m., and

while I usually would start making mimosas, I have to be at Marie's in a couple of hours before heading to the studio."

"Then just FaceTime," she said as my phone sounded, alerting me that she was trying to connect. I accepted and set my phone up on the outdoor coffee table and snuggled back on the couch, making sure I was in front of the lens.

"So what the fuck is going on that has you so upset?"

"I don't know." I groaned, knowing that wasn't really true. "Dan and I barely talk. Last night was the first conversation we've had in almost two weeks and he hadn't texted in a week. It didn't go well at all, Jos."

I stopped talking and just cried, swiping furiously at my cheeks. This next part was going to be harder to say than I initially thought. The last thing I wanted to do was put any ideas in her head about Dan possibly being untrustworthy, but I also needed to bounce this off my oldest friend.

"I asked him if he could come visit for our anniversary. We need some time together, even if it's only a few hours. Of course, it's not going to happen right now, though he did say he was going to try to carve out some time to visit soon. What really killed me was at the end of the call I over-heard Kelly ask him if he was ready to watch a movie."

I stopped there, not knowing what else to say. I

couldn't give voice to my worries or suspicions, I just couldn't. I knew Josie would connect the dots and get where I was going with this.

"Who the fuck is Kelly?"

"The only woman on his four-person team."

"Have you met this woman?"

"No. I don't even know what she looks like. I can't bring myself to ask Dan what she looks like or if she's attractive. I don't want him to think I don't trust him or I suspect something."

"But you do. Suspect something, right?"

"Jos, I don't know. I want to trust him, I do. On the one hand, it sounded pretty casual and for all I know, the other guys were there too. On the other hand, he's working extremely long hours, day in and day out, surrounded by only three other people, one of them this woman. I don't like what I heard, but I also don't want to jump to conclusions."

Josie didn't say anything at first. She was deep in thought, so I just waited her out.

"Ros, I don't think Dan is cheating on you. He's honest to a fault, and I can't imagine him carrying on with someone else and not confessing to you immediately. With that said, it doesn't mean I think everything is okay with you guys. There are obviously some issues and you guys are barely communicating at all, even through text. That's not okay. You know this. You don't need me to tell you."

"I know, Jos. I just have no idea what to even do about this while we're so far apart and trying to put on a happy face and pretend like all is well is starting to kill me. I think at this point I'm going to have to put talking to Dan on hold until we can speak face to face. This isn't a conversation we can have on the phone or FaceTime, you know?"

I was done talking about it. There was nothing I could do until some unknown date in the future and dwelling on it wasn't going to solve anything. I shook off the negativity before changing the subject.

"So when are you bitches coming to visit me?" I asked, smiling and knowing this would get Josie off the topic of Dan and me.

Josie's face dropped. "Actually, it's one of the things I've been trying to talk to you about. I don't know if any of us are going to be able to get out there anytime soon. Scarlett has some family drama going on she hasn't wanted to talk about, so she's been pretty MIA too. Cynthia just can't get the time off work."

"Is Scarlett okay?" My stomach twisted as the guilt of being a shit friend took over.

"Yeah, Scarlett is okay, just going through some stuff."

"What about Cynthia?" The knots in my gut tightened.

"I guess they laid off like half her division and now she's doing the job of three people on top of her own. She wants to quit, but you know Cynth, it will never happen." Jos shrugged at this, since this kind of stuff happened to Cynthia often. "As for me, things are just crazy right now at the center. It will calm down eventually, but with all the time I took off for the holidays, I need to focus a little more energy here. I'm hoping I can get back out there in May or June. Do you think you guys will still be there?"

"I'm not sure. The plan was for six months to a year, so it really depends on how the project goes, though they're running behind and we are getting closer to that year mark, so it's pretty likely I'll still be here. Don't worry if you can't make it though, I totally understand," I replied with a smile I was sure she knew was fake and for her benefit. As difficult as it was to hide things from Josie over the phone, in person or on camera, it was nearly impossible.

"Well, fine, I guess I won't come again!" she replied in mock indignation and outrage, then dissolved into a fit of giggles when she realized what she'd said.

"Awww, c'mon, we both know you are always willing to come again," I choked out through my laughter, shaking my head at her. We seriously had the sense of humor of middle-school boys, immature and full of silly innuendos. We both continued to laugh for another few minutes.

"Okay, hon, I just saw what time it was and I really need to go. I'm super bummed about you guys not being able to visit. I know I owe the girls a call, but I really don't want to pretend everything is going okay here with Dan, so I'd rather not make those calls right now. Would you please just do it for me?" I begged her.

"Yeah, yeah, I get it. Just this once though. I'll let the girls know you're going to call in a few weeks when things 'calm down' for you, okay?" Jos replied using air quotes.

"You're the best, love you forever!" I said, blowing her air kisses.

"Love you too! Ciao!" she said, blowing kisses back before disconnecting the call.

I sat there for a minute, staring off into the distance. I knew I shouldn't have felt it, but all I could find myself feeling at the news my closest friends wouldn't be able to visit was complete and utter relief.

TWENTY-FOUR

I DIDN'T SEE Archer again until the next night. I could have used his comfort after my call with Dan and then Josie, but I just couldn't bring myself to contact him. He would have wanted to talk about everything that had happened over the last day, and I just wasn't ready for it after talking to Josie.

He knew me well enough to know staying away was the best thing for me at the moment. He was around—I could feel his presence all around me, not intrusive, but calming, peaceful. I was unsettled and confused and incredibly fucking sad, but strangely, I also felt safe.

"Ros, how are you this evening?"

Archer had somehow snuck up on me, and I almost jumped out of my seat on the couch in front of the fire. I wasn't used to him appearing without me calling to him first. He must have sensed that I likely wouldn't have

CECE FERRELL

called him that night either, though I needed my best friend. I also belatedly realized he had called me Ros for the first time.

"I'm so sorry I startled you. Please, forgive me," Archer said, taking a seat on the other end of the couch and turning to face me.

"You're fine. I just wasn't expecting you and I was zoned out," I replied, waving away his apology, turning to face him.

"Zoning out? You've used this term a few times, but I've never had it explained to me."

"Oh, I was lost in thought, daydreaming. I wasn't concentrating on anything specific, but I wasn't fully present either. Does that make sense?"

"Yes, I understand. So, would you like to talk about what happened with Dan and the phone call?"

He wasted no time in dropping the small talk to get right to the point. I had spent the last day thinking about this, trying to decipher what the call could have meant and how it made me feel.

"Do we have to?" I joked, though it sounded far too sad and bitter to be taken as one.

"I think you'll feel better if you do talk about it. Would you prefer to speak to Josie about this?"

"No, no. I'm sure you already know I talked to her. I'm absolute shit at talking about my feelings with anyone. The conversation didn't go very far, and I know Josie had about a million more questions."

"I didn't know you had talked to Josie about this. I'm not around all the time, Ros," he replied with a grin.

I was speechless for a moment, stunned both by his statement and by the emotions his smirk stirred up in me, in places I shouldn't have been feeling anything from him. I looked away, trying to gather my thoughts, considering how much I wanted to share.

"I'm confused. And not all of it is due to the phone call. I always thought I was satisfied with the nature of our relationship and mostly happy with things. When we moved here, I became more and more aware of all the things that haven't been working in our marriage. It's killing me. I can't do these separations anymore. Now there are these calls where I can hear this woman in the background. I don't want to assume anything is going on, or assume he is unfaithful. But I have to follow my intuition, and I know something is off."

I dropped my head into my hands, covering my face and the tears tracking down it. Archer just let me ramble on, not interrupting me or asking questions, just letting me think through what I was feeling, letting me get it all out there. I should have felt ashamed for just spilling it all without a filter, but Archer never made me feel that way when we talked. He made me feel safe, like being honest was something I would never be judged for.

Air gusted by me, then a light hand caressed my back in a calming way. I turned my head slightly, peeking out of my fingers to see Archer sitting right next to me, rubbing my back. At that moment, it was exactly what I needed, what I hadn't known I wanted.

I woke with a start, sprawled on the couch with the fire still burning and a throw blanket I usually kept on the back of the sofa covering me. I groaned, stretched, and looked down at my phone. I'd only been asleep for a couple of hours. I looked around the room and found Archer sitting in the armchair.

"I'm so sorry I just passed out on you. I didn't get much sleep last night, and I feel pretty emotionally exhausted right now." I stretched again and rubbed my eyes, trying to will myself to wake up. "Have you just been sitting there all this time?"

"Yes, you were so upset when you fell asleep, I didn't want to just leave you."

"Will you need to go soon? I'm sure just sitting there probably took all your energy."

The hope that maybe he could stay for a little while longer dripped from every word. The thought of being without him right now wasn't a pleasant one.

"No, I mostly just sat there, so I didn't need to use as much energy."

"Archer, how does this whole energy thing work? I've noticed lately that you're able to do more than you were when I moved here. You can touch me now, and the amount of time you're able to be around is a lot longer than before too."

"I wish I had a concrete answer for you. You're the first person I've ever reached out to, so this is all new to me. I've been thinking about it, and I've concluded that it's like a muscle. The more I use it, the more I touch, the longer I'm in contact with you, the stronger I get, the more energy I have and can use. Is it the actual reason? I don't know, but it's the only thing that makes sense to me."

I nodded my head in consideration. His theory was as good as any other. I guessed we would see if it continued to be true.

"I have an idea, Ros. Instead of us focusing so much on all the negative things going on, how about we focus on something positive instead?" He stood up and walked over to me, sitting on the same couch I was while I curled my legs underneath my butt and settled into the corner of the sofa to give him more room.

"What did you have in mind?" I asked, curious.

"How about you tell me about the things that work well in your relationship with Dan, the good things."

I rested my elbow on the arm of the couch and then my head on my hand and looked at him, thinking about what he was asking. I figured it was as good an idea as any, and really couldn't hurt me any more than I already was.

"Hmmm. We have a lot of the same interests. We both love to hike and be outdoors. We enjoy watching movies together, even if we don't have the same taste. We tend to get along pretty well. When we're together, we rarely fight or argue."

"What else?"

"I dunno. We always just clicked. We both love to travel and explore new places, even if we don't get to do it often. Or at all really. And physically, we are very compatible," I finished before I realized what I had said and started to blush fiercely. I could feel the heat creep up my chest, neck, into my face and the tips of my ears. It was one topic we had never broached and almost felt forbidden in a way, given our magnetic connection.

"I am so, so sorry."

"Rosalind, it wasn't *that* long ago that I was alive," he replied, his voice still full of humor and laughter.

"It was, though! And you said before sexual relations outside of marriage weren't common!" I'd never realized until now just how curious I was about this topic.

"So I wasn't entirely accurate when I made the state-ment. I suppose I said it to get us off the subject. It was only a hundred years ago, Rosalind, people had sex back then. We even used the word 'fuck.' People have been having sex outside of marriage since the beginning of time, why would you think it was any different when I was alive?" he asked me, straight-faced but barely able to contain the laughter dying to spill out of him.

"I don't know, Archer, I guess it was something I never put a lot of thought into until I met you, and then you basically told me that sex outside of marriage wasn't super prevalent and was scandalous, giving me the impression you were a virgin. Since, you know, you never got married."

It was such a stupid conclusion to have jumped to. I was beyond curious to know if he was, in fact, a virgin.

"So were you a virgin? I mean, it's only fair to know since you know I wasn't one when I got married."

I smiled at him, but it had to be the most awkward smile in the world. My palms were sweaty, and I was nervous, but I couldn't put my finger on why. It wasn't like this was a conversation I had never had before, with both men and women.

He looked me dead on and then gave me a sexy smirk which then transformed into a full-on, devastating smile. I felt that look in my chest, in my stomach, between my thighs. That smile and the look in his eyes should have prepared me for his answer.

"I was called a bon vivant or a playboy. Can I just say,

I hated both of those terms? People also gave me far more credit than I deserved back then. I was nowhere near as active as the rumors said I was."

My shock must have been splashed across my face because he laughed at me again.

"No, Ros, I was not a virgin. Sexual affairs happened often. We may not have been as open about our liaisons as people are now, but they most definitely happened. My first fiancée was a virgin, and we never did 'sleep together' as you would say. My second fiancée Helena and I did have a fairly passionate sexual relationship."

I quickly snapped my jaw shut after I realized my mouth had been gaping open in shock. It was way more information than I'd been expecting. There were so many things I wanted to ask but wasn't sure I would ever be able to get the words out of my mouth. I also couldn't ignore the stab of jealousy at his last revelation.

"Out with it, Rosalind, what do you want to know? You can ask me anything."

"I don't even know where to begin, Archer. I'm still in a bit of shock." I was embarrassed as hell for some reason, and feeling the blush in my cheeks.

"Just ask the first thing that comes to mind."

"How old were you the first time?"

"I was seventeen. She was older," he replied, no shame in his answer.

"How much older?"

"She was twenty-four and very uninhibited. She taught me a lot about women and their desires and how to please them. I don't know if I would have been so eager to learn if I had met her when I was older. How old were you?"

"I was fifteen. He'd been my boyfriend for over a year. I thought it was love and we would be together forever. He stopped talking to me a couple of months later, and it destroyed me. I can definitely say I learned very little about sex itself from him, and like most first experiences, it wasn't great."

"That's a damn shame, Ros."

"How many partners have you had?" I asked quickly before I could let myself think too hard about it or talk myself out of asking.

He leaned back and threw his left ankle over his right knee, considering how he wanted to answer the question, looking as though he might not want to respond to the question.

"Enough, but not too many. How many for you?" he asked right back, his voice full of humor and challenge.

"Enough, but not too many," I promptly responded. Archer laughed at that and his laugh helped relieve the tension.

"Do you miss it? Being able to touch, to feel, to be physically intimate with someone?" I asked after our laughter had subsided. He looked down at his lap for a moment before looking back up at me, piercing me with the intensity in his gaze, making it impossible to look away.

"Do you miss it, Rosalind? Of course I miss it. When I look at you, in the moments I'm not struck dumb by your beauty and all you are, I miss it intensely. To know I will never share that with someone again, it's only a dull ache, after all this time. But there are times when I see you, and the dullness fades away and becomes an intense pain, a fierce longing. I don't think the desire to be intimate with someone ever goes away. I know it never did in life, and now I know desire even more acutely in death."

I leaned back, feeling both stunned and on fire. Archer's words touched me, affected me in a way I had never felt before. A warmth spread throughout my entire body, threatening to set me on fire. The desire he spoke of was in every cell of me, trying to fight its way to the forefront.

I had denied my attraction to him for a while, telling myself it was silly to think I could have feelings for a ghost, or they only existed because of my loneliness. After what Archer had just said, and what it made me realize I was feeling, I knew for sure those were excuses.

Loneliness was something I hadn't felt for at least a few weeks. I also cared about Archer in a way I had never cared for someone before. The realization scared me more than almost anything ever had in my life.

There was nothing left for us to say. My emotions were far too close to the surface, and my thoughts too scrambled for me to add anything else to the conversation. If I vocalized any of the things stirring inside, I would ruin our friendship right there. It was a line I wasn't willing to cross, a loss I wasn't willing to bear yet.

We sat there in silence for what felt like forever. Eventually, my eyes fluttered closed, and became harder to open back up. I felt a soft caress on my cheek, smelled the comforting scent of ocean and sandalwood, and sighed deeply as a whispered, "Good night, my dear Ros," sounded in my ear. Sleep hadn't come so sweetly or quickly in a very long time.

TWENTY-FIVE

OUTSIDE OF A FEW quick daily text messages to make sure I was okay, Dan and I hadn't had a real conversation since the last disastrous phone call. As much as I wanted to talk and ask him what was going on with his co-worker, I just couldn't bring myself to do it.

Every time I fought with myself about the pros and cons of calling to talk about it or not, my conclusion each time was this was a conversation best left until we were face to face. I didn't want any misunderstandings or miscommunications to happen, so I continued to wait until he had time to come home for a visit.

Archer and I continued to spend time together every night. We kept to our routine of watching movies or listening to music, but not once did we have a real conversation. It was like we were both tiptoeing around the can of worms we had opened with the sex conversation.

I didn't want to acknowledge any feelings the discussion brought to light, and I got the impression Archer was doing everything he could to make me comfortable by not bringing up anything that could go there as well. While a part of me appreciated the effort, I missed the easy friendship we had experienced before the conversation. I missed being able to share parts of ourselves we hadn't shared with anyone else.

One night after watching a dark drama flick, Archer looked over at me and asked, "What do you think your biggest flaw is?"

It was the first time in a while either of us had brought up a topic more than superficial pleasantries, and while I knew the question would stir up a lot of emotions, I was grateful for it. I wanted to have deep, meaningful conversations with him. My soul craved it and at this moment I realized just how much I missed the way our friendship had been.

"My inability to talk about my feelings openly. Or at all."

"Really? I don't see it at all, Ros."

"I know, you're the first person I've ever been willing to open up to completely. If Dan or Jos had asked the question, I would have made a joke of it and changed the subject. I deny my feelings and bury them deep. It's so much easier than the alternative."

"What's the worst thing that could happen if you did talk about all the things you bury?" The tenderness in his voice almost undid me.

"The worst thing is… if I were to feel the full weight of the sadness and despair and grief and couldn't get out from under it ever again. Now, what is your biggest flaw, Mr. Perfect?"

I turned the question around on him to shut down any further digging. As much as I was willing to reveal to him, I didn't want to drown in my emotions right then. I also wanted to know what flaws, if any, he had. The moniker I'd just given him seemed closer to the truth than not. No one was perfect, but I had yet to see anything in him I would consider significantly flawed.

"Which one do you want, Ros?" he spat out bitterly. When his gaze met mine, I could see it wasn't directed at me, but I was still taken aback. "I was a flawed man. In my father's and my brothers' eyes, I was too sensitive. I felt things too deeply for their liking. I had too much empathy. A man didn't talk about his feelings, didn't think about others' feelings."

"But those aren't bad things to be, Archer."

"No, but those qualities made me weak, to them. My father and brothers hated my successes because of it. They believed my emotional nature should have made me a failure, so they set up situations to ensure that outcome. Instead, I excelled at every challenge. Every sector of the business they placed me in, I exceeded expectations. You would think my father would have been proud, right?" He barked out a laugh. I was stunned and before I could think of an appropriate response, he continued.

"I was being exiled to Seattle, though no one outside the family knew. The rest of society figured my father was sending me to conquer the city. And you know what, Ros? I fucking would have."

"Oh, Archer," I said in understanding. I had no other response.

"I was what you would call a workaholic when I was alive. I didn't love the work I did, but I excelled at it. I thrived on the challenges continually thrown at me, and not just because there was some part of me that wanted to find the thing that would make my family proud."

"What did Helena think of you? She loved you, right?"

"Helena hated how much I worked. We fought about it constantly. She hated me for the time I spent away from her, but she loved the things I was able to buy her and the life this work ethic would have afforded her. I would have made a terrible husband, Ros, make no mistake."

"Archer, I don't believe it for a minute."

"No, I would have. Ros, I've had over a century to think about the life I was living, about the mistakes I made. It took decades for me to realize I hated the life I was living. It was a joyless kind of life, working harder and harder to impress a man who would never love me, to provide for a woman who would never have been happy with me. The constant striving for more wealth, more power, more land. Just more. It was an empty, barren life I lived. There was no joy in it at all. I think it's part of why I was so eager to come here, why I connected so much to this land. I experienced a sense of peace here. It would have been a simple life, away from all the things I never realized while alive I had grown to detest."

"What would have brought you joy, Archer?"

He tossed a rueful smile my way and ran his fingers through his hair.

"A woman who understood me and wanted the same life I did. A woman to be my equal, a partner. Creating a family with her. Having a home filled with children, laughter, and happy noise. Those were the things I didn't realize until it was far too late I needed and craved."

We sat silently as I absorbed all he had said. I couldn't help but imagine him getting to live the kind of life he had deserved, no matter his flaws. I was filled with sorrow over the realization he would never have those things.

"What is your greatest fear?" He threw the question at me, and I knew he no longer wanted to dwell on the wounds he had revealed.

"Death," I replied without thinking. "Oh my God, that must sound so stupid and ridiculous to you," I gasped, covering my mouth with my hand. He laughed, and it warmed me in a way only he was capable of doing.

"No, Ros, not at all. You're still living, and it's perfectly reasonable to be afraid of dying. I think it's good to have a healthy fear of death. I know it may seem like I'm still living to some degree, but every moment of every day I am reminded of all the ways in which I'm not alive, of all the ways I'm not living. What exactly about death scares you?"

"So many things. The main thing though? I'm afraid of dying before I have kids. I want to be a mom so badly."

"So why don't you have them?" he asked, as though it were the most logical thing.

"When Dan and I were having all those big conversations about our relationship dealbreakers, kids wasn't one of them. But the longer we go without even talking about having children, the more I begin to think maybe he's changed his mind, or maybe he could live without being a dad. I don't know."

"What else, Ros?"

"I don't know. Being a shitty mom. I'm terrified of it. My mom was pretty amazing when she was alive. I mean, don't get me wrong, she wasn't perfect, and I hated the way she and my dad handled their divorce. She wasn't there for me at all. Neither of them was."

"How old were you when that happened?"

"I was ten. But I look at it through the eyes of an adult now, and I understand they were both going through a hard time, they were both hurting so much. Once they got settled into lives as single parents, they were so much happier. My mom was my best friend until she died. I miss her every single day. I can only hope to be half the mom she was if I ever get the chance."

I brought my knees up to my chest, wrapped my arms around my legs and rested my head on my knees, looking at Archer.

"It sounds like your mother died young. How did she die?"

"Cancer. It seemed to hit out of nowhere. One minute she was fine and healthy. She lost some weight, but she was working more and a little stressed about things at work, so we didn't think much of it. Little things started happening, but they were so easy just to write off. She collapsed one day at work. They ran a bunch of tests and discovered it was stage four cancer. They gave her three months to live."

"Rosalind," he muttered.

"She chose to forgo any treatment since it would only buy her time, not cure her, and she said she didn't want her last days to be spent sick from treatments. She managed to make it six months. We did so much during that time. We traveled, got tattoos together even though I technically wasn't old enough, read as many books on her never-ending list as we could, watched as many of her favorite movies as we had time for.

"She lived in her last months, truly, beautifully, bravely. It's another one of my fears. We never found out if there was a genetic aspect to her cancer. She told me so little about what was going on with her illness and she didn't spend much time with doctors. Once they diagnosed it as terminal, she said there was nothing more they could do for her and she stopped with her appointments. I'm afraid maybe there is a genetic link, and it may be a matter of time before I have it too. What kind of person would I be to bring kids into this world not knowing? But I'm also too afraid to get tested. I'm a fucking mess."

"Rosalind, I'm sorry. And if it's any consolation, I know any child that has you as a mother would be lucky," he said, reaching over and caressing my hand.

"How about you? What are some of your fears?" I asked, eager to get some of the focus off of me, feeling raw from the fears I had never shared with another soul. He rubbed at his chin thoughtfully while laughing.

"I don't think I have any more fears. Dying has a funny way of neutralizing worries," he joked.

"I never looked at it that way. I mean, what's the worst thing that could happen to you? It already happened! What did happen to you anyway? The day you died? Do you remember anything? How it happened?"

"I don't know how I died exactly. I remember the weather was terrible. Raining and windy, no visibility. It was no surprise when we ran aground. I remember the collision of the boat with the rocks. It jerked so violently."

"Do you remember anything else?"

"No. I woke up here, on this land. This house wasn't here at the time, but I was tied to this land nonetheless. She was there on the boat. Helena. Shortly before the crash, she was standing close to a man. I don't know who he was. I didn't recognize him. She leaned into him, and it looked as though they were about to embrace, but then the collision happened. I had long suspected she was unfaithful to me, and there were rumors in our circle about it, but I was never certain. It's why I was on the steamer, you know," he said, looking up at me. The sharp edge of anger lurked in the depths of his eyes.

"No, I didn't know. I only know you weren't on the passenger manifests, but eyewitnesses, including Helena, attested to you being on board that day."

"I barely made it in time. The ship was about to depart. I offered enough money for them to let me on board. They never asked my name and I never even thought about paperwork. Helena with a man, looking far more intimate than they should have. My suspicions were correct. We made eye contact, and I knew she saw me. The collision happened soon after, and I remember nothing else."

"Do you think it was foul play? Do you think Helena had something to do with your death?" I asked, thinking through the information I had, reading between the lines of what he was telling me and what his body language was telling me.

"I don't know," he said, shaking his head before leaning over, resting his forearms on his thighs and dropping his head into his hands. "I just don't know. I only suspected her of infidelity. The crash happened so quickly, it all seemed like a convenient accident. But something has always bothered me about my last day. Yes, the thought that maybe she had something to do with my death has crossed my mind. I live with the anger of what she did to me, how she was so public about her indiscretions. Every time I think of what happened, of what I cannot remember, I keep coming back to her. What was her role, if any, in all this? I suppose I'll never know."

"It still bothers you though."

"It angers me. I try not to dwell on that day. Every time I do, I am nearly overcome with rage. Sometimes I think I can move on from this, but it hasn't happened yet. Maybe it's why I am still tied to this land and why I haven't moved on to whatever is next."

I was lost in thought, trying to fit together the pieces of what I knew from the research Jos had done and what he had just told me. There were some big pieces I was missing. Maybe he was right and he was tied to this land because he didn't have the closure he needed. Maybe I could provide him with it, give him what he needed to move on and not have to spend his afterlife alone.

I was moving the information around in my head. I knew then I was going to do what I could to solve this. It would take some work, but there were answers I needed, and I would have to start on the mainland to get them.

"Ros, did you hear me?" He bumped my shoulder with his.

"Sorry, yeah, yeah, I'm here. Just a lot on my mind and now I'm here trying to figure out what happened to you."

"You don't have to. It was a long time ago. Let's just leave it as it is." We both sat in silence for a few moments, just looking at each other, both of us deep in thought, though likely about much different things.

"Ask me again. Ask me one last time, Rosalind," he whispered, the intensity coming off him in waves.

"Ask what?"

"Ask me what my greatest fear is."

"Okay, Archer. What is your biggest fear?" I said it dramatically like I was playacting. He grabbed my hand tightly in a grip I hadn't even known he was capable of. He caught my gaze, and I couldn't look away, even if I had wanted to.

"You. You are my greatest fear, Ros. I'm afraid one day you will leave and I will never see you again. I fear I will have to live the rest of this afterlife without you in it. All of my fears involve you. My greatest fear is one I'm not ready to talk about, but it is still you."

My heart dropped into my stomach. The butterflies that seemed to take residence inside of me since I met him were set loose. I took deep breaths, trying to calm myself down. The fears I hadn't confessed to Archer? They all revolved around him as well. It was a secret I had to keep.

TWENTY-SIX

I COULDN'T GET our conversation about fear out of my head. I mostly tried to ignore and avoid thinking about his confession. I couldn't even go there mentally or emotionally. I also couldn't stop thinking about his story about his death. The more I considered it, the more I believed it was pretty likely not knowing the truth was his unfinished business keeping him tied to the living, to this land.

After stewing on the entire situation for a few days, I decided I was going to do what I could to try to get him answers. I first called Jos to ask her where she found the information about Archer and the steamer accident. I also called Scarlett up to get some advice and tips from her on how to go about finding more information.

I spent the next week researching everything and anything remotely related to the steamer accident,

Archer, and Helena. I had never been more grateful to live in the age of technology where the internet and Google were at my fingertips and so many records were now digital and easy to access if you knew where to look.

I learned a lot about Archer's family. They were still extremely wealthy and held ownership stakes in many of the businesses they'd owned while he was alive. His parents had never gotten over the loss, sadly. From all accounts, he was an incredibly distinctive and well-liked man during his life. Knowing him now, I did not doubt it, though it saddened me he never believed his father felt that way.

Helena ended up marrying the man she was on the steamer with when it crashed. Their names had been on the passenger manifests, so it was easy to put those pieces together. Archer was correct in his intuition and concern about her. There wasn't much said about the life Helena had led after her fiancé died and she married her husband.

They did end up having three children, and their youngest child, a daughter named Charlotte who was born to them pretty late, was still alive. She lived in the family home near Seattle. I made calls to arrange a meeting with her while I was out of the house. I didn't want Archer knowing what I was up to, not yet at least. I didn't want to get his hopes up.

She was in her early nineties, so there was a good chance her memory wasn't too good anymore or that she'd never known anything about her mother's life before marrying her father. I made arrangements with Charlotte's granddaughter, whom she lived with. She assured me Charlotte was eager to speak with me, and I was looking forward to the conversation as well.

I finally had a break in my schedule a week later. I let Archer know I was heading to Seattle for a couple of days but was vague about my reasons why. I didn't owe him an explanation, but if roles were reversed, I would worry and would want to know. I sent Dan a text message letting him know what was going on in case he happened to try to surprise me at the house while I was gone, though since it had yet to happen, I didn't think I had much to worry about there.

I was anxious the entire trip over, running questions I had through my head over and over again. My expectations were all over the place. I prayed I was able to get answers to the questions I had and hoped I could provide Archer with some peace and resolution to the questions running through his head for the better part of a century.

I drove into the Mount Baker neighborhood of Seattle and was completely stunned. I found myself surrounded by historic homes, several with million-dollar views. I slowly pulled up to a gorgeous Tudor Revival estate and knew this was the home Helena had lived in and raised her family in.

As I parked where Charlotte's granddaughter Emily had directed me to in our conversation, a young woman around my age stepped out of the home to greet me. I got out of the car and walked up to meet her, shaking her hand, and introducing myself.

"I'm in awe of this home, it's stunning," I gushed after the introductions were made.

"It really is something, isn't it?" she asked with affection. "It was completed in 1915, and my great-grandmother Helena moved in with my great-grandfather and their first two children. My grandmother Charlotte has lived here most of her life. Her sister and brother never wanted to live here—I'm not sure why—so she inherited the home. She is really excited to meet you. I told her you came across Helena's story and became interested and wanted to learn more. I figured you both could fill each other in on everything else."

She led me into the home and through several beautiful and well-kept rooms, almost all with breathtaking views of Lake Washington, and out onto a deck overlooking the rear of the estate, the lake, and the Cascades. Sitting in one of the chairs at the outdoor table was an older, beautiful woman, regal in stature. The woman stood, smiling.

"Hello, you must be Rosalind," she said warmly, reaching her hand out for me to shake.

"And you must be Charlotte. It's a pleasure to meet you."

A box sat on the table, along with cookies and coffee. While there was a chill in the air, it felt warm and cozy at the table. I looked up to see built-in heaters above us pumping full force. We both sat down at the table, and she offered me the coffee carafe. Once we were settled with refreshments, I turned to her and smiled.

Charlotte was in her early nineties but didn't look a day over sixty-five. She was tall, slender, and moved with fluid, graceful movements. Her back was straight with better posture than I had. Intelligence was evident in her eyes, and any concerns I had about how present or able she was to have this conversation were unfounded. There was an air of kindness and humor about her.

"Thank you so much for taking the time to meet with me, I really appreciate it."

"It's my pleasure. The older you get, the fewer visitors you tend to get, though I do have a lot of social engagements that keep me busy, and Emily's friends seem to enjoy hanging out with an old lady when they stop by too. I think it's because I mix strong drinks and tell wild stories about my youth," she said with laughter in her voice. "Emily mentioned you wanted to talk about my mother, Helena."

"Yes. I live in a home built on the land Archer Breckenridge once owned. I moved there recently and became interested in the history of the land, and its former inhabitants. It led me to Archer and Helena. I wanted to learn as much as I could about Helena, so anything you can share with me, I would love to know."

"Very interesting," she said as she lifted the lid off the box and pulled a photo out. "This was my mother." It was the same woman in the photo Jos had shown me. I picked the picture up and studied it before looking up at Charlotte.

"You look just like her," I said in awe.

"Yes, I heard it a lot growing up. It created a lot of issues between my mother and me, especially as I became a teenager." She took a sip of her coffee and looked down at the photo in my hands.

"What kind of issues?"

"My mother wasn't what you would call warm or kind. She was good at hiding her true self from people, but to the people who truly knew her, we knew how she really was. She was jealous of my youth and my looks. She was in her late thirties when she had me. I wasn't planned, and my mother always let me know how displeased she was that she was ruining her body over me, never mind the fact that she had had other children. The shaming and jealousy got worse the older we both got."

"What about your father?"

Warmth and affection softened her face. "My father, Richard, on the other hand, was a fine man. He was loving and funny but tortured. I never fully understood the dynamic between him and my mother, what drew them together. He sincerely loved her though, there was no doubt about it. He stayed with her to the very end."

She pulled out another photo and handed it to me. It was a picture of a very handsome man. Light hair, dark eyes, tall and well built. He had a warm smile and his eyes crinkled. Charlotte pulled out another photo, and it was a candid one of her parents together. They made a stunning couple.

"Dad was also from a well-connected, wealthy family. Not as rich as the Breckenridges, but he would have been deemed an acceptable match for my mother if the Averys hadn't been so close to the Breckenridges. I heard whispers here and there about Archer growing up. Initially, my mother was infatuated with Archer. I used to eavesdrop quite a bit as a child, and she was a boastful woman, proud of sharing her wicked exploits with her close friends. I'm not sure if you are aware, but Archer was previously engaged."

"Yes, but I don't know anything about her."

"Her name was Lucinda, and according to my mother, they were very much in love. Lucinda's family ended up sending her to Europe where she married someone else. Archer was quite upset. I overheard my mother tell some friends once she was responsible for it. She claimed she had arranged a meeting with Lucinda's aunt, where she gossiped about Archer and Lucinda having intimate relations. Neither family supported the engagement, so once an heir between the two was imminent if they didn't act, she was sent away and a more desirable union was arranged. That was the kind of woman my mother was. She saw something she wanted and went for it, with no concern for the people she hurt."

I sat silent and shocked. While I trusted Archer's intuition, I wasn't necessarily sold on the idea of Helena being directly responsible for his death, but after what Charlotte had just told me, I reconsidered. I sat back and considered how I would ask the next question. There was no PC way to do it.

"It looks like there is something on your mind, Ros. Go ahead and ask. If I know, I'll be as honest as I can." She smiled at me encouragingly.

"Okay. In my research, I came across an account that maybe hinted at some foul play in Archer's death. Had your parents ever talked about that day?"

I was satisfied with how I'd managed to ask. I didn't want to outright accuse her parents of being involved, and I hoped she read between the lines and had the information I was looking for. She sighed deeply, a furrow appearing between her brows as she laced her fingers together. I patiently waited for her to be ready to talk.

"My parents argued over Archer a lot. I don't know if they thought we couldn't hear or weren't listening, but I did. I was always listening. My dad held a lot of guilt in his life. It weighed him down. He was never able to be completely happy because of it—well, guilt and the poison that was my mother. As a child and teen, I knew the guilt revolved around Archer, but I never knew why. As a young woman, I came to believe it was over their infidelity. My parents began their relationship while she was still engaged to Archer. I knew it was something my dad wouldn't have been comfortable with. But again, he loved my mother, enough to stay with her through all her antics.

"One day when I was in my early twenties, I came home while my parents were in the middle of an intense argument. They didn't know I was there. My mother was screaming about Archer, about how she married the wrong man, how she should have stayed with him, how much she regretted marrying my father. He said, and I will never forget, 'How can you say that, Helena, when I risked everything for you when I killed for you?' He sounded so broken. Her response? 'If I couldn't have him, no one could. I wish I hadn't let you have me. If it weren't for Rebecca, I could have married Archer.' My father cried that day. Sobbed. It was then I realized my mother had forced my father to kill Archer. His appearance on the ship and the collision of the steamer worked in her favor, but I believe she would have had him killed no matter what.

"In her eyes, he belonged to her. She didn't want anyone else having what was hers, even if she didn't want him anymore. It was also the day I found out the only reason my mother married my father was because she had gotten pregnant with my sister, Rebecca. I don't believe she would have married him otherwise. I think she would have gone on to marry Archer. The guilt slowly killed my dad. He was the sweetest, gentlest man. I don't know how he did it, but I know it killed him. His love for my mother destroyed him."

I was stunned. She didn't continue for a while, which I was grateful for. I needed a moment to absorb what she'd just said. I had hoped to get answers, but never had I expected to find validation to Archer's beliefs so quickly. I looked up at Charlotte and she looked sad and a little broken herself.

"I didn't realize I was living with some guilt this whole time too. I never asked either of my parents about what happened, and I never shared this information with anyone. The guilt of just knowing a secret like this can weigh you down too," she said. "I know you don't have to, but I would appreciate if you kept this between us. All the involved parties are long gone, but it could still hurt all the families involved if it got out. I hope you understand." I could see the worry written all over her face.

"Oh, Charlotte," I said, reaching over and covering her hand with mine in a calming gesture, "I wanted to satisfy my own curiosity. I never planned on sharing this information with anyone." She smiled warmly at me, relief in her eyes.

"Thank you, Ros, I really appreciate it." We sat for a few minutes, eating our cookies and drinking our coffee. "Have you ever seen a picture of Archer?" she asked me suddenly, changing the subject.

"Yes, just one during some research."

She reached into her box and pulled out a few photographs. "Here you go," she said as she handed them over to me. "He was handsome, wasn't he? As good-looking as my dad was, I have to say, Archer Breckenridge was more attractive."

I looked down at the photos. One was the photo Jos had shown me. One of the others was a portrait and another one a candid.

"My mother held on to these in secret. I discovered them after her death, and I couldn't bear to part with them either. He is a part of our family history now."

I picked up the candid of him. It looked like he had been sitting for a photo session but happened to be caught laughing when he didn't know a picture was being taken. I subconsciously caressed the picture, taking in his smile, thinking about how good it felt to have the smile directed at me. Charlotte made a sound and I glanced up quickly to find her with her neck crooked to the side, looking at me curiously.

"You look as though you know him, love him even," she said.

"He resembles someone I once knew," was all I could give as an explanation. There was no way to tell her I indeed had come to care for him more than I should.

We continued to talk about her parents, her family, including her husband and children. Before I knew it, hours had passed and it was time for me to head to my hotel. I thanked Charlotte for a wonderful and unforgettable day, and she invited me back anytime I was in the area.

As I drove off, I thought about how I'd share this information with Archer, whether he would believe it or not. How did you tell someone long dead they had been murdered? By the time I headed back to Orcas Island the next afternoon, I still didn't have an answer to that question.

TWENTY-SEVEN

"WHAT DO you want to watch tonight? It's your turn to pick," Archer said as he got settled on the couch next to me.

I had gotten back from Seattle and my meeting with Charlotte a few days ago, but I still couldn't find a way to tell Archer what I had learned. I could tell he knew something was going on with me, that I was acting differently. I was cracking under the weight of the secret, but he didn't ask or push me for answers. He gave me the time and space I needed to figure it out on my own. It was one of the things I loved about him.

"Tonight, we are going to watch one of my all-time favorites. *Dirty Dancing*. Have you ever seen it, Archer?"

"No, I can't say I have," he replied, chuckling at me.

"You will love it, I promise!"

"So it's one of your favorite movies?" he asked incredulously once it was over.

"It's a classic!" I protested.

"No, Ros, *Casablanca* is a classic, *Roman Holiday* is a classic. What we just watched? It was not a classic."

"Fine, it's what we call a new classic. Did you not like it?"

"I'm not sure how I feel about it. It was silly and overly dramatic. That's what you call dancing now?"

"First off, it's emotional and a little dramatic. But it's sweet. Hello, 'nobody puts Baby in a corner!' You can't get more romantic. He loved her and stood up to her family for her! Another thing, it was the movie director's version of dancing in the 1960s. Dancing today is much dirtier."

"What do you mean by dirty?" he asked, genuinely curious.

"Well, in the movie, they considered the dancing the kids were doing 'dirty' because it wasn't like the dancing people were doing before. They danced with their bodies close together, grinding together, almost mimicking sex in some cases, but on the dance floor. That's why it's called dirty dancing. The dancing in the movie? It's nothing compared to how dirty dancing can be now."

"Show me," he demanded.

"Wait, what?"

"I want to see what dances are popular right now."

"Okay. Don't say I didn't warn you though."

I grabbed the remote and opened up the apps menu. I pulled up YouTube so I could choose a few music videos to show him. We watched some, including one showing twerking in all its bizarre and explicit glory. After the fifth video, Archer asked me to stop.

"Enough, enough. I think I've seen enough," Archer said, waving his arms and covering his eyes. I couldn't help but laugh at his antics and his faux outrage and disgust.

"When is the last time you danced, Archer?"

"It's been over one hundred years, Ros, duh," he said in a serious voice.

One look at his face showed he was anything but. I burst out laughing again. The more time we spent together, the less formal he sounded and the more modern idioms he picked up. Never in a million years would I have expected to hear the word "duh" come out of his mouth.

"Okay, here we go. Stand up." I reached out for his hand, beckoning him to join me.

"What are we going to do?" he asked as he came to stand beside me.

"We're going to dance. Like in the videos we just watched."

I smiled a huge, bright smile at him, excited by my idea. He looked much less thrilled.

"Look, just stand there and follow my lead. I'll even turn one on for you to watch if you need guidance."

I pressed play and danced around him, making sure I never made contact with him, while he stood still, looking at me and the TV. After the second song, he finally started to move with me.

He was a pretty decent dancer, finding the rhythm of the songs quickly, becoming more comfortable with fluidly moving his body as more songs played. I reached out to him, surprised when my hand made contact with his very solid body. There was never any telling when he would have enough energy to be more than air, but it was happening with much more frequency and for longer periods of time.

The minute he realized it too, he grabbed my hips and pulled them up against his. We danced close together, our bodies brushing against each other. He looked down into my eyes, his gaze so intense I couldn't look away. It was heated with barely contained lust.

Our bodies were connected, moving in sync, and desire rose up inside of me, threatening to take me over. My heartbeat raced, and I placed my hand against his chest, where his heart would beat if he were alive. I opened my mouth to say something, but there were no words.

"I feel it too," Archer stated simply.

We continued to stare at each other, our bodies joined from the chest down, barely moving now. I don't know how long we stayed like that, letting the tension build around us, threatening to light us both on fire with its fierce intensity. The playlist I had set up ended, and silence surrounded us. It worked like a bucket of ice on me, waking me up from the trance desire had put me under, and forced me to take a step away from Archer and out of his grip.

He also took a step back and shook his head, rubbing the back of his neck. He looked away, deep consideration on his face. When he turned back to me, his stance was more relaxed and the lines beside his mouth deepened into a smile.

"So we've tried your version of dancing, which was interesting. Are you willing to try what we called dancing during my time?"

His smile and enthusiasm were contagious, and while I was still filled with nervous, electric energy from our last round of dancing, I was eager to have him show me something from his past. The other truth, one I wasn't willing to admit even to myself, was that I wanted an excuse to get close to him again.

"Sure, why not. But just know, you may have quite a bit of teaching to do for us to get to the dancing part."

He told me a few songs to put on a playlist, and the

music began. He took hold of my hand, wrapped his other arm around my waist, and pulled me closer to him, but not so close that we were touching anywhere else.

"Just follow my lead, and you'll be okay," he said with his natural confidence.

Two songs in, and I could see his faith in my ability start to wane. I'd taken ballet and contemporary dance classes growing up, so I had a sense of grace and rhythm, but anything like ballroom dancing and I was a lost cause. I was too stuck in my head, trying to count steps and anticipate moves.

We stopped for the third time and Archer attempted to tell me again what we were supposed to be doing and implored me just to let him lead. He was so patient, and he tried so hard, but I thought even he was starting to see his efforts might have been in vain.

"Let's try just one more song, and I will teach you a different dance. This one should be easier for you."

A new song began, and we started again. The look of concentration and determination on his face and my utter inability to get any of the steps correct or let him lead caused hysterical laughter to well up in my body, bursting out. I couldn't hold it in.

His shock at my sudden and loud chuckling caused him to stumble during a semi-tricky move, causing my leg to get caught at a weird angle around his, and with the momentum we both went down, landing in a heap on the ground. All was silent after our fall for a moment, but one look at his face and I dissolved into a fit of giggles again. It only took a moment for him to join me.

We sat there, a tangle of limbs, laughing until we could barely breathe—well, until *I* could barely breathe. We both quieted down, and I looked up at Archer as I caught my breath.

I continued to stare at him, and then I blurted out, "You were right, you know. About Helena. You were right about it all."

I threw my hands over my mouth to keep any other words from spilling out. I hadn't planned on saying anything tonight, but my mouth had other plans, and now the words were out and I couldn't take them back. I knew our fun and happy night was about to take a nosedive into the deep and heavy.

"What do you mean, Rosalind?" he asked, confused.

He scooted back and untangled himself from my arms and legs before rising. A tense, anxious energy radiated from him, enveloping the room as he paced. I could tell he wasn't sure if he even wanted to hear this, but the words were out there now, so I knew I had to just get it over with.

"When I was in Seattle, I met with Charlotte, Helena's daughter. We talked a lot about her mother and father, and what happened the day you died."

He fell hard into the armchair like he was unable to

carry his weight. "What was said?" he asked so quietly I nearly didn't hear him.

I looked over at him. He was becoming less solid by the minute. This conversation would take out all the energy he had left. I couldn't help but wonder if it would also give him all the reason he needed to move on and disappear forever. As much as I wanted to be selfish and keep him here with me, he deserved to know—he deserved a chance to move on and not be tied to this place for eternity.

"We talked about a lot of things. Charlotte is wonderful. A kind, lovely woman. She's Helena's youngest daughter. She didn't have a great relationship with her mother; she said Helena was a jealous, cold woman. Helena liked to brag to her friends about the malicious things she did, and she argued a lot with her husband. Charlotte had overheard a lot of stuff growing up."

I stopped and looked over at Archer, concerned about how he was handling all this. He looked stricken and sad, and all I wanted to do was wrap my arms around him and comfort him. I knew just by looking at him he was fading, so physical touch probably wasn't an option.

"Go on."

I took a deep breath before continuing, knowing I was about to wreck him, knowing I had no other choice.

"Helena was responsible for the end of your first engagement. She wanted you and spread the rumor among Lucinda's family that you were engaging in a sexual relationship. She knew this would be what they needed to send Lucinda away."

His eyes looked wetter than normal, and I guessed he would have cried then if he had been able to.

"I... I didn't know. I don't know how I was so fooled by her."

"You obviously had a gut instinct something was off with her though, because you've thought all this time she was involved in your death. You would've never even considered it if you really believed in your heart she was a good person."

"Perhaps."

"The man she was with on the ship, his name was Richard. They were having an affair, and she later went on to marry him. She was pregnant with her first child the day you died."

Archer looked absolutely shell-shocked at this information, and in that moment, I wanted to take it all back.

"Keep going," he ground out between his teeth, the muscles in his neck corded in tension.

"She realized she was stuck with him and would have to marry him. Instead of letting you go, she decided if she couldn't have you, no one else would either. I'm convinced she was mentally unstable. She persuaded Richard to kill you."

Archer interrupted with a string of curses under his

breath that I couldn't make out. I flinched at the rage that came off him in waves.

"Keep. Going. Rosalind."

I didn't want to, but he deserved to know it all. "Archer, you being on that ship was a coincidence she worked in her favor. Charlotte never heard how it was accomplished, she only knew he did it for Helena, and he regretted it every day of his life. The guilt never went away, it slowly killed him, and because of what they did, you were always present in their marriage. It wasn't a happy one, and it seems like Helena did not lead a happy life, no matter how it may have appeared."

I looked at him, and he sat bent forward with his arms resting on his thighs, his head between his hands, his hands tugging at his hair. A thick silence sat between us for a few minutes, and when he realized I had nothing left to add, he raised his head and looked at me with the most tortured and sad eyes, his anger somehow spent.

But I also saw something else there too. Relief and acceptance. He finally knew the truth. I sensed he would find peace in it. We continued to sit for what could have been hours. I never checked the time; it wasn't important. I just waited for him to be ready to talk.

Eventually, he got up, straightened himself out, and walked over to me, placing an airy kiss I barely felt on top of my head.

"Thank you, Rosalind. Thank you for getting me the

answers I couldn't get for myself, for granting me the closure I never thought I would have."

Archer smiled at me as he dissipated and I was left with his unique scent, something so patently him even death and time couldn't erase its essence. I'd come to crave that scent, to love it, to despair of it when it came and I knew it was only a matter of time before it was gone completely.

Tears fell and covered my cheeks. I was emotionally exhausted and scared. I didn't want to believe it but had to accept this might have been the last time I would ever see Archer, if the information I gave was what he needed to move on. Something essential inside of me began to crack and break apart at the thought that I would never see him again. I knew even then those fissures would never be repaired.

TWENTY-EIGHT

AN ENTIRE DAY and night had passed without me seeing or hearing from Archer. It was scaring the shit out of me. What if I had provided him with the closure he had needed during our last conversation and now he had gone into the light, so to speak? The thought I would never see or talk to him again broke me. My heart splintered further apart with each minute that passed without me hearing from him. Archer had become so important to me, my best friend, someone I didn't think I could live without.

I was exhausted and wasn't up for hanging out, and I wanted to give Archer whatever space he needed to process what I told him, but I also desperately needed to know if he was still here, how he was doing, if he was handling all the information. I rolled onto my back, grabbed some pillows from the other side of the bed to prop under my head, and decided to talk to him.

"Archer, you there?" My voice trembled.

"Yes, Rosalind, I'm still here." It was so strange hearing his voice without seeing him, and I didn't think I would ever get used to it.

"Oh, thank fuck! I was so worried you were gone for good."

"No, I'm still here. There was no bright shining white light or someone from my past to meet me."

Archer tried to make a joke of his situation, but there wasn't anything funny about it. He went quiet after this, and I couldn't think of anything else to say, and I couldn't tell from his voice what he was thinking or feeling. So I just lay there and waited.

"I want you to know I'm relieved to know what happened to me. While it's good to know how I died, to not have it hanging over me anymore, I don't think closure was what I needed to move on from here."

Archer paused again for a moment, and I got the impression that he was trying to gather his thoughts, trying to figure out a way to articulate all the things he must have been feeling since my revelation.

"Maybe there isn't anything that will allow me to leave. I'm fine with the possibility now." There was a finality in his voice, a true acceptance of his circumstances.

I couldn't help the smile that took over my face. My heart seemed to grow and expand in my chest. A light-headed sensation followed quickly on its heels. Sweet relief at the knowledge that Archer wasn't going to up and disappear left me replete.

I lay there in contented silence, sleep starting to take over me, when I felt a breeze pass over me. My eyes fluttered open in time to see Archer appear in the corner of my room. I sat up quickly, covering myself with my sheet out of instinct before I realized that I was fully, if lightly, clothed in a lacy camisole and panties.

"Sorry if I startled you," he said as he made his way over to the armchair and plopped down in it, leaning back and resting his ankle on the opposite knee. "I just wanted to see you and make sure you were doing okay with all this. I don't think we've ever let more than a day pass without seeing each other."

"I'm so sorry, Archer. With everything I dropped on you last time, I just wanted to give you space, let you figure out what you were thinking and feeling without having to feel like you had to discuss it with me, you know?"

"I *do* know and I appreciate it. I'm grateful you went to find the information. You didn't have to, and you will never know how much it means to me."

Archer paused there and a contemplative, almost troubled look passed over his face. He wasn't as happy as I would have anticipated he'd be after learning the answers to questions he'd been asking himself for decades.

"Ros," Archer began before stopping.

He broke eye contact, looked down and covered his mouth as though he wanted to hold the words in a little longer, as though both restraining them and releasing them were physically painful. He dragged his hand down his face and sat up, spine straight and stiff, decision made.

"Do you ever think your mom is around you? Do you ever feel her presence the way you did mine?" Archer finally managed to force out of his mouth, words tinged with apology and regret over questions he knew would be a knife to my chest.

I flinched and my throat tightened painfully. Archer leaned forward, his arms dropped to his thighs, and he pinched the bridge of his nose before his eyes lifted to mine, remorse etched into their depths. Still, he didn't retract the question and the heavy weight of the silence pulled me down into myself and my thoughts.

"Ros?"

I shook my head and closed my eyes, trying to find a way to talk through the grief gripping my throat like a vise. I swallowed reflexively, and then again. I just continued to shake my head, not necessarily a denial of his questions. My bed dipped then under the weight of another body sitting upon it. The light pressure of finger-tips gripped my face, caressing my cheek before exerting more pressure and gently forcing my face up.

I inhaled deeply, finding comfort in the scent that was all Archer, the one that was now tied with the feeling of home. I found courage in his nearness, a safety in his presence next to me, solid and as real as anything I had ever felt before. I took a deep breath and opened my eyes to that pair of green ones I'd come to adore. The tender-ness and understanding I found there gave me the push I needed. I nodded my head at him and opened my mouth.

"No, I don't think she's around me at all. I've never felt her around. I can't tell you how many times over the years I wished for it, prayed for it. That she could just come back for one more conversation, that I could tell her I loved her one more time."

Archer leaned in toward me and swiped under my eyes, wiping away the tears that had begun to fall. "Do you still wish she were around? Now that you know me and know it's possible?"

I sighed and shifted so close to Archer that we were now touching, connected from waist up. I leaned over and rested my head on his shoulder, still not used to how solid his body sometimes felt, but deriving comfort from his proximity nonetheless.

"When you and I first met, I searched for her in

everything. I figured if it were possible for ghosts to exist, it wasn't that farfetched that maybe she was here and hadn't found a way to make contact. But the longer I went without getting any sense of her presence, the more I thought about what it would mean if she *were* still here."

I turned to face Archer, compelled to look into his face when I said this. "It would mean she didn't move on or have any real peace in the last eleven years. It would mean that she had some kind of unfinished business. And I know for a fact that she had accepted her death, and I don't think she had any regrets at the end. So no, I don't wish she were still here. I wouldn't wish that for anyone, Archer." I grabbed his hand and squeezed it then, needing to be connected to him.

"If you died now, would you have unfinished business? Would you be able to say you left the world with few regrets?" Archer's voice was barely above a whisper breathed into my ear, his words made rough by pain.

I looked away, over his shoulder, out the window and into the mist-filled night. I considered his words carefully, knowing the truth that hid too close to the surface. I thought back to our conversation about fear and knew he had to have seen so much more of everything I tried to deny and ignore than I had ever wanted.

It all began to build: the grief, the pain, the fear, and the regret. So much regret. As the tidal wave of the emotions I suppressed for the better part of a decade pressed upon me, I broke and became the flood.

My bed shifted as Archer moved, and I couldn't help but wonder how this was possible, how he had gained so much power and strength that I could feel him as though he possessed a living body. Strong arms wrapped around my waist from behind and pulled me until I hit a solid mass. Legs bracketed mine and he rested his chin on my shoulder. Archer's scent enveloped me and somehow his body surrounding mine warmed me from the inside.

"Shhhh, Ros. It's okay. It's okay."

The tenderness that laced his words did what nothing else was capable of doing. It calmed the raging storm inside of me, and slowly, as he held me tightly, the sobs subsided into quiet tears tracking down my face. And still he held me.

Then the words I'd held inside for eleven years but never spoken spilled out past my lips. And I didn't regret them.

"I have so many regrets," I said in a voice that could barely be called a whisper. It didn't matter how quietly I spoke, I knew Archer would hear every single word. "I miss her so much, Archer. So fucking much. The pain, it never goes away. So I push it down, as deep as I can. Then I cover it with anything that I think will keep the thoughts of her at bay."

"Does that work for you, Ros?"

"No, it never works for long, and then I feel like I'm drowning all over again. Why, Archer? Why does it hurt so much? Why does it hurt the same as it did the day she died?" My voice cracked under the weight of all my pain.

His arms tightened around me. "I don't know. Have you ever talked about her or her passing?"

"No, not really. I always shut it down. My father never wanted to talk about it, and as time passed, it just became too hard to talk about. Now every time my mom is mentioned, it's like a wound being ripped open all over again, only I discover it was never fully healed and it's just festering and infected."

"Let's start to treat and heal it. Let's start with your regrets. What regrets do you have in regard to your mother?" Archer's voice was all gentle inquiry.

"I feel like I've been living my life in a way she wouldn't have agreed with. She was so brave, adventurous in her own way. And honest. She was so honest. She would hate that I was living half a life, too afraid to take the risks necessary to have the life I want. I regret the choices I've made, or really, the choices I've abstained from making at all."

"It seems to me that you *have* been taking risks lately, you have been making changes to your life," Archer said in my ear.

I thought about all the choices I had made, beginning with taking the leap to come to this place, and I knew he was right. I wasn't sure if I could even count those as regrets anymore.

"Yeah, I guess you're right."

"What else, Ros?"

"The test."

Those words were the only ones I was able to get out before a new wave of tears began. Archer said nothing in response, he just nodded his head. He never forgot a word I'd said in any of our conversations, so I knew he knew exactly what I was referring to. We both sat in the silence and let those words and their implications hang in the air.

My hair stirred with what could only be described as an exhalation. "What about the test scares you, Ros?"

I breathed in deeply.

Once. Twice. A third time.

I wasn't at all surprised that he knew it was fear that held me back. "I can't help but wonder why my mom never got the test. It wouldn't have made a difference either way, her cancer was terminal. I sometimes tell myself that if she didn't need to know, I don't either. But I know I haven't had the test because what if I *am* genetically predisposed to it? What happens then? Is it just a matter of time? Will I never realize my dream of having kids because I'm afraid of passing it on to them? Maybe not knowing is better."

Archer reached up and cupped my face, turning my head toward his until we were only breaths apart. "You will never know unless you talk to a physician. I'm sure the test exists so that you *can* take measures to prevent it from happening. This will always hang over your head if you don't get it done."

He paused there, and fear flashed in his eyes before he shuttered them and hid it away. "Ros, promise me. Promise me you will get this test done. Your mother would never have wanted you to live with this kind of fear in your life."

His pleading, the urgency in his voice moved me in a way I never knew possible. I nodded my head then, agreeing without considering the ramifications of the decision, but knowing that only Archer could make me see how right this choice was.

Before I could speak my assent out loud, he leaned forward and kissed my forehead before resting his against mine. In that moment I had the sudden desire to wrap my hand around his neck and bring his lips to mine. I gasped at the sudden impulse and moved my head away from his, breaking the contact I refused to admit I wanted so badly.

"What else, Ros? What else do you regret?" Archer's

hand fell away from my face and wrapped back around my waist.

"I regret not talking about her for so long. I've hidden it all away, only acknowledging her in scheduled moments. I cut Josie out from that part of my life, even though my mom was such a big part of her life too. I've kept her memory locked up so tight, and it still hurts, and I don't even understand why I did that anymore."

"You did it because you were young when you lost her and you didn't know any better. But here we are, and I would love to hear about your mother. So let's topple another regret. Tell me about her."

I pulled myself from his embrace and turned to face him, my knees up against my chest and my arms wrapped around my legs. Archer smiled that beautiful, heart-stopping smile, and I couldn't help but return it.

"Her name was Hanna, and she was amazing. She was understanding and kind. Oh, and funny. She was so damn funny. It was like she had a joke or humorous response to just about any situation. Her laugh was the best I'd ever heard. It sounded like home."

The more I talked about my mom, the more I shared with Archer, stories and traits, anything and everything I could think of, stories I hadn't even known I remembered. It all came spilling out of me and he soaked it all in, only interrupting to ask questions or clarify something he didn't understand.

With each word that left my mouth, a weight lifted gradually, until I felt a new lightness that was so unfamiliar, but felt so right. And that? That was something I knew I would never come to regret.

TWENTY-NINE

"HEY, I'm gonna take a break for a bit, kay?"

I laid the book I was reading to Archer on the floor and stretched out on the couch, plopping my feet on his lap. There was a new intimacy between us, a comfort that came with so much time spent together and secrets shared. It wasn't a leap for me to call Archer my best friend and mean it.

"Sure. Would you like me to take a turn?" he asked as he placed his hands on my ankles.

We realized a few days ago that he had no problem resting a book on his lap and reading from it. We still weren't sure how this was all possible, how he grew stronger with each passing day, how his once-insubstantial form was now a very real body much of the time we spent together. Certain activities still zapped him of his energy more than others, and he still needed rest, but I had a feeling that if someone came across him, they would think he was alive.

I was about to respond when my phone rang on the coffee table. I was going to ignore it until I saw it was Dan calling.

"It's Dan. This could be quick, or it could take a while. I never know." My conversations with Dan now exclusively took place through text message, so the fact that he was calling made me think this was more than the typical messages he sent.

"It's okay, I know you're tired, I'll see you tomorrow," Archer said as he waved before disappearing.

"Hey," I said as I answered the phone.

"Hey, babe. How's it going?" Dan sounded exhausted. There was something else in his voice that gave me an uneasy feeling.

"It's going. I haven't been sleeping well, so I'm pretty exhausted and was about to go to sleep. How are you? You sound tired too."

"Yeah, I'm pretty wiped. I have some news though. I'm coming home in the next week."

"Wait, what?" I asked, sitting up quickly. "You mean for a visit?"

"No, Ros. For good. I'm shutting down the project. I know it's sudden and I know it's earlier than expected given all the delays and issues, but I'm ramping down right now. I'll explain later. Rogers said we can stay in the house as long as we need to. I thought we could use this time as a vacation before we head back to Santa Barbara."

"Wow. That's just… a lot of information to take in. I thought I'd have more time here. Shit, I'm going to have a lot of work to do to turn over my program." I realized I didn't sound excited, no matter how much I wanted to feel it.

"I know. There's a lot for us to talk about," he said and sighed deeply. Something was bothering him, weighing him down.

"Is everything okay?"

"Yeah, yeah. It will be. We'll talk when I get there. I love you. I'll see you soon, Ros."

"I love you too," I responded woodenly.

Dan hung up, and I sat there for a good five minutes with the phone in my hand, just staring at it. I should have been excited about Dan being done and coming home, and about the fact we would get time together to work through all the things that weren't working for us.

It hit me like a ton of bricks. This also meant my time with Archer would be coming to a close so much sooner than I'd expected. The prospect of losing my best friend was something I was incapable of processing.

"Ros, what's wrong?" Archer asked.

I wrung my fingers in my lap and looked down, uncertain how this conversation was going to go down, unsure of how I was going to say all the things I needed to. The tears stung my eyes, and blinking them wasn't helping to hold them back this time.

As I sat there in silence, feeling the tension rolling off Archer, who was sitting so close to me, waiting for what I was going to say, my throat ached with all the unshed tears and all the unsaid words were fighting and clawing their way to the surface, desperate to be let out.

"Dan is coming back."

He turned and looked away, tugging on his hair in frustration. He groaned, and it was so painful to hear.

"When?" he barked out.

"I don't have an exact date, but he said in the next week."

The tears were starting to slip down my face. I didn't even bother wiping them away. There would be no point.

"Is the project over? I thought it was going on for another two to three months."

"I don't know if it's over, he was vague about the details. I only know he's coming back, and then we're leaving. Going back home." I said the last sentence so quietly it was almost a whisper, but I knew Archer would hear me.

"Fuck, Ros. *This* is your home."

I couldn't hold it in anymore and a sob broke loose. In an instant, I was in Archer's arms, my face pressed against his chest where his musky scent I loved so much was even stronger. I wrapped my arms around his waist and was surprised by how solid he was. So much more than I had grown used to.

"Shhhh. Shhhh. It's going to be okay. I promise," he whispered, stroking my back.

"No, it's not. You don't understand. My heart is fucking breaking right now. You feel like home to me, Archer, but this isn't my home. Not anymore."

"Rosalind," he said so firmly I looked up at him.

The fierceness in his gaze ripped me apart. He grasped my face in his hands, ever so gently rubbing away my tears with his thumbs.

"I've been beating around the bush with this, not being entirely honest for fear I would lose you, and out of respect for your marriage, though your own husband doesn't appear to hold the same respect for it," he said bitterly. I opened my mouth to defend Dan, but he cut me off, not allowing me to even get out one word.

"No, Ros, it's the truth, and deep down you know it. The truth I've been withholding, that fear I never confessed? It's that I'm in love with you. I love you in a way I've never loved anyone, in a way I never thought was possible, and it's the scariest thing I've ever experienced. You are everything to me. And I… I fucking love you. I didn't mean to, but I do."

A single tear tracked down his cheek and the honesty of his words was written all over his face, in his eyes. I had been noticing the more time we spent together, the more movies we watched, the more music we listened to, the more books I read to him, the more he spoke as though he'd been alive just a year or two ago. He didn't sound like he had lived a hundred years ago—what little had remained of his vocal habits from that time had now gone.

I knew this was a bizarre and inappropriate time to have the realization. As I was lost in thought, his grip on my face tightened slightly, but not painfully, and I looked in his eyes again to see them flame with love and passion and lust.

Before I knew what was going on, his lips slammed down on mine in a heady, demanding kiss. It somehow managed to be both tender and harsh at the same time. I could miraculously feel the wet trail his tongue left behind as he licked my lips.

Archer bit my bottom lip, making me gasp, and as my lips parted to release the air, he thrust his tongue into my mouth, seeking and finding my tongue as he deepened the kiss. It went on forever and for only a second before it ended. We were both panting, staring at each other. I finally broke.

I couldn't continue to deny to myself that I loved him. I was in love with him. I probably had been for far longer than I cared to admit.

I realized that when people talked of soulmates, of one eternal love, this was what they were talking about. A love that lit you up from the inside, that set you on fire. A love that was so different from everything and everyone else, you knew you would never meet anyone like them again. A love that fulfilled and sustained you in ways you didn't know possible. That made you stronger, braver, better in every way.

This was what Archer did to me. He challenged me to be the best possible version of myself. Urged me on and supported me, always assured me he was there, even when I couldn't see him. This was a love there would be no returning from. I would never be the Rosalind I'd been before I walked onto this island, before I walked into this house.

And I knew there was no future for us. There was no future for lovers when only one person of the couple was actually, physically alive.

"Archer, I love you too. More than you will ever know." I took a deep, ragged breath, unable to say anything else.

And there was Dan. The guilt was nearly crushing. What kind of person, what kind of wife did it make me, that I had fallen in love with someone who wasn't my husband? I might not have chosen to feel this way, might never have consciously sought this out.

This love had come over me like a tsunami, suddenly and with little warning, all-consuming and devastating. I might not have been technically unfaithful until this moment, but my heart now contained another, and because of it, guilt surrounded me, closing in, making me feel claustrophobic even in the largest of spaces.

I still loved Dan. I was still *in love* with him. He was an amazing man and right for me in so many ways, except all the ways that truly mattered. The ways in which Archer had invaded my heart and taken over. If I didn't know how to explain to myself how this had happened, how was I going to make sense of this to Dan or anyone else?

This had to come to a stop. The only way this ended was with me walking away from Archer and him accepting it. The mere thought of never seeing him, feeling his whisper of a touch, hearing his laugh or words, his sweet deep melodic voice, smelling the scent that was uniquely his. Losing all of those things forever killed me, filled me with an acute pain in my stomach, a combination of heartbreak and dread and guilt.

"Archer... I think I need some space. This is too much right now. I need to figure out how to process this all," I said in the tiniest voice, so quiet I began to think he hadn't even heard me. Goose bumps erupted as his kiss landed on my cheek before he moved next to me.

"I understand, Ros. I'm here, just call me if you need me," Archer said as he faded away.

The end was inevitable—the only thing I could do was start the breaking now in hopes it would hurt less with the pain spread out.

THIRTY

I DIDN'T SEE Archer once over the next week, didn't even attempt to speak to him. It was a fight with myself every minute of every day to not reach out, but I had to get used to life without him in it.

I kept myself busy by focusing on my art program. In addition to running my classes, I was starting to do all the things necessary to transition the program over to a new director. I held interviews and chose two different local artists to run the program together. One would be in charge of the children's and teens' program, and the other would be in charge of the new adult program that would be starting in the next month.

The first gallery show fundraiser for the program was also scheduled for the month after I was going back to Santa Barbara, so I remained in charge of planning and hosting, but the new director shadowed me to ensure the transition when I left was as seamless as possible for future shows.

I was grateful for the chaos during the week Dan returned. I was struggling with letting go of my program and having to say goodbye to the students I had come to know and love. My only solace was I'd already started making plans to start up a chapter in Santa Barbara.

The crazy amount of work also helped keep my mind off of Archer and my upcoming reunion with Dan. We had discussed staying in the house for six weeks after he came home to give me the time needed to tie up all the loose ends with the program as well as time to train the incoming instructors and program director.

MarisCorp was understanding and great about the extra time we needed in the house. Dan had hinted that Liam Maris wanted to potentially contract him for another project planned for the following year, but it was all he had said about it.

Dan was due back in two days, so I was just curled up on the sofa watching an old black-and-white movie I had never seen before to pass the time. I was zoning in and out, barely paying attention, struggling to stay awake. I must have drifted off.

"I've missed you, baby," a voice whispered in my ear. I jolted awake, jumping up and screaming before I saw it was Dan.

I threw my arms around his neck, holding him

tightly. Dread flooded my stomach as I realized his embrace didn't feel familiar. He didn't smell familiar.

This was the first time he had returned from a project where I didn't recognize him in the bone-deep way I used to. He didn't feel like home. Tears pooled in my eyes, falling over and tracking down my cheeks. Dan pulled away and reached out to wipe them away.

"What's wrong, Ros? You aren't supposed to cry at my return," he joked, but something in his voice sounded… off, not right.

"I don't know. You've been away for what feels like forever. Everything just feels strange."

It was probably the closest to the truth I would be able to get with him. I dropped back down on the sofa, pulling my knees up to my chest and wrapping my arms around them. Dan recognized my attempt to protect myself.

He pushed the armchair in front of where I was sitting on the sofa and sat down. He leaned forward, resting his forearms on his thighs, and clasped his hands together. We just sat there, staring at each other.

I looked at him closely, seeing the tension in his neck and shoulders, how rigidly he held them. He had more wrinkles than I remember and had a little more silver at his temples than he had before the start of this project. The exhaustion was written all over his face. I couldn't imagine how bad the stress was on this assignment if the effects of it were manifesting themselves physically so quickly.

I looked into his eyes and saw more strain, worry, and an emotion that looked a lot like guilt or regret. We both knew we needed to talk, but neither of us wanted to be the first to start. Hell, maybe we didn't know how to start after all the distance between us.

"You know, Ros, I thought you'd be happier to see me, more excited to go back home to Santa Barbara. You don't even seem excited to see me at all." He was being defensive, which was so out of character for him, and it instantly threw up a red flag.

"Dan, I'm excited to see you. Not as excited about going back to Santa Barbara. You just woke me up too. You know how I am when I'm woken up out of a dead sleep."

"We haven't seen each other in months, Ros. I get that it's late, but this is all you can muster?" The anger in his words smacked me awake. I couldn't understand how something so small had escalated within him so quickly.

"I don't know, babe, we're going to have an adjustment period. We always do after you get back from a project. You know we have a lot to talk about when it comes to us and what our marriage is going to be like, moving forward. I just don't think this conversation should happen tonight."

He swore and shook his head before lacing his fingers

behind his head. "This was not what I expected to come home to. I expected a warm welcome, like I usually get. Why are you so distant? So cold? Are you pissed at me about how this all panned out?"

I saw red and the rage exploded out of me. "Are you fucking kidding me, Dan? Do you want to have this conversation right now? It's two in the damn morning. Nothing good will come of us having this conversation tonight. And fuck yeah, I'm a little distant. None of this went as planned. I get that work was a shit show, but you stopped communicating with me, Dan. Fuck!"

He got up and started pacing. His tension and nervous energy ramped up with every step he took. He must have crossed the living room four or five times before he stopped dead in his tracks and turned back to me, giving me a strange look filled with contemplation and something darker and more troubling.

"You've changed, you know?" We both knew it was more of a statement than an actual question. "I don't know when it started, but you've changed while I've been gone," he continued.

I still couldn't tell by the tone of his voice if he considered this a positive or negative thing. Then I considered the fact he had been AWOL for so long he wouldn't even recognize if I had changed. It didn't alter the fact that he was right.

"Yeah, I guess I have changed. But you know what, you've changed too. What happened, Dan?"

He shook his head in response, but said nothing.

"There's been a difference in your voice the last couple of times we talked, Dan. I brushed it off, figured I was just being paranoid. But now you walk in here, and the negative, nervous energy is coming off you in waves. I can see something is wrong. What the hell is it? Why do I sense guilt or regret or remorse just as much as I can see the stress?"

I looked up at him in time to see him take a step back and bend over to grip the back of the chair in front of him. It looked like someone had punched him in the gut. He walked back over to the armchair and fell into it. He looked so broken, so different from the Dan I last saw.

"I'm so sorry, Ros. I fucked up."

He dropped his head into his hands, gripping his hair and refusing to make eye contact. It hit me then that this was bad. Whatever he was going to say would be so much worse than I was ready for.

"The project was fucked up from the start. I shouldn't have been surprised when Maris transferred the project to the facility on his private island, I should have anticipated it, but it blindsided me. I was lonely and bitter. We were working crazy hours, sometimes working three days before going back to our quarters to sleep."

"But—"

"No, Ros. Just let me get this out. It was just the four of us, and we got really close. I mean, how could you not get close when these are the only people you're seeing or talking to all day, every day for months? We would all spend what little downtime we had together as well, as a group. Kelly and I got close. We're really similar, almost like she's me in a woman's body. She sort of became my best friend. The more we worked together, the closer I got to the team and Kelly, the easier it became to handle the distance between you and me. Then it became easier to just not call. Fuck, I'm sorry, Ros, I really am. I did everything wrong here."

He looked up at me, eyes rimmed in red, stricken. I couldn't miss the fear written all over him. He was pleading with me to listen, to understand, to forgive with this look. I waited him out in silence so absolute I could hear the rain falling outside. I knew more was coming.

"One night we were hanging out, just the two of us. We would do that occasionally, usually just bitching about the project and watching movies. Well, the night was going as usual, but we fell asleep on the couch. I woke up to her lying on me. I went to stand up, to put distance between us, when she leaned in and kissed me. I… I let her do it. I kissed her back for a few seconds. And then for a few more. Soon I forgot why we shouldn't be kissing at all." He stopped there, avoiding my stunned gaze and refusing to say more.

I inhaled sharply and tried to take a deep breath but my chest seized and tightened painfully. My lungs, my chest constricted and then I was suffocating, being crushed under the weight of all the words Dan hadn't said. I was dying in the lines he was expecting me to read between.

I'd heard people talk about how a broken heart could be physically painful, how you could feel it viscerally, each valve crushing or ripping apart, making you feel like death would come after the torture of feeling every soft, vulnerable part of you shatter into pieces. I'd never believed that. I'd always thought it was just an exaggeration, a way to analogize the emotional pain of losing something that meant everything to you.

In the moments I was left to leap to the conclusion Dan hadn't drawn for me, I knew that I'd been wrong all along. How foolish I had been to think a broken heart couldn't be felt physically, especially considering what it had felt like when my mother had been ripped from my life.

"What. The fuck. Happened, Dan?" The words were like sandpaper against my vocal cords as I forced them out of my throat with all the willpower I had in me.

"Fuck, I'm so fucking sorry, Ros. I never planned it, I never wanted it to happen, and I regretted it the minute it did. God, please, believe me, Ros, please forgive me. I had us work triple time and arranged to bring in a couple of extra people from the company to help finish this project on an accelerated timeline. I knew I needed to get back to you as soon as possible. I knew what was going on with us wouldn't be fixed with us apart all the time. Ros, could you please just tell me what you're thinking?"

The desperation in his voice affected me more than I'd expected it would, but I was still shocked by the implication of what he was admitting.

"Dan, I don't give a fuck about the project. I want to know exactly what happened. Did you fuck her?"

He said nothing. He just continued to hold his head in his hands. I waited for what felt like forever but likely was only minutes. Dan finally allowed his gaze to reach mine and before he even nodded his head, the truth was written all over his face and in the anguished glint of his eyes.

An agonized gasp rang out in the room. Dan slammed into the back of the chair he was sitting in and I realized the sound had come from me. I turned away from him then, walked over to the nearest wall and slid down it until my ass hit the ground.

"I fucked up, I know it, and I'm fucking sorry, Ros. I switched her work schedule so we barely worked together after and only when others would be around. I didn't want her to think this was something I was willing to entertain again. I know I fucked up by letting it happen, and I'm so. Fucking. Sorry. Tell me I can fix this. Please, Ros. Tell me what I can do. I don't want to lose you."

His voice broke on the last word and tears fell down his face. I didn't think I'd ever seen Dan shed even a hint of a tear in all the years we'd been together.

I knew then that he was being honest about this only happening once. Dan was one of the most honest people I knew. He could have kept this all quiet, never told me, and I would never have known. I also knew that I couldn't be around him right now. I was seconds away from losing the thin thread of composure I was holding onto, and I wasn't willing to let him see that snap.

"I believe you, Dan, but I can't do this right now. I don't even want to look at you. You need to leave. We can talk tomorrow, but I can't do this tonight. No, I *won't* fucking do this tonight."

The words came out slow and calm, so steady and even that it almost scared me. Dan stood up and made his way over to me, reaching out his hand to help me stand.

"No. I can't. I don't want you anywhere near me right now, not when all I can picture is your hands on her body."

He stumbled backward the moment the words left my mouth, reacting like I had struck him. His face was still wet with the sheen of the tears he hadn't wiped away and he nodded his head with resignation before turning and walking back out the front door.

As the door slammed shut I wrapped my arms around my knees and dropped my head to rest on them. As the full reality of what just happened hit me, tremors wracked my body and a sob broke free. As the pain took over my body, another emotion crept in, spreading through my veins like poison.

Guilt.

As angry and shattered as I was by Dan's confession, I knew I was worse than him. Not all of the blame rested on his shoulders. I'd kissed Archer. Worse yet, I'd fallen in love with Archer. As much as I wanted to rush out the door and lay bare all of my faults and wrongdoing to Dan, how would I make him understand that while Dan had given his body once to another woman, I had lost my heart to a ghost?

THIRTY-ONE

I WOKE up a few hours later to Dan wrapping his arms around my waist and pulling me into him. His bare chest warmed my back first, then his bare legs came into contact with mine. The painful sobbing after his confession earlier had worn me out before I fell into a fitful slumber. I must have been way more exhausted than I thought, because I hadn't even heard Dan come back into the house.

He kissed the back of my neck, featherlight kisses. It felt so good, and it had been so long since I had felt his touch that I moaned despite myself before I pushed him away.

"Dan, no! I said you could come back in the morning, not sneak into bed when my defenses were down. Get the fuck out, now!"

I didn't recognize the raspy, raw sound of my voice. I

turned over onto my back with my eyes closed. The thought of even looking at him made me sick to my stomach, disgust and guilt warring with each other, creating a whirling pool of nausea.

He leaned down and kissed the corner of my mouth. Before I could push him away, my sleepy daze fell away, and I realized the kiss didn't feel the way it used to. The pressure and feel of his lips were different.

I inhaled and my nostrils filled with Archer's scent. My eyes flew open, only to find Archer looking down at me, his body touching the length of mine, sturdy and solid.

"How?" I gasped out.

"I don't know, Ros. We've both witnessed my strength growing and my ability to take form for longer periods of time, but I have no logical explanation for why this is possible. I don't know how this is happening, but I'm not going to second-guess it. Tell me no, tell me to stop and I will."

I stroked his cheek, unable to believe this. There were so many thoughts, so many emotions raging in my body. My mouth only uttered one word.

"Stay."

The smile that broke out across his face shattered me into a million pieces. He put those pieces back together when he leaned down and kissed me. The minute his lips touched mine, all thoughts about how this was possible, all potential protests flew out of my mind.

I gasped, feeling breathless, and he took the opening, plunging his tongue into my mouth. Mine met his, and I deepened the kiss. I grabbed his hair at the nape of his neck, surprised by how soft and silky the strands felt in my fingers.

He groaned at my touch as warmth and wetness dripped down my thighs. My heart thundered at the reality that somehow, I was getting the one thing I wanted more than anything else in the world.

Archer peppered kisses down my neck, alternating between light, airy ones, gentle bites, and strokes of his tongue to soothe the pain from his teeth. The alternating sensations of pain and tender kisses drove me crazy, made me even wetter. He began making his descent down my body. Kisses fluttered along my collarbone before I reached down to lift my camisole over my head.

A growl ripped out of Archer, and my eyes flung open at the sound. His gaze was feral, hunger and love written on the planes of his face. He grasped my hands, intertwining our fingers. I watched as he continued to kiss down my body, his tongue dipping out to taste the valley between my breasts. He placed a searing kiss on my left breast as he squeezed my hand and his whispered "I love you" tickled my skin, exactly in the spot I knew he could feel my heart racing.

All because of him, all for him.

He lowered his head to my breast, taking the hard tip of my nipple in his mouth. His tongue circled the peak before he bit down gently, tugging it with his teeth then sucking it back into his mouth. He switched to my other breast while playing with the first with his fingers, alternating between pinching it and running his thumb over the tip.

I moaned, arching my back, craving his touch everywhere. His touch ignited a fire under my skin, the flame roaring through my veins and burning my skin. I already felt so close to the edge, so close to just plummeting over it simply from his touch and his kiss.

I ran my hands over his shoulders, through his hair, gently raking my nails down his arms. I couldn't get enough of touching him, of the feel of his skin under the tips of my fingers. I cataloged the dip and bulge of every muscle, each freckle painted across his skin, taking snapshots of his glorious body I could hold onto for the rest of my days.

"So beautiful," he whispered reverently as I ran my hands down his back, loving the feel of the hard muscles moving under my hands.

He kissed his way down my stomach, circling his tongue around the indentation of my belly button, the light caress of his fingers over my stomach eliciting goose bumps all over my skin. I felt his lips curve up into a smile against my lower stomach before placing a kiss there.

He settled down between my legs and looked up at me as he grasped my thighs and set them on his shoulders. His smile turned devilish as he lowered his head and placed a kiss on my swollen clit. His tongue darted out and licked my slick slit, from my core to the swollen bundle of nerves that wanted all of his attention, in one long, firm lick. Archer moaned against me, the vibrations causing my back to arch off the bed as my hips bucked.

His mouth felt like one erotic, unending, blissful kiss against my center. He didn't stop until my thighs were shaking, until I was gasping and on the precipice, his name a prayer and a plea on my lips. Archer sent me plunging over the edge and continued to lick me as I came back down from my climax.

"You taste so much better than I imagined, Ros," he whispered against me.

He rose up on his knees, and I took in his body for the first time, appreciating the beauty of it, trying to ingrain the image on my consciousness. Archer crawled back up my body, spreading my legs further with his knees. He lowered himself to my body, and his cock surged forward toward my entrance.

He placed his arms on either side of my face and kissed me hard, passionately. He looked into my eyes as he hitched my thigh up around his waist with one hand

CECE FERRELL

and caressed my face with the other. His eyes roved all over my face, taking me in, memorizing how I looked in this moment we both knew we wouldn't get again.

"I love you so damn much, Rosalind."

He intertwined our fingers together as he thrust himself into me, hard and deep. I moaned as he filled me. He paused for a moment, giving me time to adjust to his size. Soon he began moving inside of me in a slow, hard rhythm. He looked into my eyes the entire time. I couldn't look away, I was mesmerized. My hips moved in sync with his, grinding against him.

My heart could hear the words his spoke with each thrust. *I love you, you will always be mine, it will only ever be you.*

Mine responded with each grind against him. *I won't forget you, you'll always have my heart, I love you.*

Archer picked up the pace and pushed into me harder and faster. He changed his position slightly, rotating his hips differently, and he hit a sweet spot inside of me that elicited a loud moan at the same time the base of his cock ground against my clit. Archer kissed me fiercely and I tightened around him. He groaned, his control starting to slip. Seeing his loss of control pushed me over the edge, and I came hard, spasming around him.

He rolled us over, changing our position. He sat up, pulling me into his lap, so I was straddling him. He

302

wrapped his arms around my back and pulled me close to him, so close my chest grazed his. He smiled the sweetest, sexiest smile at me and I could feel my lips spread in an answering smile. He leaned in to kiss me, our lips barely touching.

"God, I love you, Archer. I love you so much," I whispered against his lips. His answering moan vibrated against mine. I raised up my body, dropping myself back onto his length, letting him fill me as I rearranged my legs so they wrapped around his waist. We sat like this, with me in his lap, chests pressed together. He gripped my waist and started to thrust underneath me.

Archer looked into my eyes again as I moved with him. His hands controlled my movements, and we continued our slow, steady pace. Our eyes never wavered as we continued to kiss. I caressed him every-where my fingers could reach. I thought we knew in the moment this was our one chance, our one time to be together. We didn't take it for granted, we savored every single moment.

Archer's movements quickened, his thrusts hitting deeper. I adjusted my movements to match his, feeling his body tense, getting closer. He ran one of his hands up my body, grasping my breast and pinching my nipple before continuing on its path up. He caressed my neck, then reached up to push a strand of my hair behind my ear before cradling my face in his hand, pulling me closer to kiss me deeper, harder.

It was maybe the sexiest thing I'd ever experienced. Another orgasm built inside of me, and I moved faster, kissed Archer more fiercely, chasing the release only his body could promise me and never wanting it to end.

"I'm right there, Ros," he said in a tortured voice. "Come with me, Ros. If you can, please."

The urgent demand pushed me over the edge, and I came, looking into his eyes, watching his face twist in pleasure as he climaxed inside of me, filling me with his hot release.

He collapsed on top of me and turned us to our sides, so we were facing each other. "Hey," he said, caressing my face, rubbing his thumb along my kiss-swollen bottom lip.

"Hey," I said back in a husky, sated voice.

"I love you, Ros. Don't ever forget that," Archer's deep, melodic voice whispered in my ear.

I nodded my head. I couldn't find the words to express all I was feeling at the moment. Elation, satisfaction, peace, confusion, and fear. I couldn't even begin to wrap my head around how this was possible.

I knew that any minute guilt would fill my veins. With all the thoughts racing through my mind, all the emotions I couldn't articulate, I wouldn't allow myself to regret these moments I'd shared with Archer.

I hadn't done this for revenge, some need to get back at Dan for what he had done. I'd allowed this because I loved Archer more than I had ever loved anything or anyone, and I wanted the memories of this one night I got with him for the rest of my life.

As he placed a kiss on my head, light as air, his breath a warm caress on my skin, there was one thing I knew without doubt. So I spoke the words out loud again before he had a chance to disappear, because I knew it would be impossible for him to maintain enough energy to stay any longer after what we had done.

"I love you too, Archer. Always."

THIRTY-TWO

BANG. Bang. Bang. Bang. Bang.

I opened my eyes and then winced as the bright, mid-morning sun hit my face. I massaged my temples, wondering what could have happened between when I finally fell asleep last night after Archer left and now to cause a headache with this kind of banging, pounding pain in my head. Then I heard a frustrated, muffled male voice and I knew that the banging wasn't coming from my headache after all.

I rolled out of bed, grabbed my robe from the bench in front of it and shuffled to the front door as I wrapped it around my body. I swung open the door just as Dan was about to start another round of knocking.

"Finally. What happened? I even tried calling you and it went straight to voicemail," he said, his voice raspy with lack of sleep, his hands curled into fists so tight his knuckles were white.

"I forgot to charge it. It's probably dead. Why didn't you just use your key?" I stepped aside so he could make his way into the house. He walked in with tentative steps, his discomfort radiating from every inch of him.

"After what happened last night and how you told me to leave, I figured it was better if I didn't just walk in. I wasn't sure if you would want to even see me today."

I rubbed at my forehead, avoided eye contact and tried to figure out what I wanted, figure out if I was even ready to talk all this out with him. As much as I would have loved to pretend that nothing had happened last night, between Dan's confession and my own indiscretion, I knew that I couldn't. It wasn't fair to either of us and it would be better to decide where we went from here sooner rather than later.

"Do you want me to leave? I can find a place to stay if you would rather not have this conversation right now." Dan stepped closer to me, but stopped right before making physical contact. He held out his arms, a wordless request to come closer.

Guilt and bile surged up from my stomach into my throat and threatened to spill out all over us both. I shook my head no, denying his request. I looked up at his face just in time to witness the flinch of pain. It hit me then that this look was only a hint of what would likely be there by the time this talk was through. My chest ached, the thought of hurting Dan causing a very real pain in my body, regardless of his own lack of innocence.

"No, don't go. We need to figure this all out." I made my way to the sofa in the living room, but Dan interrupted me before I made it there.

"Ros, could we go somewhere else to do this? Maybe go for a walk or something? I don't know why, but I think this would go better outside."

I thought about it for a minute. I considered declining. Insisting that we stay right here, but I was starting to feel suffocated by all the secrets and lies living in these walls.

And then it hit me that it was very likely that Archer would be a witness to all of this if it happened in the house. He was good about giving space and privacy when needed, but would he be able to say no to the temptation to secretly have a front-row seat to what could be the demise of my marriage?

"Sure, I know a pretty quiet area we can go to for some privacy. Just let me get changed and we can drive over."

Dan simply nodded his head before walking out to the balcony. I went to our room to change and throw my hair up into a messy bun, too keyed up and anxious to even consider spending more than a minute or two on it. I took a quick look at myself in the mirror in our closet and barely recognized myself. My skin was too pale, my eyes had dark circles underneath, and there was a wild glint to my eyes that I had never seen before.

"Get it the fuck together, Ros. Just tell him. All you have to do is say the words. 'I cheated too. I'm sorry.' You can do this," I whispered to myself in the mirror.

I needed the practice and the pep talk, though I was fairly sure it wouldn't make one damn bit of difference. What did I say to Dan when he started asking questions about who and how and why? I couldn't tell him the truth. I just had to hope the confession alone would be enough.

We parked near the shops and made our way to the same rocky beach where I'd had my breakthrough months ago. As I paced along the shore, it hit me that the place that had witnessed me come alive with purpose and passion would also be witness to the potential breakdown of my marriage. I swallowed hard, an attempt to keep the fear and pain down before it all erupted out of me in a flow of words and confessions I could never take back.

The crunching of rocks and shells under a heavy foot alerted me to his growing proximity, and before I was even close to being ready for this talk, the warmth and tension of his body made contact with my back. I turned and glanced at him over my shoulder, hesitation clear in his eyes. I didn't know if he was hesitant to start this or hesitant to reach out to me. I didn't know if I would have accepted that touch from him, if I could have accepted it. I did know that in no way did I deserve his touch or comfort.

"Ros. Fuck, I still don't know what to say. I'm sorry. I'll never stop being sorry." He thrust his hands in his hair, leaving it in disarray before dragging his hands down his face.

"Dan. Just stop. I... I..." And there I stopped.

I turned away from him and looked out over the water again. It was breaking me that I was about to cause him even more pain than he was feeling now. Pain he'd rightfully earned and deserved, but it would never sit well with me to see him hurting, no matter the cause.

"Ros, just tell me what you're thinking. Ask me whatever you want and I'll answer it. If you need more space, I'll give it to you. Whatever you need, just tell me. I just don't want you to walk away from us. I know I fucked up, but we can fix this. Please tell me you want to fix this."

Now.

Now was the time to tell him, to lay it all out there. I turned around again and took him in, searched for the love I'd always assumed would be evident in his face, his gaze when he looked at me. There was every chance in the world that this would be the last time I would see him look at me like this, even if it was all dampened by the turmoil roiling around him.

"Before you say anything else, I have something to say, and I need to get this out before you say anything." I paused and he nodded his head as his body stiffened, his attempt to steel himself for what I was going to say.

So I loaded that gun, I cocked it, and I pulled the fucking trigger.

"I fucked up too, Dan. I—I cheated too."

My words rang out, cutting through the sound of the water lapping at the shore, and I saw the moment they hit their target. He stumbled back and gripped his mouth in agony and disgust. He turned in circles, both hands gripping the back of his neck. I just stood and waited. Waited for his judgment, his pain, his hate. I deserved it all. More than he did.

Because though he'd fucked another woman, I'd given my heart to someone else. And of the two sins, mine was definitely the worst.

THIRTY-THREE

"ARCHER," I called, standing out on the balcony. My arms, encased in a thick sweater, were wrapped around my stomach.

It had only been a day since I'd last laid eyes on him, since everything in our lives had imploded, but it seemed like even longer. Dan had come back to the house last night, though he was staying in one of the guest rooms. Archer had to be aware of all the tension going on in this house, though I wasn't sure if he was still around or was just pretending to be gone. I hadn't felt his presence in any of the ways I was used to in the last day, and I'd be lying if I said I wasn't worried.

I walked over to the balcony railing and leaned on it, looking out into the water. This would be the first time I'd tried talking to him or seeing him during the day, and I wasn't even sure he would show up at all, if he were able to. For all this time that we'd known each other, for all the years and years he'd been a ghost, we both still had almost no clue how it all worked. I continued to wait until I sensed his presence behind me, until I smelled that scent of his I loved so much, the one that now smelled like home to me.

"I'm here, Rosalind," he replied, heartbreak written across his face, etched deeply in his eyes. I wondered what he had overheard in the last day, and the pain I was causing him shattered another piece of me.

"I wasn't sure if you were still around or if you would even come."

"I stayed out of the house to give you space, but I couldn't bring myself to leave altogether. I've been here, but at a distance, in case you changed your mind." The undeniable hint of hope rang out in his voice, and it broke my heart even more, especially knowing what I'd come to say.

"How, Archer? How did you do it? And why did you do it?"

I couldn't mask the edge of accusation in my voice, even though I know he wasn't solely at fault. He flinched as though I had struck him and I could see the buildup of what looked like unshed tears in his eyes. My question needed no further clarification.

"I don't have an explanation. I don't know how, you already know that. I know there is no excuse for what I

313

let happen. After you told me you would be leaving and wanted me to give you space until then… You never wanted to see me again…"

He paused, dragging his hand over his face roughly. "In that moment, I'd thought I lost everything. When I woke up next to you, for lack of a better word, it was like a gift. I needed to see if you wanted this too, wanted us. If you did, I wanted to feel you, to share that moment of love and intimacy with you at least once. I'm sorry… No. If I'm honest, I'm not sorry. I wish I were, for your sake, but I can't be sorry about what we shared. I'll never regret it."

I had no idea what to say after, and I almost forgot why I came out here to talk to him in the first place. I dropped down onto the outdoor sofa and leaned over, resting my elbows on my knees, putting my head in my hands. I wanted to scream, to cry, to relive the last almost year of my life.

Archer came closer. His warm comfort washed over me when he placed his hand on my shoulder, gripping me tightly. It was like our time together continued to change him, empower him. As much as I wanted to feel the comfort of his presence, I shook him off, knowing it would lead to nothing good and wouldn't change what I came here to say and do.

"Did you do it for revenge? Because you were pissed

at Dan for admitting what he had done?" I asked, hearing the desperation in my voice.

I didn't know why I needed answers from him, why I was so intent on trying to place the blame on him as though it would ever alleviate my guilt. I was just as guilty.

"Ros, no. You know me better than that. I love you, Rosalind. I love you with every fiber of my being. I will always love you until I cease to exist in any way. I did it without considering the ramifications it would have on you, on us."

He turned away from me, gripping his hair before running his hand through the rest of his hair. He was right. I'd known the minute the question had left my mouth revenge had nothing to do with this just as it had nothing to do with why I'd gone along with it.

"God, I'm so sorry, Archer. This isn't your fault. I'm to blame. I wanted it just as much as you did and I said yes. I asked you to stay… and I want you to know that it wasn't revenge for me either. I just… I just need you to know that."

We sat there in silence, the tension building between us. Finally, I looked up, staring at his back, rigid with the emotion of what we both knew was going to be goodbye. My throat ached with the weight of holding back all the words I needed to say, words I didn't want to speak.

Archer had turned to face me, but his body was no less rigid, and his hands were now balled up into fists, as though he needed to do it to keep himself from trying to touch me. We were only a few feet apart, but he felt miles away from me in that moment. He opened his mouth to speak, but I cut him off before he had a chance to get one word out.

"This isn't even what I came here to say. Archer, I'll be leaving in a week. For good. Dan and I are going back home to California."

"What? Are you serious, Ros? What about what happened? What he did?"

As he said the words, my mind went back to what had happened yesterday.

"I fucked up too, Dan. I—I cheated too."

He stumbled back and gripped his mouth in agony and disgust. He turned in circles, both hands gripping the back of his neck. The wait for whatever he would say in response felt like an eternity.

"What the fuck, Ros? You're fucking with me right now, right? You're just trying to show me how you feel. Tell me that's what that is." His voice shook with rage and disbelief and it scared me more than anything else. Any hope I had that we could move past this died.

"No, I'm telling the truth. And I'm sorry, Dan. I'm so sorry." My voice broke on the last word and then the tears came.

"Fuck! When? Who? C'mon and tell me, Ros. I want to

hear this. How long has it been going on? What fucking right did you have to kick me out last night when you were hiding this shit from me? When you had secrets of your own?"

Dan screamed, raged at me. He threw his arms out in a "come at me" gesture, but he never came any closer. My presence was repellent to him in that moment, and when my gaze finally met his, when he looked at me with hurt mixed up with loathing, I knew it likely wouldn't change anytime soon.

"Dan, you don't want the details just like I don't want the details about you and Kelly. It happened once. Only once. It won't ever happen again, I promise. I just need to know where we go from here." The lies tasted terrible in my mouth, but it was all over, and I didn't believe that being completely truthful helped anyone.

"I can't do this, Ros. I can't even stand to look at you right now." His voice was an eerie, scary calm. Without a second look, he turned and walked off the beach and away from me.

He came back to the house later that night, broken and exhausted. I knew I had to have looked the same way when he flinched at the sight of me. The one thing I was surprised to see was the regret and apology written all over him. I knew those emotions had to be all over me as well. He sat down on the coffee table across from me, resting his arms on his thighs, and looked up at me.

"Ros, we both fucked up. I don't know how the fuck we got here, I don't know how we could even get past this... Fuck, I don't know anything right now. But I know I want to try. I *want to leave this fucking island, I want to go back to our home and I want to try to fix us. Do you think that's even possible?" he asked when his eyes finally met mine.*

"Ros. Rosalind!" Archer's voice, louder than normal, broke through my thoughts. "Are you all right?" he asked, stepping closer.

"Yeah. No. No, I'm not okay. Nothing is okay right now. I told Dan yesterday what happened between us, Archer. I told him that I slept with you."

I paused then, needing a break, not knowing what else to say. I gripped my arms even tighter around my body, trying to contain all of the emotions that wanted to spill out of me, my body taut and rigid with the effort.

"What did you tell him? He knows and you're still leaving with him?"

Archer's face was pale with shock, his body as tight and stock-still as mine. I ran my fingers through my hair in frustration. This was so much harder than I'd expected. I just needed to say it and get it over with. There was no way to sugarcoat the truth, and he deserved nothing less than it.

"I just told him I slept with someone else. I couldn't give him the details. He would never understand, he—"

"You didn't tell him that you love me? That it was more than just the act?"

"No." A single, whispered word that held my apology and shame over hiding the full truth from Dan.

"Dan and I talked last night. We decided to try to work through this, to fix everything that's broken. I owe that to him."

The words were out, and while I wanted to feel some sense of relief, instead my chest ached with a crushing sadness. Archer bent over with a gasp, my decision a blow to him.

Before I processed his movement, he was right beside me. His thumbs whispered against the skin under my eyes. I almost questioned what he was doing before I realized I had been crying and he was wiping away my tears. He was devastated but was still trying to take care of me, comfort me.

"Ros, I want to ask you to stay. I'd beg if I thought it would work, and I've never begged anyone for anything before. I wish I had the answers to make this all better. I wish I knew a way for us to be together. Though it would kill me if I were still alive, I know I have to let you go," he whispered, holding my face in his hands.

His grasp tightened, and when I looked at him, his body looked just as real and present as it had that night. I turned my face into his hand, kissing his palm. The faint intake of his breath resounded in my ears, a barely audible gasp, wholly unnecessary, but there all the same.

He wrapped his hand around the back of my neck and pulled me closer, so close our lips were only a breath apart. I looked up from his lips into his green eyes, and I cried.

I tried to calm myself so I could memorize his beautiful face, every contour and line. So I could remember the exact shade of green of his eyes in this moment. I wanted to remember the look of love, passion, desire, and loss all so plainly evident in his eyes, each emotion warring with the other. He closed the distance between us and crashed his lips against mine.

I deepened the kiss without hesitation. I knew I should have stopped, that it was wrong, but I also knew this was the last kiss we would ever share. The damage had been done weeks ago, one last kiss wasn't going to make it worse.

So I enjoyed that kiss.

When Archer ran his tongue along the seam of my lips, I moaned, opening myself up to his invasion. I ran my tongue along his, returning the kiss, savoring it. As our tongues tangled, he groaned into my mouth. Heat pulsed between my thighs and I knew my underwear was soaked. I leaned my body against his, dying for the contact.

I reached up and ran my hand through his thick, soft hair, shocked I could do so, that I could feel the strands, that I could feel his hard, solid body move against mine. Soon I was backed up against the house, my body caged in by his, the evidence of his desire rubbing against me, the only thing separating us the thin material of my leggings and the thickness of his pants. He reached down, gripping under my thighs and lifting, and I answered by wrapping my legs around his waist, grinding against his hardness, seeking the friction his body was providing.

"Rosalind," he whispered in an agonized voice full of lust.

Hearing his voice worked like a bucket of ice water. I pushed against his chest, and he looked into my eyes. The moment he recognized I wanted space something changed in him, a resigned acceptance clouded over the lust raging in his gaze just moments before. He released my thighs, gently putting me down.

He didn't move back more than a step though. His arms still caged me in, his forehead dropped to mine, and we stood there gasping, chests heaving, trying to calm our raging bodies down. I would have gone there again with him, given in to what we so desperately wanted.

His growing strength, the change in the things he was able to do, and the love and connection that tied us together were all the reasons why I needed to say goodbye and walk away now. There was no future in this, no future with a ghost. How could there be?

I reached up and placed my hand against his cheek. When I opened my eyes and took in his face one last time, I could already see the faint hints of transparency start to seep back in. What we just did must have exhausted his energy, and he was starting to fade out again. He turned his head, placing a warm, tender kiss to my palm before wrapping his hand around mine and squeezing it. He looked back into my eyes and nodded his head.

"I love you so much, Archer. I will always love you," I said, another sob racking my body. "There is so much I want to say, but I can't find the words," I whispered, my body shaking.

He pulled me into his arms and ran his hand soothingly along my spine. I shivered with the pleasure of his touch, goose bumps appearing all over my body.

"Try, Rosalind. Please just try. I need the words. I don't care if they'll wreck me," he whispered into my ear.

I shook my head and gripped him tighter. My hold on him started to give way and I knew that soon, very soon there would be nothing left to hold onto but air, the memory of his body, and all the feelings I couldn't escape.

"Fuck. I'm sorry. I'm sorry I'm hurting you. I'm sorry that there isn't a future for us. And most of all..." I stopped, breathing deeply, nearly gasping and trying to get a handle on the chest-crushing, soul-decimating pain running through my body. "Most of all I'm sorry that I still love Dan. I hate saying that to you, because you deserve so much more. But I owe you the truth, and the truth is part of me still loves him and wants to try to make things work. And I'm sorry for that, Archer. I really am."

"Ros, stop. I know you love me. I know this isn't easy, for either of us. I know you love him. I also know there's a tie connecting our hearts together, and nothing will sever that. Not time, not death," he whispered in my ear, somehow knowing exactly what I needed to hear to walk away and let him go.

He tightened his embrace, holding me for what felt like forever. I clung to him with my face buried in his chest, taking in his scent, knowing I would never smell anything better again in my life. We both pulled back and looked at each other one last time. He leaned in, placing a kiss first on my lips, then on my forehead, before he let go of me and stepped backward.

He faded more with each footstep away from me he took. I raised my hand to wave. He waved back as his face broke into a broad, beautiful, breathtaking smile.

His eyes were bursting with love, and I laughed through the tears still falling, grateful I was able to see this smile one last time. His smile didn't waver before he faded completely, disappearing forever. I tried to comfort myself with this final memory of him.

THIRTY-FOUR

SOMEHOW DAN and I were able to wrap everything up that we needed to in that week. It wasn't as difficult as I had expected to train and pass over all my preparations for the program and the showcase to the new coordinators. I would miss the children I had taught but tried to console myself with the fact that I would get to meet more when I started things in Santa Barbara. I couldn't replace those kids, but what other option did I have? Dan said that most of the project was wrapped when he had returned home the night that everything fell apart. Everything he wasn't able to finish in the last week he could do remotely.

Saying goodbye to Marie and the book club ladies was far more difficult than I had anticipated. These women were one of the biggest reasons this island had felt like home to me, and Marie had become so incredibly important to me. She was my best friend and mom stand-in all at once.

I knew we would stay in touch, but my days wouldn't be the same without her stories, her kitchen filled with delicious foods and warmth, and her beautiful laugh. The ache from walking away from her was almost as bad as the one that Archer had left in his wake.

In that last week, I hadn't seen or felt Archer once. I both hated it and was grateful for the distance. We had said goodbye, I didn't think I was capable of anything more than that. I grabbed my purse from the kitchen countertop and took one last look around the first floor of the house that I had fallen in love with. It felt stupid to be sad over leaving a place I had been in for a year, but I was attached all the same.

As Dan and I made our way to the front door, ready to cross the threshold and leave for the last time, something crashed to the floor behind me.

"What the hell was that?" Dan asked as he turned around. I could already see it was a book lying open.

"It's just a book. How about you go ahead to the car, and I'll be there in a second after I put it back." I was already walking toward it.

"Okay. Man, that was strange," Dan muttered to himself as he left the house.

I bent down and grabbed the book, flipping it over to see what book it was, making sure not to lose the page it had fallen open to. I knew there was a reason for it landing on the page it had.

City of Glass.

I walked over to the kitchen island, setting the book down and skimming over it. A passage instantly jumped out to me. I sighed deeply. He knew. He was aware of how much I loved the book series, knew the quote would resonate with me.

"Oh, Archer," I whispered. I left the book open on the island and made my way back to the front door. As I stepped out of the house, I turned around and took one look back. "Even after this life, I will love you too."

I closed the door behind me and walked away, somehow strong enough to not look back.

THIRTY-FIVE

KNOCK. Knock. Knock.

"I'm coming, I'm coming. Hold your damn horses!" Jos shouted while making her way to her door.

I couldn't help but smile as I stood on her front porch waiting. I'd decided back in Washington that I would just wait until I got back home to surprise her.

Home.

This place surely didn't feel like home anymore to me. I knew what that felt like now, and home was back on an island, traipsing around with a ghost.

Time. You just need time, more than a day back here.

Those were the words I kept repeating in my mind, hopeful that one day soon I could convince myself of their truth.

"What. The. Fuck!" I turned back toward the door at the sound of her voice. Damn, I had missed her so fucking much. I barely had a chance to shoot her a grin before I was pulled into her embrace. "Seriously, bitch! What are you doing here and why didn't you tell me you were coming?"

"I wanted to surprise you," I replied, still stuck in her death grip.

"C'mon, we haven't talked in like three weeks." Jos released me from her hold before grabbing my hand and pulling me through her door. "How's everything? Did Dan finish the project?" she asked rapid-fire before turning back to me.

One look at me and the smile melted off her face and was replaced with a look of concern. I knew then that the thin veneer hiding my emotions was completely transparent. Jos always read me so well, I shouldn't have been surprised. "Ros, what the hell happened?"

I tumbled down onto one corner of her sofa, sinking into the soft cushions and pulling a throw pillow onto my lap.

"What didn't happen?"

The minute the words were out of my mouth, I knew I had fucked up by not planning out what I wanted to say before I had even knocked on her door. I couldn't just tell her what Dan had done. It wouldn't have been fair to reveal his indiscretions without admitting my own, but Jos would jump all over that and be pissed I hadn't told her sooner.

I just wasn't ready to go into details about Archer and me, and I wasn't sure that was a truth I could or would ever admit in full to anyone. I couldn't lie because Jos read me better than anyone out there. She would know I wasn't telling her everything. I decided to go with as close a version to the truth as I could stand to tell.

"Did Dan come back with you? Is this just a visit?" I knew she was going to hit way too close to the truth if I let her keep asking me questions.

"Yeah, Dan's back too. The project is pretty much done."

"So what's wrong? Why do you look like someone killed your kitten?"

I winced as I braced myself to say the words I was already regretting. "Everything is fucked, Josie. I'm going to say this and I want you to let me just say it and not interrupt, got it?" Jos rolled her eyes at me but nodded her head in agreement. "Okay. Dan cheated on me. He fucked someone he worked with." The words rang out like a shot.

"What in the actual fuck, Ros?" she screamed before clasping her hands over her mouth to prevent any other words from slipping through. I threw a dirty look her way that said, *You promised*, without having to say anything. That was the beauty of our friendship. Words weren't always necessary. She got the message.

"It was just the once, and before you ask, yes, I

329

believe him. He's fucking wrecked. But that's not the only issue." Her eyes widened at that. "I cheated on him too." I forced the words past the sudden lump in my throat, pushing the confession past the ache that threatened to close off my airway and vocal cords.

"Ros, you're kidding, right?" She jumped out of her seat and sat next to me, wrapping her arms around me, but not so close that we couldn't see each other's faces.

"I wish I were. And before you ask, it was just some random guy I met and it was only once. I told Dan though, so yeah, we both fucked up pretty bad. But he still wants to work things out and I want to try too."

The final words came out with a gush of air from my lungs. Relief and anxiety all twisted up together in my gut, the perfect cocktail of my undoing.

"God, there's so many things I want to ask you. I want to know everything about this guy and how it all went down. I still can't believe you."

"I can't, Jos. I really don't want to talk about it. I met him at a really weak moment and I made a mistake. I'm never going to see or talk to him again, so I just want to move past it."

My tone brooked no argument and my words were close enough to the truth that I could tell Jos bought it, even if her natural desire was to keep badgering me with questions. It hurt to say what had happened with Archer was a mistake, but in some ways, especially for what it meant for my marriage, it *was* a mistake.

"Okay. Maybe not today, but one day soon you *will* give me all the details about this. My question right now is, do you want to work things out with Dan? After all of this, don't you think it's a sign? Maybe you should just cut your losses and walk away?"

I sighed and grasped the pillow tighter. I wasn't sure how to answer that honestly without getting into all the details about Archer, how to tell her how conflicted I was feeling when I'd left so many pieces of my shattered heart behind in another place, with the ghost of a man who wasn't the one I'd made vows to love and honor eternally.

"Yeah, I do. We've already decided to go to marriage counseling. We need this if we're going to be together and we should have done this a long time ago. Jos, I can't help but think that if we had tried to fix all of these things before we left, none of this probably would have happened."

I had been thinking about that a lot over the last couple of weeks. Ignoring all the issues between us had left our marriage wide open and vulnerable to any threats from the outside, left us too weak and alone to fight them off. And in they'd come in the form of a sexy co-worker and an irresistible spirit.

Realizing all of this, admitting my role in all of it to

myself had been devastating. I could withhold some of the facts from Dan, but I couldn't hide them from myself. Revealing the true nature of my betrayal would only hurt Dan more, and despite his role in this, he didn't deserve it. I would have to learn to live with only the pieces of my heart left.

While regret plagued me, I still couldn't bring myself to regret Archer. If anyone ever asked if I could go back in the past knowing what I do now, would I change anything, would I keep it from happening knowing I could have a whole heart, I knew that I would rather live in fragments having known the kind of love that existed between Archer and me.

THIRTY-SIX

"OKAY, so last week we met briefly to get acquainted and lay out what our goals and expectations were for our sessions. Now that that's out of the way, I'd like for us to dive right in this session. We'll start with talking about how you both are doing and how the last week has been. Usually I find that starting the sessions with that often segues into the bigger issues we are trying to resolve. Ros, how was your week?"

Dan and I had been back in Santa Barbara for nearly three weeks. It had taken us a couple of weeks to finally get into marriage counseling with a counselor recommended by a friend. Neither of us had been in any kind of therapy, so we didn't know what to expect.

In that time, we had barely spoken to one another. Everything between us was so awkward. We walked on eggshells around one another and the air practically vibrated with the tension humming between the two of us whenever we were in the same room, something we both had been avoiding since returning.

We also were sleeping in different bedrooms. I couldn't bring myself to touch him, to initiate any kind of intimacy whether physical or emotional. Dan didn't seem eager to breach the void between us either.

So here we were, sitting in a comfortable if sparsely decorated office of a well-regarded marriage counselor, someone we were hoping would salvage the wreck our relationship had become, and I had no clue what to say.

"Umm, it was okay, I guess. I'm just trying to get back into the swing of things here."

"And how is that going for you?" Susan, our therapist, asked.

She adjusted her tall, willowy frame in the armchair she sat in across from us, crossing her legs and tapping out what I assumed was a quick note on her iPad before looking back up at me with a warm smile that was meant to put me at ease.

"I'm not sure, actually. I feel this strange mix of things. It feels like nothing and everything has changed all at the same time, if that makes sense. I've been gone for a year and life here went on without me, and I'm not sure how I fit into things anymore because everything is different. At the same time, everything looks the same and there's a feeling of... I don't know... comfort, I guess? Familiarity? This place. It feels like home and it feels foreign."

"That's understandable, Ros. You've gone through two moves in a year and a lot has happened during that time. We will delve a little more into these discordant feelings soon." She turned her body slightly to Dan, giving him the same smile she had given me. "Dan, how was your week?"

He just sat there staring at his hands that were hanging between the space of his spread knees. And we waited. Susan didn't interrupt or ask him any questions, she just sat back and gave him time and space to gather his thoughts, like she could see the tumult going on in that head of his.

Eventually he sat back, resting his hands on the armrests of the chair he was sitting in. It hit me then that we were sitting in two different chairs, separated by a small table where a tiny potted succulent and a box of tissues sat. I didn't know why that struck me as strange, but for some reason it did.

"I don't know. It wasn't good. Nothing's been good lately. I wish we were past all of this shit, you know? I feel like a stranger in my own home. Sometimes I just want to reach out to Ros, pull her in my arms, kiss her. Then I think of what I did, how bad I fucked up. I think about what she did, and I start to feel sick to my damn stomach and then the urge dies. I've been throwing myself into work, hiding out in my office, doing every-thing and anything to take my mind off the fact that this shit is fucking killing me."

He spat the words out like he'd tried to swallow them down but they tasted so bad that he couldn't stomach that.

"Ros, have you noticed this? How do you feel about what Dan said?"

How did I feel? I didn't think I could even put into words what was running through my head, all the discordant thoughts.

"Confused. Of course, I feel the distance between us. But this didn't start recently. This has been going on for a long time. Every project, every month Dan's gone, the distance grew a little bit more until everything fell apart in Washington. By that point the divide was too vast."

I hesitated, waiting for the strength, the courage to say the things that I had been avoiding over the last year.

"I didn't notice that things weren't working between us, that they hadn't really been working for a while until we started to prepare for the move. Things had always been this way from the start. It was our normal, it was my first real relationship, so I thought this was how it was supposed to be. I loved Dan and I knew how much his career meant to him. But as we prepared for the move I realized how much things weren't working for me."

I stopped trying to gather the last of my thoughts, and turned to Dan.

"I jumped at the chance to move because I thought it would give us more time together, time we needed to reconnect. The opposite happened. It wrecked us."

Dan just continued to stare at me, his anger and pain impossible to hide, practically radiating from him.

"No, Ros. We ruined us. We did this together. And I… I don't know if we can fix it. Half the time I don't know if I *want* to fix this."

I couldn't break his stare, and I couldn't say another word because Dan was right. In a hundred different ways over all our years together, instead of creating something, building a strong relationship and a life together, we'd been putting on a good show, avoiding the real hard work that was necessary to create something lasting.

He was right, our denial of truth and reality had destroyed us. The thing that broke me apart even more was the fact that I wasn't sure if the damage was repairable either.

THIRTY-SEVEN

KNOCK, knock, knock. Knock-knock-knock.

I groaned and flinched against the brightness of the sun glaring into my eyes. I didn't know who was at the door, but based on the insistence and cadence of the knocking, they weren't going to just go away on their own.

Another near-sleepless night filled with regret, unease, and nausea that I'd tried to chalk up to anxiety had plagued me. I rolled over, considering getting out of bed to answer the door, when my stomach rolled and threatened to upend itself in protest.

Maybe it wasn't just anxiety causing my symptoms. I tried to count back to when they'd started, and realized that between my stomach issues, my fatigue, and the occasional bouts of vertigo, there was a really good chance I was sick.

"I'm coming, I'm coming. Hold your damn horses," I called out as I pulled on my favorite robe and shuffled through the house to the front door.

"Fuck, Ros, you look like shit!" Jos exclaimed as soon as I opened the door. She swept by me and made her way to the living room.

"Yeah, like I've been telling you, I'm not feeling well. I think I might actually be sick. I'm probably gonna have to suck it up and go to urgent care." I plopped onto the other end of the sectional, pulled a throw blanket over myself and tried to find a comfortable position.

"Dude, you've been saying you're sick for the last month. I thought you were just trying to avoid me. What's going on?"

"I dunno, Jos. I think Dan and I have reached our limit. I don't think there is any way for us to work through this."

There was an inexplicable sense of relief in admitting the truth that I had been hiding inside out loud.

"No. I don't mean between the two of you, though we will get back to that. I mean what are your symptoms? Why have you been so sick for the last month?"

"Oh. I don't know why. I thought it was just all the changes, the emotions of trying to salvage everything. Now I'm thinking it might be something serious. Maybe it's IBS or something. I've been nauseous, I've thrown up a few times. I get dizzy here and there. I've been crazy exhausted."

"Maybe it's morning sickness," Jos joked. I tossed a pillow at her head.

"You'd love that! There's no way…"

I laughed out before stopping myself. I thought about how long I'd been feeling off. Then I tried to remember when I last had my period. I'd been so caught up with the implosion of my marriage, the move back here, the therapy that I hadn't even realized the last time I had my period was… over three fucking months ago. Before we left the island. Long after Dan and I had last slept together, but shortly before Archer and I had.

But that wasn't possible. He wasn't even alive.

Yeah, but you also didn't think ghosts were possible. And you really *didn't think you could actually have sex with one.*

Fuck.

I was going to be sick for sure. I got up and ran to the bathroom, barely able to contain the vomit until I reached the toilet. I emptied what little was in my stomach and slumped against the wall, my head resting on my bent knees.

"So maybe your marriage isn't over quite yet. Nothing brings a couple together like a baby, right?"

I yanked my head back and looked over at Jos in the doorway, her eyes alight with humor and empathy.

"Think Dan will be happy? You guys wanted kids,

right? I know the timing is shitty, but—" She stopped mid-sentence as she assessed the look on my face, the guilt and shame that must be written all over me. "Rosalind. Whose baby is that?"

My head dropped back to my knees and I took in a deep, painful breath. The weight of what I'd done, the consequences I'd been living with and the ones that I would now have to face, the secrets I'd been keeping from Josie crashed into me like a wave, threatening to pull me under and drown me in all the mistakes I'd made, all the pain I'd caused.

"Not Dan's," was all I could manage to get out in a ghost of a voice that didn't sound like mine.

"What the fuck haven't you been telling me?"

She didn't even try to hide the accusation and hurt. I knew it was finally time to be honest with Jos. Even if it meant she thought I was crazy. Even if it meant laying myself barer than I had ever been.

"So much, Josie. So. Damn. Much. I don't even know where to begin." Even I could hear the agony and vulnerability in my voice.

"Start at the beginning. Take your time."

"I met someone in Washington."

The words rushed out of me, my shoulders sagged as my spine relaxed, the weight of my secrets starting to lift off of my body. I looked up at her then, not at all surprised to see her jaw dropped open in shock, a million questions threatening to spill out, evident in the strain of her narrowed eyes. I continued before she could utter a single one of them.

"Jos, I will tell you everything, I promise, but I need you to not say anything and just let me get this all out."

She snapped her jaw shut with an audible clicking of teeth and nodded her head, encouraging me to continue. I knew that I would need to get this out as quickly as possible if I stood any chance of her not interrupting me.

"Remember when you came to visit and we did that research on the man who used to own the land the house was built on?"

She nodded slowly, squinting, and I could almost hear her brain working to figure out what this information had to do with my cheating on Dan.

"And you remember how you kept joking that all that weird shit happening in the house was him haunting me?"

Another nod.

"Well… it was. Him haunting me, that is. I know how this sounds, Jos, I do. But I promise, I'm not crazy and I'm not joking. Archer was haunting the house."

I stopped there. I couldn't help but wish that the explaining was done, that all my secrets and truths were already laid bare.

"He was lonely, and Dan was gone and I was lonely, and we began to spend time together. And, Jos? He was so amazing. *Is* so amazing. I fell in love with him, and then I left him. I left him there to spend an eternity. Alone."

It all hit me in that moment. The wave threatened to drown me where I sat. Every single emotion I'd been trying to deny and avoid, everything I'd spent the last three months trying to bury, it all came back, so much more painful than before.

Instead of diminishing while I kept it all under wraps, the pain just multiplied, compounded to a level that now felt unbearable. How could one person hold all this pain inside their body? How could one person feel this much agony for the rest of their life? These questions kept running through my head, but it came up with no answers.

"Okay, so you fell in love with a ghost. Pfft. That part I get. Well, I don't *get* it, but I see what you're saying. What I don't get is what this has to do with the likely bun in your oven?"

I broke then. At the gentleness in her voice, the lack of judgment. At the love all over her face, at the warmth in her smile. Sobs racked my body and I believed in that moment that the tears would never be exhausted, that tremors would persist until I ceased to exist in this body.

"Shhh, shhh." It was all Jos uttered, as she came to sit beside me and wrapped her arms around my body.

Those words and the comfort of her embrace were all I needed.

"We… we slept together. Don't ask me how, neither of us could figure it out. But it happened. His body was real, solid. It felt like any living person would feel. And we slept together, and I cheated on Dan. We didn't use a condom. Now I'm pregnant, and somehow, Archer is the father." My body shook with the effort to breathe normally and get myself under control, and I managed to force out past my diminishing sobs.

"Holy. Fuck. I know you didn't want me to say anything, but those are the only words that seem appropriate right now. Holy fuck. Leave it to you to get knocked up by a fucking hot-ass ghost. You always were an overachiever."

A giggle escaped my mouth, and then another, and another until I couldn't stop and my body was shaking from mirth rather than misery. Jos had given me the one thing I never expected to feel: comfort and hope.

"So, what are you going to tell Dan?" she asked as our laughter subsided, bringing me back down to earth.

"I don't know. Nothing?"

"Dude, you guys are still living together, don't you think he'll start to notice the adorable little bump I'm sure you're bound to get sooner than later?" Again, there was no judgment to the question.

"Jos, I don't want to tell him. I don't think it's going

to work out. We're at an impasse with therapy. He can't get past what I did, he still wants the details I obviously can't give him. Never mind that he's just as guilty as I am."

"Maybe with more time?"

I shook my head in defeat. "No. On top of all that he's pretty much never home. You would think that all the discussions we've had about his career being a huge obstacle in our marital happiness would have brought about some change. But no, he's gone more than ever. There isn't an us and there hasn't been for a while, and this should hurt so much more than it does."

There it was. The truth I had been avoiding for months, maybe even years. And it didn't even hurt. It just felt like another fact, a foregone conclusion.

"You're going to leave him? Are you sure about this, Ros?" she asked, her arms still around me, stroking my arm.

"I don't know. I think we need to have a talk though and see where we go from there."

The last piece I had been holding in fell out of my mouth and into the weighted atmosphere of the room already too full of confessions and truths laid bare. I wanted to pack away all the emotions again, tie them up tight inside so that numbness could take the place of being torn apart by the aftermath of my choices and mistakes.

I was beginning to realize though that if I had any chance of being whole again, of living a good, happy life, I had to feel everything that threatened to wreck me. I had to own it and deal with it, stop living the way I had for most of my life. I owed it to myself.

I looked down and gently caressed my lower abdomen. Yes. I owed it to myself to put the work in and repair all the shattered pieces of myself. And I owed it to this sweet little miracle, this amazing little life that was growing inside of me.

THIRTY-EIGHT

I FLINCHED at the thundering sound of the front door slamming. It had been three hours since our appointment ended in screams and tears (screams on Dan's part, tears on mine). Three hours since the end of what was very likely our final marriage counseling session.

Dan hadn't even come home the last three nights, ignored every single text message and voicemail and email I sent him, so I'd been thoroughly surprised when he walked into our therapy session. I had been fully expecting to go it alone.

Regardless of what I had said to Jos nearly two months earlier, I was finding it difficult to pull the trigger on my marriage and walk away. A part of me still wanted to see if we could make things work, believed that we could make things work. We truly loved each other, and I'd always assumed that love would be enough to carry us through whatever storms we faced. Sadly, it looked like we had been in different boats the entire length of our relationship, barely grasping each other's hands to stay connected.

There was also the matter of the baby I was carrying that was definitely not Dan's. Right after Jos left that day I'd called my OB/GYN and got in that week, where they'd confirmed that I was indeed about three months pregnant. (I also took the test to see if I had the cancer gene mutation and was relieved to discover that I wasn't genetically predisposed.)

Dan and I hadn't been together physically for well over six months, so there was no denying that I was living a reality I never considered possible: pregnant with another man's child. With a *ghost's* child. I still had no answers for how that was even remotely possible, but at this point it didn't matter, the damage was done.

Seeing that tiny speck of a baby on the ultrasound screen had been surreal and beautiful, all at once. It was a sucker punch at first. I'd had it in the back of my mind that it might be possible for this all to have been a massive mistake. I expected them to move that probe through the warm jelly they glopped on my belly and to tell me there was nothing there at all, that their test had been wrong.

The minute that little gummy bear in my womb had appeared on the monitor, the moment the rapid whoosh,

whoosh, whoosh of the heartbeat hit my ears, reality hit me like a freight train, panic and denials rising up in my throat. They were quickly replaced with an immense amount of love and a fierce desire to protect. I'd known then that this baby was going to reshape my entire world.

"Ros, did you even hear a single word I just said?" Dan asked, the undertone of anger causing me to recoil.

"No, I'm sorry. Can you please repeat it?"

"No, I can't. I'm done with this. Even when you're here you're not really here. Your mind is somewhere else. Is it with him? All these times you drift off, are you with him?" He paced the living room, hands gripping his beautiful hair, each word cutting me open.

"Dan, no. I wish you would believe me, trust me."

We both paused for a moment, stuck in a stare-down, our wills, our wants, our feelings fighting against each other silently. Disbelief radiated off of him. Of course, it was too much to ask for him to trust me when I had betrayed him.

Then I fully processed exactly what he had just said, and I couldn't stop the anger that threatened to erupt, suddenly and with little warning. In the deluge of guilt I had been drowning in since that night with Archer, I kept forgetting that I wasn't the only one who had fucked up. I wasn't the only one who had betrayed our vows.

"You have some fucking nerve, Dan. Some fucking nerve!" I shook my head in disgust, turned and stalked over to the window, unable to look at him without wanting to rip into him.

"What the fuck is that supposed to mean, Rosalind?" His voice boomed out as he stalked toward me and stopped suddenly just a few feet away.

"You know exactly what it means." My voice was deadly quiet, the rage I had been suppressing for so long betrayed by the tremble I couldn't hide.

"No, I don't!" He gripped my shoulders and the heat from his hands and body felt like acid burning through my skin. I spun away from him, then turned back to face him and knew this was it. The moment when everything imploded.

"Dan, you can't possibly be serious! Let's just not mention the fact that you fucked someone else too, okay? Let's just completely avoid that. How about we talk about the fact that you are never home? Ever. That this has been going on since we've been together. It's no wonder we are where we are right now, we never even got a chance to build something solid and substantial because you were always gone from one project to the next!"

"You knew that, Ros! When we first started dating, you fucking knew. You accepted it, said you were okay with what that would entail. For years you were fucking fine with it. And now all of a sudden everything is falling apart, and it's my fault? I'm supposed to take all the blame?" The words seethed out.

I opened my mouth to respond but then closed it with an audible snap. He was right. He was so damn right. He couldn't shoulder all the blame in this. It wasn't fair and it wasn't right.

I was just as much to blame for his career creating a wedge in our relationship. His job, while a major issue, wasn't the main one. It was our lack of communication. We'd never known how to communicate effectively, and it was obvious now that nearly five months of marriage counseling hadn't changed that.

"You're right, Dan." I slid down into the nearest chair and pulled my knees up to my chest. "You're completely right. It's not all your fault. Your job isn't fully to blame. It hasn't helped things, but it's not the main issue. We've never been good at communicating. We both let your career become this third entity in our marriage. Those things we can change and fix with time and effort."

I paused, taking a deep breath and readying myself to say the inevitable. To finally tell him what I'd been thinking about for the last couple of months. Either he would respond well and we would continue to try, or things would go the way my gut was telling me they would, and one of us would be walking out of this forever.

"Dan, we've been doing therapy for months now. You say you want to work it out, to get past this, but you spend even more time away from home than you did before and you've completely shut me out—"

"Ros—" he cut in, trying to shut down whatever else I had planned to say.

"No, you will not interrupt me. You will listen to what I have to ask and then we will talk about this, okay?"

Dan sat down on the sofa across from me and curtly nodded his head.

"I've been working at this and it just doesn't feel like you've put in the same effort." I held up my hand for him to stop as his eyes hardened and jaw set with indignation, his mouth opening to argue. "That isn't a judgment or a placement of blame. It's simply how I see it. Maybe I'm wrong, but it doesn't feel like it. It feels like you're just going through the motions right now. Do you even want to continue working on this with me? Do you even want to be married to me anymore?"

My voice broke on the last question, and I shut up then and waited for him to answer the questions I'd never thought I would ask.

I watched as different emotions passed over Dan's face. As his jaw ticked with the tension of clenching his teeth to hold back the angry words dying to spill out.

The amount of control he was exerting was impressive. And heartbreaking.

How had we gotten to this place? I couldn't help but ask myself that question for the millionth time, even though the answers were laid before us now.

"Fuck, Ros," he groaned out as his head fell back against the sofa. "Fuck." I continued to give him the time and space he needed to figure out what he needed to say. "No. I don't think I do. I just can't get past what you did. And before you say anything, I know I fucked up too. But you haven't given me any answers, and every time I close my eyes, I see you fucking another man. Every time I pass a man in the street who looks at you, I wonder if that could have been him. If that was the man who had his hands all over my wife. If that was the man who had been inside what was mine."

"Dan—" I tried to interrupt.

"I'm sorry, I'm so fucking sorry I cheated on you. And I know you're sorry too. But I just don't think I can forgive you. I can't even forgive myself."

And there it was. The truths we'd been avoiding.

The end of our marriage.

Over with a handful of soul-crushing words.

Everything after happened in a haze. I nodded my head in assent, letting him know I wouldn't fight him on this.

We talked out how the dissolution of the last eight

years of our lives would be handled. I would stay in the house until it sold. He would move out that weekend. It was all so matter-of-fact, clinical almost. Dan walked away that day with a lightness in his step and relief in his eyes.

My body sagged against the wall in relief that he never noticed the baggy sweater that covered the tiny swell of my stomach as the door shut behind him. And as the reverberations of his departure went through me, all I felt was hollow.

THIRTY-NINE

THE WIND WHIPPED my hair around my face as another wave hit the shore, sending a spray of mist from the ocean over me. A shiver ran through my body, and I pulled my sweater tighter around my body to ward off the chill in the December air.

I closed my eyes and inhaled deeply, yearning for the briny scent of the ocean, the smell that reminded me so much of the one I missed. As much as I loved it, the ocean was no replacement for what I truly wanted, for the thing I would likely never have again, though it did soothe some part of my mangled heart.

I didn't know what it was about the ocean, but it always called to me, the waves crashing like a siren's song to my soul, beckoning me back home to where I belonged.

"Ros, it's fucking freezing out here. What are you

doing?" The warmth of Josie's body as she dropped down onto the sand next to me began to thaw my frozen arm and leg. She threw a blanket over both our laps and I leaned over, resting my head on her shoulder. I simply shrugged in response as her rumble of laughter moved through me. "Nope, not good enough. Talk." Jos wrapped her arms around my shoulders and squeezed.

I had a feeling I knew what she wanted to hear, but I wasn't ready to say the words out loud. So I sat and let the silence settle between us. God love her, she let me sit with my thoughts, allowed me the time I needed to formulate what I wanted to say.

"Do you ever come to the beach and the minute you set foot on the sand you feel like you're home? Like all the answers are there just waiting for you to discover them?" I turned then and looked at her, willing her to understand.

"Is that why you've been out here every night for the last couple months? You think you'll find the answers to your problems in the waves?" Jos asked, voice barely audible above the crashing of the water at the shore.

"I tried going out during the day, but this town is so small and I was always seeing people who didn't know Dan and I had split up. Trying to explain that was difficult enough. Now that I'm showing? I just couldn't do it."

Jos hugged me to her body again, and I knew that she

got it. "Dan still doesn't know I'm pregnant," I whispered, part of me hoping she wouldn't hear.

"Oh, Ros. You're hiding out, then?"

"Yeah. I guess I am."

And it was true. I had begun hiding when I realized I could no longer hide the child growing inside me. I didn't go out during the day, I had my groceries delivered, I only ventured out when necessary after dark and to places that I wasn't likely to run into anyone Dan or I knew.

My now nightly trips to this secluded strip of beach? Those too were a necessity.

Sometimes I dreamed, hoped that Archer would figure out how to leave that piece of land he was tied to and find me on this beach. That we would come full circle and figure out a way to make this work. Some nights I even convinced myself that he was there, lingering nearby, that the scent of sandalwood and musk mixed with the salty ocean breeze wasn't just my imagination yearning for something that wasn't possible.

"Are you happy, Ros? Really, truly satisfied here? Because I have to say, it doesn't seem like it. You came back from that island a different person, and yeah, I know that was bound to happen with everything you've been through, but you're like a shadow of your former self. You've been walking around here these last few months like a ghost. Tell me, are you happy with your life right now?"

Jos' words would have been ironic if it weren't for the fact that she knew that a ghost was at the root of what I was going through. I sat and considered her question, not sure how to put into words all the thoughts tumbling through my mind, all the feelings coursing through my veins.

"No," I whispered before turning to face her. "No, I'm not happy. But I have no idea how to fix this. I don't think there *is* a way to fix this. My marriage is over, and I know that didn't happen overnight or even in a year, but it's done and I have so many regrets about that, all this guilt that just threatens to tear me apart."

I couldn't help or hide the tremble of my voice, so I closed my eyes and took deep breaths.

One breath. Then another.

Attempts to calm down the roiling inside that threatened to drown me completely. A moment to gather the strength to say what else I needed to say, the words I needed to hear uttered out loud.

"Now I have this baby coming, and I want so badly to be excited and happy about it. Every time she kicks and moves or has hiccups I smile so big it hurts my face, and the wonder and joy of her existence fills me to the brim. And then the crushing reality that I'll be raising this child alone with no concept of how to tell her who her father is sets in and depletes every last bit of that joy. My child will never know how amazing her father was, and it breaks me to know that Archer will never know how amazing a father he would have been. And I have so many regrets about that too, though I cannot for even a second even muster one bit of regret for the child we created."

I was done. There it all was, laid out in front of us, ready for Jos to soak in the truth of my situation, to come to the conclusion that there was no straight line to happiness for me anymore. This was my new reality, and all I could do was find a way to accept it for what it was, and find a way to move on without breaking myself or my daughter.

"Okay, bear with me for a minute," Jos began, shifting her body so she no longer had her arm around me and was now mostly facing me, her legs curled up underneath her. "If we lived in a perfect dream world, one where anything was possible, what would you want?"

I turned away from her and back to the ocean. I had never even bothered asking myself this question because I knew that I didn't live in a perfect world. I lived in a world where shitty things happened. Where girls lost their mothers far sooner than they were ready to. Where marriages fell apart and burned to ash, even with hard work. Where somehow a woman got knocked up by a ghost. My wildest dreams coming true wasn't even an option to consider at this point.

I also knew that Josie wouldn't let this go until I answered, so I humored her. "Perfect world?" I asked and looked at her out of the corner of my eye in time to see her nod. "Okay. It would be me living on Orcas Island again, for good this time. Archer and I would have found a way to be together and raise a family. I would take over Wild Art and consider expanding it into Seattle. And I would create my own pieces. I would finally live the life I never dared to hope for."

I trailed off there, considering if there was anything more that I wanted to add, any other long-forgotten or abandoned dreams I could find a place for in this dream world I was creating. I avoided eye contact with Jos, not wanting her to see how much this pained me, how even just imagining this created an ache in my chest.

"And that's what you really want? In your heart of hearts?" Jos asked, breaking through my turbulent thoughts.

"Yes. More than anything. But what good does it do to dwell on what I can't have?"

My hushed words were quickly carried away by the wind, and I wasn't sure if she was even able to hear them.

"Rosalind, why not? Why *can't* this be your reality? You're no longer married. While you've been teaching again, you aren't really doing anything you can't do there. So what that Archer is a ghost? He was real enough to get you pregnant. I don't see how you both can't find a way to create a life together as well."

She stopped ticking her points off her fingers there, giving me a moment to take in what she was trying to say. Jos turned to me then, forcing me to face her, and took my hands into hers. I recognized the strain around her eyes, the furrowed brow, the defiant tilt of her lips. She was about to hammer home her point, and she wanted my full attention.

"You know what you want. You know, deep down inside, what feels right for you. When are you going to start giving yourself permission to trust those instincts? When are you going to give yourself permission to go after the life you want, judgment of others be damned?"

Each word made impact like a punch to the gut, rocking me to the core. My hands became slippery with sweat, Jos tightening her grip in response. She wanted an answer, one I wasn't sure I could give her right this moment.

She waited a moment, then another. She searched my face for clues to where my thoughts were, and then she nodded, a resigned smile on her face, a signal that she had found what she was looking for, even if it wasn't what she wanted.

"That sounds so much like something my mom

would have said." I let the words slip out onto the wind, not sure if I said them loud enough for Josie to hear. Her responding gasp a second later was my answer. We let the words hang there in silence for a minute. Then another.

Finally, Jos let out an incredulous laugh. "You're right. That *is* something your mom would have said. I think a lot of my good advice comes from her."

"I think so too." I turned then and smiled at her. The disbelief and joy in the wide smile she returned let me know she understood the importance of this moment.

"She'd be really proud of you, you know? I know it seems like everything is a mess right now, but you've changed so much over the last year and a half. You've taken so many risks that the old Ros never would have even considered. I know she would be so proud of you, and so happy that you're going to become a mother."

"God, Jos, I hope so. I can't wait to pull out her old recipes and bake with my daughter. I can't wait to share with her the old movies we used to watch. Remember classic movie nights? I can't wait to share that with her. And vacations, adventures. Mom was amazing, and I hope I'm even half of that for my girl." I didn't even bother wiping away the tears that made my cheeks even colder in the wind. I was no longer willing to hide my emotions or my memories.

"Just about every night was classic movie night at

your house. I can't wait to do those things with you two, too."

I looked over at Jos. Her cheeks were wet with her tears and made red by the cold ocean breeze. "We should start writing down the stories about my mom we want to share with her, so we don't forget anything." Jos squeezed my hand tight in agreement.

It was then I pulled out my phone and played with the screen until I pulled up the photos. I scrolled through until I found the one I was looking for. Jos and I standing in front of Sleeping Beauty's castle at Disneyland, smiling at the camera with baby faces and eyes squinting in the bright sun, wrapped in the arms of my mom who was sporting her own massive smile. What couldn't be seen was my dad behind the camera.

Jos inhaled sharply, covering her mouth. "Ros, where did you get this? I remember that day." She looked up at me with glassy eyes, fully recognizing how important this was. Some things had been lost during my parents' divorce, several photo albums included.

"My dad. I went and saw him. We talked for a bit and he gave me albums of photos he'd found in a box."

"When did this happen? What did he say about that?" She gestured at my protruding belly with my phone still clasped in her hand.

"It was a couple of months ago. I knew it was long past time to start repairing our relationship. Oh, and he doesn't know about the baby yet. I was able to hide the belly. I'm not ready to explain all this yet."

"Why didn't you tell me sooner? Have you seen him since?"

"I don't know. I'm still trying to work out how I feel about it all. I haven't seen him since then, but we do talk on the phone once a week." I shrugged, unsure what else to say.

"Well, it's a really good start."

Jos handed back my phone and threw her arms around me and gave a tight squeeze. I thumbed through my phone and handed it back to her, wanting her to see the photos I'd saved on there from our childhood. She glanced at me with a bright smile, tears pooled in her eyes and threatening to fall at any moment.

We sat without talking, huddled close together for warmth, the waves crashing on the shore and the wind rustling the palm fronds the only sound. Jos and I scrolled through the pictures, exchanging smiles and looks full of the memories we shared.

"Okay, babe," Jos began after a while, handing me back my phone and placing her hands on my belly. "It's fucking freezing out here. Let's get my precious niece home before she becomes a little ice cube in there."

She helped me up and we walked hand in hand to the street where our cars were parked. I almost asked if I could spend the night with her instead of returning to the cold, empty house Dan and I had shared before he moved out. I almost asked, but stopped myself at the last minute. I needed time alone with my feelings and thoughts, time to make sense of everything, to find a way for my heart and head to sync.

As I drove home, Jos' words reverberated through my mind, on a constant loop.

Why couldn't I give myself permission? Why had I been denying myself permission for so damn long? What did I have to lose?

It was in that moment, when I truly asked myself those questions, that I realized what I should have a long time ago: if I stayed, I had nothing to gain, but if I took the risk that didn't look so much like one anymore, I could gain everything I ever wanted.

So I jumped.

FORTY

AS MY CAR made its way up the drive, I had a flashback to another day not that long ago when I'd been traveling this path for the first time. In some ways, it felt like just yesterday, in other ways it was like years and years had passed. I came around the final curve and the vegetation cleared and made way for the house that felt more like a home than anyplace else I had ever lived.

The surprise, joy, and hope I'd felt the first time I made this drive were all present now. The tightness in my chest that sent icy tendrils through my veins was all new. My body grew colder as I got closer to the house, my anxiety reaching all-new highs.

What if Archer didn't want to see me? What if he didn't want a life with me, with our baby?

All of these what-ifs, so many fears and worries were on a constant loop in my head, had been since I set foot back in Washington. There was so much at stake and for once in my life I hadn't considered what the alternative would be, what my course of action was if this failed.

I put the car into park in the driveway and took a deep breath. I had spoken to our contact with MarisCorp and she'd let me know the home was empty and I was welcome to walk around. I got out and stretched my aching back and rubbed under my massive belly.

Another thing to be nervous about. What would Archer's reaction be when he saw me in this state? Would he know it was his child I carried inside my body? Would he just assume it was Dan's and wonder why I had come at all?

I slammed the car door and forced myself to take that first step. And then the next. I made my way to the front window, cupped my hands around my eyes and looked inside. The furniture was covered with drop cloths and even from my limited vantage point the layer of dust over some of the surfaces was obvious. No one had lived here since we had moved out.

I didn't have the keys to the house, but I knew I wouldn't need them to get Archer's attention. My presence there alone would be enough. I also didn't think I was capable of taking one step into that house again, not after all that had happened, no matter how much I loved the place.

I followed the stone step path around the side of the

house, being careful to watch my step. I could be clumsy on a good day, but considering the extra bulk on my frame, all it would take was one careless step to cause me to come crashing down. Once I made it to the back and the balcony off the main floor, I stepped to the railing and looked up.

Dusk was fast approaching, and the sky was on fire, shades of pink, lavender, orange, and red painted across the darkening sky in streaks. Out over the water the signs of an incoming fog could be seen in the distance. I knew the visibility would be gone within an hour or two, so I soaked it all in, knowing my time on the island could be short-lived.

As the sky darkened into a deep blue, I glanced at my phone and realized nearly an hour had passed as I waited for Archer to sense my presence.

"Archer? Are you there?" I called out in little more than a whisper.

I could have shouted out to him, but I knew from past experience that it wasn't necessary. If he were here, he would know. He would sense me, he would hear my whispered words.

I closed my eyes and waited. I tried to feel him, searching with my senses for his presence. I inhaled and exhaled deeply, trying to calm the growing unease inside of me, the feeling of nausea and fear clawing its way through my system, up my throat. I tried to ground myself to this place that used to feel so right, hoping with a heart that was starting to burn to ash that I hadn't lost him.

I kept my eyes closed for what felt like hours, trying to feel that energy that always flowed and arced between us, that electricity that used to spark to life the minute I set foot on this land and we were in close proximity to one another, that unnamed thing that I'd tried to ignore and deny for so long. I opened my eyes to the twilight sky when I realized that it wasn't here.

He wasn't here.

I had waited too long, so trapped in finding reasons why this could never work that I'd missed all the reasons it could. A fierce kick rocked my abdomen from the inside and I heaved out a ragged sob. My hands found their way onto my belly, caressing it, an attempt to soothe our child while my insides quivered and quaked like a boat caught in a tempest.

I'd been so caught in all the things that were wrong, things that didn't matter, and I'd lost it all in the process.

Somehow, I made my way back to the car and collapsed into the driver seat. I gripped the steering wheel and rested my head on my hands. Soon enough my hands were wet with my tears and my body continued to shake with the sobs I could no longer find the strength to contain. How would I move on from this?

How could I live with a hole the size of Archer etched into the very fabric of my being?

How? How? How?

The words were an endless refrain in my head, replacing the previous what-ifs that had taken up residence there.

Eventually an incessant ringing broke through the mournful melody in my head. I glanced at my phone sitting on the passenger seat. Josie was calling. I let it ring through to voicemail as I wiped away the wetness on my cheeks and tried to calm my ragged breaths. After a moment it rang again, and I reluctantly answered it, knowing Jos wouldn't stop calling until she reached me.

"Hey, babe, I just wanted to check in with you and see if you made it there okay," Jos said the minute I picked up the call.

"Jos, I fucked up. I fucked up so bad. I waited too long. I left him, and I waited too long, and now he's gone. He's fucking gone, Jos." I managed to force the words out through the contracting of my throat before I broke down all over again.

"Whoa, whoa, whoa, Ros. Slow down. What do you mean? Where are you?"

"I'm here at the house and he's not here. I've been here for hours and he's not here, Jos. He's gone. He's. Gone."

Broken. I could hear it in my own raw, raspy voice.

"Ros, what do you mean he's gone?" She couldn't hide the disbelief that tinged her voice.

"I think—I think he moved on. I think once I left, he moved on… for good."

I shook my head as I uttered the unthinkable in a hushed voice, as though saying the words out loud finally made them real. Jos didn't say anything and the silence just stretched between us.

Finally she said, "What are you going to do now, Ros? Where are you gonna go?" Her voice was as quiet as mine. A respect and finality ran through her words.

"I don't know. I made plans to stay with Marie. I guess I'll go back there for now. But tomorrow? The next day? I don't know, Jos. I just don't know."

"You can always come back here. We'll have the baby together, raise her together. We can do that, you know? We can make our own family, Ros. I am your family. Don't ever forget that, okay? You say the words and I'll be on the next flight out there."

She stopped there, her voice made jagged by the tears she didn't even try to hide. There would never be a world where we both existed that I wouldn't love her, where we wouldn't somehow find each other and form a bond stronger than blood.

"I know. I love you, Josephine."

"I love you too, Rosalind. Call me after you get settled at Marie's."

Instead of going straight to the inn, I decided to drive to the only other place on this island I'd always felt drawn to. I pulled into Eastsound and parked a few blocks off the downtown area, still populated with people on their way to and from a late dinner. I walked toward the small strip of shore that I'd found my purpose on, the same place I'd witnessed the beginning of the end of my marriage.

The fog I had spotted earlier in the evening had already rolled onto shore, leaving visibility at a few feet. I wrapped my arms around myself and sighed as the heaviness of disappointment weighed me down. I couldn't help but wonder if a clearer night would have provided the relief and cleansing my battered heart needed. I sat on a large, flat rock and closed my eyes, listening as the waves hit the shore.

I shivered as the air gradually cooled. I stood, released a long breath and opened my eyes as something inside of me jolted and pulled taut, like an invisible rope sitting coiled inside of me was being pulled tight.

I gasped as what felt like a million sensations hit me at once: a magnetic pull toward the water. The racing energy of electricity skating over my skin, making the hairs stand on end and my heart race. The heady scent I'd missed so much hitting my nose and drugging me with its familiarity.

All of these sensations hit me as a figure took shape

through the mist. A figure that appeared so achingly real I nearly cried in relief.

My eyes slammed shut in self-preservation. I knew once I opened them the feelings would all dissipate, and what I imagined to be there would be gone. A moment passed, and then another, but still the feeling persisted.

"Well, finally," a deep, melodic voice breathed into my ear with a warm gust of air.

My knees buckled and my inevitable collapse was only stopped by strong, warm arms banding around my body, right under my chest and above my pregnant stomach.

These words, the first Archer had ever uttered to me, were reverberating through my mind.

My eyes flashed open and I looked up into the most beautiful pair of green eyes I had ever seen in my life.

"Archer," I managed to gasp out before everything went black.

FORTY-ONE

I WOKE up shivering on a hard surface in an unfamiliar place. I tried to sit up but was stopped by something strong banding around my midsection.

"What is going on? Where *am* I?" I said aloud to myself.

"Ros, are you okay?"

That voice. That deep, melodic voice that I now only heard in my dreams. And in that moment it all hit: me on the beach in Eastsound, the cold, damp air. Thinking Archer appeared there when I'd known he was gone. Yet here he was, his arms wrapped around me while we sat on a rock on the beach.

I turned to him them, his arms loosening their hold, but not breaking their embrace. "You're here. You haven't left." I couldn't hide the astonishment, the hope in my voice.

His eyes crinkled as they smiled, and it was a sad thing, that smile. Not the one full of joy I had been so used to. His hand snaked up between us, cupped my face, and caressed my cheekbone. I closed my eyes and nuzzled into his touch, a feeling of rightness, of warmth, of *home* seeping into me.

"Of course I'm here. Where else would I be?"

"The other side? That bright white light to oblivion?" I tried to joke, but I choked on the words so thick and sharp with all the things that remained unsaid between us, with all the things that had happened while we were separated.

Archer shook his head at me. "No, Ros. There was no bright white light, no paradise for me once you left. I fear there never will be. I considered, for a time, trying to seek you out, to make sure you were doing well. I couldn't bring myself to do that. I knew that if I found you happy with Dan, it was something I couldn't stand to see."

He paused then, and I wondered why he wasn't as happy to see me as I was to see him. His words made it sound as though he still loved me, but his actions, the emotional wall he seemed to have erected in my absence said something entirely different.

It was when I looked down at his arm still wrapped around me, resting on the swell of my stomach, that I realized where his thoughts were. His eyes dipped to mine, then down to my belly, and back up to my face. He smiled, but it didn't even begin to reach his eyes.

"How long are you here for, Ros? Did Dan come with you?" His voice dripped with anguish even while he tried to sound happy for my current situation. It was obvious he thought Dan was the father and that our time really had passed.

"I don't know, Archer. Forever, maybe," I said with a shrug, trying to send him a message with my eyes, urging him to read between the lines. His face broke at my words though, heartbreak in every cell of his body.

I shifted then, turning into his lap, and grasping his face in my hands. I nearly jolted at the electricity that sparked as our bodies connected, that ever-present current that hummed between us. Relief flooded my body with warmth that this part of our bond remained unchanged. I had to resist the urge to lay my lips upon his. The fight against my instinct took everything in me.

"Archer, it's just me. I'm here alone. I came for you, if you'll still have me." It came out as a statement, but it was just as much a question.

My heart pounded, threatening to beat right through my chest. I had been gone for nearly seven months, and I didn't think Archer had fallen for someone else during that time, but I was worried that it was enough time for him to change his mind about me, about us. There wasn't any logic to the thought, but it was there nonetheless.

He pulled back and his eyes searched my face frantically, disbelief written all over it. "Repeat that, please."

The first tear fell. Then the next. For a minute, I wondered if I had made a mistake. Then I thought back through what it had taken to get me to this moment and I knew that even if this ended poorly for me, even if Archer walked away from me, this risk I'd taken was not a mistake.

I smiled through the tears. "I'm here to stay, Archer. This is where I belong, and I hope that you'll be by my side."

Archer's lips quirked in a faint smile and it was obvious he still didn't quite believe me. He looked down at his hand on my stomach again and his expression dimmed. "And what about Dan, Ros?"

"We're done, Archer. The divorce will be finalized in a month. So what do you think?" I didn't want to let on that his reluctance to give an answer was killing me, that the hope I'd had at his appearance on the beach was slowly starting to fade.

"I... I don't know, Ros. I don't know what to think."

Archer turned his head, breaking my hold on him. My hands fell down into my lap and I looked down, unsure of where to go from here. Maybe I needed to give him time to think through this all, to wrap his head around it. Springing something like this on someone wasn't always the best idea, but here I was and I couldn't undo it now.

"Ros, what about the baby? Is Dan fine with you moving so far away with his child? How will that all work out?"

My head jerked up suddenly as my eyes searched his face. It was there. I swore I heard it, the hint of hope underlying his questions. I stood up and walked to where the water met the shore.

In all the things I'd planned when I came back here, I'd somehow forgot to even consider how I would explain to Archer the truth of my pregnancy. How had I not even considered that this man might not even believe that he was, in fact, the father?

I closed my eyes and breathed in deeply, exhaling slowly. I would throw the words out there with the understanding that this could end badly for me. It was the only way I could think to move forward and I was done living half a life, letting fear rule over the things I truly desired.

My skin sparked to life as the scent of sandalwood and tobacco wrapped around me. A second later I felt the weight of Archer's very real, present body behind mine, the featherlight touch of his fingertips brushing against mine. That magnetic pull, the thread in me connected to the one in him. I opened my eyes then and straightened my spine.

Now was the time. And for better or worse, I was ready.

I turned to Archer then, taking him in fully one last time before I let the last truth fall from my lips. "The baby isn't Dan's, Archer."

He gasped, took a step back, nearly stumbling before he righted himself. He rubbed at his chest as though it pained him, with a look of agony on his face. I realized then with horror that he'd taken the leap I hadn't intended.

"Archer," I began, arm outstretched I took a step toward him. Thankfully he didn't continue to retreat. "This baby isn't Dan's. It isn't anyone else's, either. Archer—this baby is *yours*. Somehow, and don't ask me how, I can't even begin to explain it, we created her that night. She is just as much yours as she is mine."

I stopped myself then. I let my arm drop and I bit my lip to keep more words from pouring from my lips. I watched as the emotions crossed his face: disbelief, hope, anger, fear, and something else I couldn't put my finger on. I wished I could skip this part, take away the hurt and pain I was sure he was feeling. Archer shook his head and turned away, walking up the shore away from me.

My eyes welled up and I didn't have the strength to wipe them away. My body began to shake and my chest tightened painfully. I knew this was the risk, that he wouldn't believe me or want what I wanted anymore, and while I had tried to prepare myself for that, there was no way to anticipate this kind of pain. My stomach jolted, and I looked down to see my daughter begin to kick around, her foot or hand pushing outward through my skin. I grunted as she hit what felt like my ribs.

I looked up then to see Archer right in front of me, silently reappearing in that ghostly way of his. His eyes narrowed on my stomach and looked back to mine in question, so many questions.

"Are you—? Can I—? Ros…" He looked so confused and he couldn't finish one sentence.

I gave him a tentative smile, my heart too battered to hope this was the turning point. I reached out and grabbed his hands and placed them on my stomach. He trembled slightly under my hands as I held them to my abdomen, shifting every few seconds in an attempt to figure out where she would move next. It only took a few minutes before she kicked again. He looked up at me then, such wonder written all over his beautiful face, so many more questions lingering in his eyes.

"I know this seems crazy, Archer. I didn't believe it myself at first. There is no other explanation. You are the only person I have been with in well over a year. I don't know how this is possible, but she's real and she's *ours*."

I waited him out, letting him process all of this without saying anything else. I didn't want to influence his decision in any way, this had to be something he truly wanted.

"She's… She's mine? Truly, Rosalind?" Archer's voice shook with yearning as a tear slipped down his face.

I nodded then, smiling through my own tears, smiling so big my face hurt with it. "Yes, Archer. She's yours."

Before I had time to process it, I was wrapped up in Archer's embrace, my face in his neck, inhaling his scent that I had missed so much. I gripped him back, hoping that I never had to spend another night without this, that I never had to know what it was like to not have him in my arms and by my side.

Archer pulled back then and wrapped a hand around the nape of my neck, gently caressing the pulse beating in my throat. "And you, Ros? Are you mine, too?"

I broke then, my knees buckled and the tension in my chest eased in relief. "Yes, Archer. I'm yours. Always, only yours."

Archer smiled at me then, that breathtaking smile that finally made its way to his eyes, those beautiful green eyes crinkling with unrestrained joy. He kissed me, a deep, soul-shattering meeting of our lips that breathed life back into me.

With our lips melded together and his body fused to mine, I knew with complete certainty that I had finally returned home.

MY DEAREST CHILDREN,

I know this is really your mother's story as much as the story of our love, but I couldn't help but share some of my thoughts with you as well. I know your childhood was unconventional, to say the least, but I hope in all that craziness you saw the love too. The love I have for your mother and the love we both have for you three.

When you've been dead for one hundred years with no company other than that of those who live their lives around you with no notion that you even exist, it gets lonely. It also gives you a lot of time to think about things. To dwell on all of the things you did wrong in your life, all of the things you'll never get to have or experience. It's more than enough time to drown in your regrets. I had many regrets, and as I watched people live and the world change, I found myself wishing to just disappear forever.

One day, long after I had given up hope for ever having peace in my afterlife, the door to the home where I had lived for a century swung open, and I heard a voice that made my heart tighten in my chest, made my entire body feel as though it were floating and rooted to that place, all at the same time. Feelings I hadn't ever experienced in life, let alone in death.

Then I saw her face and it was all over for me. I never believed in love at first sight. After all that I had experienced and years of solitude spent so close to the living, but just distant enough, I'd never expected to ever experience love. I thought surely, I would never know the inexplicable joy and agony that are hallmarks of losing your heart to another. But for some reason, the universe felt it right to bestow upon me someone so unreasonably perfect, and it was in that moment I knew I'd spent all those years alone for a reason.

The first great joy of my life, on either side of death, was meeting your mother, loving her, getting the chance to call her my beloved, creating a life with her. My second greatest joy was witnessing the miracle of each of your births. Getting to see you grow, learn, fall down and make mistakes, getting to witness you all live.

I will never be able to describe to you what it felt like the first time I beheld each of your little faces, red and screaming upon entering the world. I will never be able to put into words how my heart filled to bursting when I smelled your skin and kissed your cheeks. What it was like to see so much of your mother in your faces and see the green of my eyes blink back at me. I hate to even rank these things, as though there is any way to compare these very different joys.

The three of you, along with your mother, brought me back to life in a way I never knew was possible. You all allowed me to live and love in ways I never had before, never should have been able to. Every moment with you all has been a miracle of epic proportions. That you all manage to exist is a miracle, and while I will never have any answers for you as to how that is possible, I simply know that it is.

There will come a day, and if you are reading this, that day may have already come, when your mother and I will no longer be around to share life with you. I only hope that you all are grown when that happens, that our loss will not be a devastating one to you all. I would love to say we will still be around to watch you all have careers, fall in love, and raise families of your own, but that is a promise I cannot make.

If you are reading this, I believe that your mother and I have somehow found a way to move on to whatever else lies on the other side of death, through the mist and veil of life here on earth to our hereafter.

I love you with all of my heart, always. I hope you will continue to feel the love your mother and I spent our lives trying to give you every single day of your own lives. Lana, Clark, and Grace, all of my heart, all of my joy, all of my love to you. Always.

Love,
Your dad, Archer

STAY CONNECTED

There are lots of ways we can stay in touch!

Join my Facebook reader group, one of the best ways to connect with me and other readers: Cece Ferrell Books.

Stay up to date with new releases, giveaways, and other fun stuff through my website:
www.ceceferrell.com

You can also find me on the following sites:

ACKNOWLEDGMENTS

This is so surreal, being at the point where I am writing
the acknowledgements for my first book. I first began
writing Through the Mist in 2012 and there were points I
never thought I'd be here, hitting publish for the
first time.

There are so many people that helped me along away to
get to where I am now. I know I'm going to forget some
of you here and I just hope you know it isn't intentional.

To my mom and dad, thank you for being the best
parents a girl could ask for. You guys have always
supported every single dream I had, never once telling
me they were impossible, always asking what you could
do to help make them come true. I know how rare and
special that is and I will always be grateful to you both. I

am here right now, realizing one of my oldest and biggest dreams because of you guys!

To my husband Josh, you are simply amazing. Your endless support and encouragement through this process means more to me than you will ever know. You have been there for me every step of the way, pushing me forward when I was determined to stop, always believing in me, pulling my weight at home and with the girls when I couldn't be pulled away from this book. I saw everything you did to help this dream come true for me, and I cannot say thank you enough. Baby, we finally made both of our dreams happen!!!! You truly are my rock. I love you so much.

To my daughters, I know you both are too young to read this, but I hope one day you will. Thank you for being the best kids a mom could hope for. Thank you for inspiring me to follow my dreams every day. I hope one day I inspire you both to chase your dreams too. I love you with all my heart.

To Collette, thank you for being the best friend a girl could ask for and supporting me in ways I never expected. You read my book when I was on the verge of giving it all up, and your love and excitement for this story and these characters gave me much needed hope. I love you.

To Juliana, thank you for being my best friend, my sis. Your love, support, and encouragement means the world to me. I love you and am so grateful to have you in my life.

To Laura and Marika - my girls, my best bitches, my #hmc crew. There will never be enough words to thank you both for all you've done for me. I don't know how I got so lucky to meet you both, but I'll always be grateful that we did. Thank you for everything. I love you guys and now you're stuck with me!

To Danielle, thank you for our long talks, late night convos, and texts. I've loved getting to support each other through this part of our journey and I'm so grateful for you kind, supportive words. I can't wait to read Beau and Jules' story!

To all of my beta's: Krista, Larissa, Brooke, Kristine, Greg, Bella, Rebel, Laura, and Marika. Thank you, thank you, thank you. It is because of your time, effort, and feedback that Through the Mist is where it is now. I couldn't have done this without you guys and I am eternally grateful.

To my editor, cover designer, and proofreader - thank you for the fantastic work you've done for me. My book baby is shiny and beautiful because of your hard work.

To my Adams Mom Crew, thank you for your support and community. Thank you for letting me talk your ears off about this book. Thank you for just being there and putting a smile on my face when I need it. I am so lucky to have you all in my life.

To Bella Love, Auden Dar, Cassandra Robbins, Leslie McAdam, Mara White, HB Jasick, Mia Miller, Krista Sandor, Kelly Violet, Jami Denise, and so many other author friends that I'm blanking on right now - thank you all for your support, chats, and encouragement.

To all my friends and family who have supported me through this journey, to all of you that shared my posts and info about my book, who messaged me or shared kind and supportive words, to all of you who pre-ordered my book or plan on buying it - I'm not going to even try to list you all because I know that there are so many of you that I would assuredly forget someone. Please just know that I've seen all the love and support and I am so incredibly grateful to each and every one of you. Thank you.

And finally, to you, dear reader. Thank you for taking a chance on me and on this book. Your support in buying and taking the time to read my book means everything to me. You are a part of me realizing this dream. Thank you.

Constellation

A second-chance romance, coming in 2019

One look.
One touch.
One night.

That's all it took to change everything.
Three months of bliss before it all disappeared.

Weeks into months into years of breaking apart under
the weight of loneliness.
The pressure of responsibilities.
The soul shattering reality of life.

One touch.
One look.
One afternoon.

That's all it took to bring our world crashing down around us.

Regrets? They are a brick wall between us.
Would I change a thing?
Not for all the stars in the sky.

ABOUT THE AUTHOR

Cece Ferrell wrote her first story at the age of eight, which sparked a passion for the written word. An intense fascination with stories from the past led her to getting her B.A. degree in Renaissance Studies from the University of California Santa Barbara.

Cece loves: words, especially of the four letter variety, snark, tea, all things crafty, and flawed characters who love passionately. She is a sucker for a great smile and thinks there is almost nothing better in the world than dessert.

Cece resides in Southern California with her husband and two little girls who keep her on her toes. When she's not writing, Cece can be found reading voraciously, having adventures with her family, or binge watching Netflix with her husband.

Made in the USA
Las Vegas, NV
21 October 2021

32763223R00223